The Guardians of Rockport

The Collapse

©2022, David Jones

ISBN: 978-1-66785-371-0

ISBN eBook: 978-1-66785-372-7

GUARDIANS OF ROCKPORT

THE COLLAPSE

DAVID JONES

CHAPTER 1

Doug Chapman sat in his home office sipping his third cup of coffee. During his last medical checkup, the recently retired Wisconsin state trooper was scolded for consuming too much caffeine, an unfortunate habit that grew out of a career of public service working odd hours and in typically bad weather. As he scrolled through the various current events articles on his computer, he was annoyed he now needed reading glasses to make out the small text on the screen. At fifty-four years old, he was starting to feel his age. The progression into the retirement phase of life was furthered by the fact he would soon be a grandfather. While he was elated his daughter Maddy was pregnant, the title of grandpa was just one more reminder that he was getting old.

As he read the news, he was rightfully worried about the future his grandchild would inherit. The headlines were sobering as each one presented a darker outlook than the last. Regional conflicts in both Europe and Asia had been escalating rapidly and placing the rest of the world into turmoil. The North Atlantic Treaty Organization, NATO, was a paper tiger at best, while the United Nations had grown so corrupt, they served no real purpose. No longer able to remain on the sidelines, the United States was now on the verge of entering the wars in both theaters. Most of the participating countries were motivated by their own financial interests, which allowed global tyrants and dictators to thrive unchecked. The tens of millions of refugees displaced by these conflicts had contributed heavily to the global economic instability.

Even in the small town of Rockport, Wisconsin, unemployment was growing rapidly, and the impact of the economic crisis left store shelves lacking most items. The supply chain had been so heavily influenced by international trade that its collapse was crippling. Over the past few decades, America had grown far too reliant on cheap goods from China and petroleum from the Middle East and Europe. Overregulation led most industries to rely on foreign manufacturing rather than making their products domestically. When the cheap foreign labor and inexpensive products were suddenly unavailable, domestic manufacturing was not in a position to pick up the slack. This led to the rapid collapse of the supply chain in the US.

Even if the products could be manufactured entirely in the United States, the huge spike in fuel prices made it impractical to transport across the nation to the store shelves. The government chose to combat the problem by simply printing more money to defray the cost of goods. This unsustainable tactic eventually led to hyperinflation and a sharp spike in interest rates. That, in turn, led to the housing and stock market crashes. Over the past few decades, America had built a house of cards on an unstable base. When the base gave away, the house collapsed.

The rapidly growing problem was that people were afraid of what the future had in store for them. Divisive politics and a biased media had been pitting large groups of Americans against one another for years. Under the new economic strain, people were at a breaking point. Civil unrest was rampant in cities across the nation, and it was only a matter of time before it moved closer to small-town Wisconsin.

Doug turned off the computer and sat back in his chair to reflect. While pondering the world situation, he cast his eyes over the walls of his office. The room was filled with thirty-four years' worth of photographs, awards, and shadow boxes from his military and law enforcement service. Each individual photograph and memento held a special memory for him, and like many combat veterans, he internalized. Doug was very proud of his service, but his memories served as both a badge of honor and a constant reminder of survivor's guilt. His fourteen years as a state trooper followed after his twenty-year career as a special agent with the Air Force Office of Special Investigations (OSI). Doug had served all over the globe, investigating felony crimes and conducting counterintelligence and antiterrorism operations. Having served as the special agent in charge of the Antiterrorism Specialty Team (AST) based out of Germany, Doug and his fifteen-man team operated in multiple high-threat locations, including special missions in both Iraq and Afghanistan.

One photograph on his wall caught his eye in particular. It was a photo of him standing alongside his best friend and former Air Force buddy Matt Johnson. The photograph, taken seventeen years earlier, captured an era that seemed like such a long time ago. Yet he would relive the horrors of that deployment often when he closed his eyes. The two men were standing in front of a large insurgent weapons cache they had just captured with an Army Special Forces team. They were grinning and smoking celebratory cigars, as was the custom after successful operations on the AST. Matt would be severely wounded a few short days after that photograph was taken when an insurgent bullet would shatter his left femur, ending his military career. Doug was completely lost in thought, reliving that same battle he had fought in his mind so many times over the past two decades. No matter how much he visualized taking out the insurgent gunman before Matt was shot, his wishing could never alter the reality of what had transpired. As Doug relived the horrors of placing a tourniquet on his best friend's leg, a strange beeping noise was present in the background. Moments later he was brought back to the real world by the sound of his wife, Penny, yelling down the stairs, "You have a fire call!"

Doug had joined the Rockport Volunteer Fire Department along with his son-in-law, Mark, five years earlier. Mark was a highly skilled, full-time firefighter/paramedic in Milwaukee and joined the local volunteer department with him as a bonding opportunity. It was also a great way for Doug to prove to himself that the aging warrior still had what it took to go through the fire academy at forty-nine years old.

Doug rushed through the house and grabbed his cell phone off the kitchen counter on his way out the door. Glancing at the phone, he wondered why he hadn't been alerted by the emergency cell phone app the department used. At least the call came through on the old pager, allowing his wife to hear it. Doug jumped into his gray Dodge Ram 1500, started up the engine, and activated the red-and-white firefighter emergency lights mounted on his dash. As he raced down the long gravel driveway from his house through a heavily wooded area and past the open gate of his property, he paused for a moment to look for cross traffic. His driveway connected directly to the county highway, a two-lane road leading to the town center, just two miles to the west.

Looking to his left, Doug observed a white Chevy Suburban with the same red-and-white emergency lights strobing on the dash as it approached his location. He recognized the SUV as belonging to his friend Brad Peterson, the Rockport fire chief, and the two exchanged eye contact and a familiar smile as the Chevy passed. This was a common occurrence as the two responded to the fire station from the same end of the town. They were good friends and had worked closely over the years when Doug was a trooper. Doug turned onto the county highway and accelerated, trying to catch up to the Suburban.

As the Hemi V8 engine accelerated, Doug turned up the fire radio and listened as the Calumet County dispatcher broadcasted an update on the incident. The call was for a structure fire involving a two-story farmhouse located at W5676 Windfall Road. The fire was phoned in by a neighbor who advised they could see smoke from the next farm over. Doug was familiar with the older couple who lived at the house, just as he knew many folks in the local area from his time as a trooper. The small farm, located on the far edge of their jurisdiction, belonged to Elijah and Linda Schmidt. Elijah was an aging Vietnam veteran and the third generation to farm that land. While Doug was not particularly close to Elijah, they did make small talk at the local Veterans of Foreign Wars (VFW) meetings. Like many veterans of his generation, Elijah was a quiet man who kept to himself. At the last meeting, Elijah brought his dog with him, who took a liking to Doug. When patrolling that area as a trooper, Doug would stop by occasionally just to check on them, as he did many of the aging residents in the county.

The fire station was just inside the center of the town, a short, two minutes' drive when responding to a fire call from his home. Doug covered that distance in short order and was only a few seconds behind the chief as they approached the station. As the station came into view, Doug could see the hurried activity of the volunteer responders who had beaten him there. Two of the five garage doors on the red brick fire station were already up, exposing engine 41 and water tender 45. Four firefighters were already there, scrambling to put on their turnout gear and board the trucks as the chief and Doug pulled in.

Getting out of his truck, Doug jogged through the open garage door of the station to a row of yellow metal cages in the back of the building. He stopped in front of the cage that contained his turnout gear, which was marked with his name on a piece of tape. Doug slipped off his shoes and stepped into the size-ten fire boots staged inside his bunker pants. Once he got both feet in the boots, he pulled the oversized protective pants up, securing the thick red suspenders over his shoulders. Next, he placed the gray Nomex protective hood over his head and neck, with his face protruding through the opening. Finally, he put on his heavy fire coat and grabbed his helmet and a canvas bag containing the mask to his self-contained breathing apparatus (SCBA). Both Doug and the chief finished gearing up at the same time, as if they were racing each other to be first. Both men were well under the one-minute requirement for state certification. Once geared up, both men boarded Engine 41, filling the last two open seats. As soon as they closed the doors, the fire engine started to roll with lights flashing and sirens blaring.

Engine 41 was the newest and primary engine at the Rockport Fire Department. While it was new to the small department, it was still twenty years old, having previously served with the full-time Appleton Fire Department, twenty-five miles to the north. The large, red fire engine seated six firefighters. The driver and chief sat in the front of the cab, while four firefighters sat in the rear of the cab, two facing rearward and two facing forward. Doug took the last empty seat on the rear driver's side facing forward. Once he was seated, he placed his arms inside a set of shoulder straps that extended from the seat. These straps connected him to the firefighter air tank and regulator located inside his seat back. Once his air pack was buckled and secured into place, he looked out the window at the quaint little town as the engine rolled through with lights and sirens roaring. As the truck left the town and sped toward the Schmidt farm, some ten miles to the south, the crew could see a large plume of black smoke rising above the tree line in the distance. All on board knew that the thick, turbulent smoke meant the fire was large and burning hot. They hoped that the Schmidts had been able to get out of the home in time as the house would most likely be a complete loss by the time they arrived.

The chief looked over his shoulder into the back of the cab and shouted over the sound of the siren. "Did anyone get the fire call on their cell phones?" Nobody had received the cell phone alarm notification, only from their pagers. Further, none of the firefighters had any cell reception at all. The chief decided to use the engine radio to check with the county dispatcher to see if there was some sort of communication issue.

"Calumet County Dispatch from Rockport chief."

"Go ahead, Rockport chief," replied the dispatcher.

"We are not receiving cell phone reception in Rockport. Is there an issue with the communication tower?"

"The cell phone outage is all over the place, Chief. We are not sure what is causing it yet. The call you are responding to came in over a landline, but those are out now as well."

"Roger that, Dispatch. Rockport chief out."

As the emergency responders approached the farm, the chief started to give tactical commands over the radio to the firefighters in the following trucks.

"Water tender 45, when you arrive on scene, immediately set up your collapsible water tank. You will supply water to the engine."

"Roger that, Chief," came the reply.

In many rural areas, there is no municipal water supply providing water to fire hydrants. In these cases, the firefighters must find water from other sources. While the fire engine can draft water from a lake or swimming pool if one is nearby, much of the time they need to bring the water in to fight the fire. This is done with a water tender truck, which transports three thousand gallons of water to the fire scene. The water is then dumped into a collapsible pool for the fire engine to draft from. The water tender will then go retrieve more water to refill the pool as needed.

The chief then looked back over his shoulder into the rear of the cab and shouted instructions to the engine company. He instructed the two rear-facing firefighters, Nick and Jessie, to man the fire attack hose. The two forward-facing firefighters, Ryan and Doug, would be responsible for any rescue operations. Doug prepared his gear to enter the structure to conduct search-and-rescue operations if the opportunity presented itself. He pulled down his protective hood, exposing his head, and pulled his SCBA mask from its container. Once the mask was secured over his face, he pulled the head straps tight to ensure a tight seal. Next, he pulled the protective hood back up over his head and neck to protect his skin from heat and flames. He then attached the respirator from the air tank on his backpack to his face mask. Reaching behind him, he turned the valve on, which allowed air to flow to his mask when he inhaled. As the fire engine neared the farm, Doug put on his fire gloves and helmet, securing the strap under his chin so he would be ready for immediate action.

As the fire engine turned onto the short access road leading to the farmhouse, Doug observed an old green pickup truck partially blocking the path. It was parked all by itself in the middle of the road. Doug recognized it as Farmer Schmidt's truck. Inside the cab he could see Baxter, the farmer's border collie, sitting alone. The black-and-white dog made eye contact with Doug as they slowly passed by. This was out of place and concerned Doug as he wondered where Mr. and Mrs. Schmidt were. The large fire truck had to slowly navigate around the parked pickup truck to continue on to the burning farmhouse. As the house came into view, it was apparent to all on board that it would be a defensive operation only. This meant firefighters would not enter the building as it was too dangerous, and the chance of survivors being alive inside was nil. The house was fully engulfed with flames, indicating the fire had already flashed over. Even a firefighter wearing full protective gear could last only a few seconds in that environment.

As Engine 41 pulled up near the burning house, the driver jumped out and placed chalks behind the tires to prevent it from rolling. He then started to operate the pump to provide water to the fire attack team from the limited on-board water tank. Nick and Jessie climbed down from the truck and grabbed the hose from the right side, extending it out so they had plenty of slack in the line to move around the fire scene as needed. Once both of them were positioned at the nozzle, Jessie gave the hand signal to charge the hose and send her the water. Once the hose line was charged, Jessie pulled the lever back on the nozzle, allowing the water to flow. The attack hose could dispense water at a rate of up to two hundred gallons per minute. As the high-pressure hose tried to push around the small-framed, 120-pound firefighter, she took a braced stance and allowed the hose to press into her torso to help stabilize the water stream. Her attack line partner, Nick, stood directly behind her, using his much-heavier body weight to assist in controlling the line.

The rescue team, consisting of Doug and Ryan, climbed down from the engine and performed a search of the exterior areas for any survivors. While it was too late to enter the burning structure, it was common for survivors to be found unconscious near windows or exits just outside the fire. Once they completed the search, finding no survivors, they assisted the attack team working to extinguish the fire.

After three hours of fighting the fire, the volunteers were completely exhausted. Just wearing the fifty extra pounds of fire gear is itself taxing, but dragging a hose line filled with water is even more strenuous work. Water weighs eight pounds per gallon, and even a short section of hose can weigh more than one hundred pounds when filled.

Once the chief declared the fire completely extinguished, he contacted the county dispatch center to request an arson investigator from the state Department of Criminal Investigation (DCI) in Madison. Anytime a fire death is suspected, the protocol was to have a state arson investigator respond and conduct the criminal investigation.

While it was not currently his duty as a volunteer firefighter, Doug was a trained arson investigator from his time in the Air Force. Even though it would take a detailed and lengthy investigation to determine the exact cause of the fire, it was apparent to Doug that arson was a factor. The burn patterns were consistent with multiple points of origin, indicating more than one fire started independently. The smell of an accelerant, likely gasoline, was present, and he had observed several empty gas cans while he was conducting his preliminary rescue search. Doug feared the worst as he had not located the Schmidts outside the house even though their truck was still there. The major question on his mind was why. Why would someone burn down the Schmidts' house, and were they inside?

CHAPTER 2

Chief Brad Peterson had served on the Rockport Volunteer Fire Department since graduating college twenty-two years earlier. A local boy, he was raised on the family farm about five miles outside of town. He was certain of one thing growing up: he did not want to be a farmer. He was a hard worker, and between the farm chores and good genetics, he grew to six feet, three inches and a powerful 280 pounds.

His size and strong work ethic made him a star football player for the Rockport High School Guardians. As happened in many small schools with few students, Brad played on both the offensive and defensive lines. Playing varsity all four years, he was very popular, which made high school one of the highlights of his life. He would go on to attend his dream school and play NCAA Division 1 football for the University of Wisconsin.

While a standout player in high school, he was only average at the collegiate level, with not much hope of a professional career. Not interested in returning to rural farm life, he chose the company of girls who were of a higher social class. In his sophomore year, he started dating Kimberly, a socialite and the daughter of a wealthy Chicago advertising executive. As opposites tend to attract, she seemed to embody the lifestyle he thought he wanted. Likewise, she was infatuated with the idea of dating someone more masculine than the men in her parents' Chicago social circle.

The two married at the end of their senior year, just days before his father passed away from a heart attack. They returned to the small town of Rockport to help his mother settle his father's affairs and put the farm up for sale. One thing led to another, and twenty-two years later they were still here. Brad fell into a teaching job at his alma mater, where he was able to relive his glory days by proxy as the head coach of the Rockport Guardians.

A few of his old high school buddies served on the volunteer fire department. Looking for adventure and to rekindle his former small-town social status, he joined as well. After just ten years he would rise through the ranks and become chief of the department.

In a small town, arson investigations with possible fatalities were not a common occurrence. Knowing that Doug had a wealth of investigative experience and a unique skill set, he thought it wise for him to take control of the scene now that the fire was out.

"Doug, I requested the DCI arson team to come up and investigate. I want you to take control of the scene until they arrive. What resources do you need?"

"Roger that, Chief. I will need help putting up the yellow fire line tape. I will photograph the scene, but I don't want to enter it and possibly contaminate any evidence, in case it turns out to be a homicide. I'm curious about the farmer's truck and dog. We should have someone check that out and see if it has any answers."

The chief replied, "Sounds good. Grab a couple guys to help you hang the yellow tape. I will walk down and check on the dog."

As Brad walked toward the old pickup that was parked in the center of the access road, he couldn't help but think it was left there intentionally. It was parked in such a way that any responders would have to encounter it but would still be able negotiate around it to get to the fire.

When he got to the truck, the dog sat calmly on the passenger side of the bench seat as if he had been waiting for him. The windows were left partially down, and two dog bowls were left on the driver's side of the bench, one with dog food and the other water. Resting on the dash was an elaborately carved wood box, not much larger than a shoe box.

After opening the passenger door to check on the dog, Brad inspected the silver tag attached to his collar to see if there was a phone number, an address, or owner information. The only information on the tag was the dog's name, Baxter. As he scratched the dog's head, the dog looked at him calmly with his big, sad, all-knowing eyes. The eyes somehow communicated that he understood what was happening.

The dog jumped down from the cab of the truck and slowly walked to the front and sat down, looking in the direction of the burned-out house. Brad removed the two dog bowls and placed them on the ground in front of him; however, the dog wasn't interested in them. As Brad walked around the truck, looking for anything out of the ordinary, he found a large bag of dog food sitting in the bed of the truck.

Returning to the cab, he took a seat on the passenger side and picked up the wooden box. Lifting the lid, he saw that the contents appeared to be random personal effects. There were a few old photographs, a stack of old letters, a music CD, concert tickets, and a couple of military medals. Glancing back up to the dash, he saw a yellow piece of paper that had been placed under the box. Unfolding the paper, he was surprised when he saw the letter was addressed to Trooper Doug Chapman.

CHAPTER 3

Penny Chapman watched out the kitchen window as her husband of twenty-six years drove off to fight a fire. She smiled to herself as she knew he would never be able to settle down like a normal retiree. She had been watching him ride off in the distance to battle dragons for as long as she could remember. Like all wives, she worried for her husband's safety, but after standing by for several combat deployments, she found the worry became a normal part of their relationship. During the last four years of their military career, Doug was the leader the Antiterrorism Specialty Team (AST) and was deployed during much of their assignment in Germany. While a special agent in charge position was typically administrative, Doug always seemed to find his way into the action.

When Doug was off saving the world in some far-off place, Penny was back at their home base holding the family together. As the wife of the boss, she was also responsible for caring for the other fifteen subordinate families who had a husband or wife on the team. The military spouses back at home were not just sitting around worrying about their loved ones; they also had to continue on with their lives as single parents much of the time. All of the many challenges that any parent experienced were only magnified in a military family. Struggles such as financial problems, discipline issues, health concerns, pregnancies, divorces, depression, and caring for special needs children still existed, but without the extended family support that many civilian parents had. The military spouse is the true unsung hero that makes it possible for their service member to be effective.

Penny had a very challenging time during the last few years of Doug's military career. She not only had to raise their teenage daughter, who had way too much of her father in her, but she also had to serve as a strong role model for the younger wives on the team. The weight of that task was no more burdensome than when a team member was wounded or killed in action. She would accompany the death notification officer and chaplain as they informed the spouse. As horrible as that duty was, Penny was the right person for the job. She possessed the perfect amount of empathy, spirituality, and faith to help these young families accept the realities of what happened while still mourning their loss. She would spend countless hours at Landstuhl Army Medical Center, assisting the wounded OSI agents and their families in a way only she could.

Thankfully, her husband understood her burden and was grateful for her sacrifices. He promised her that after they left the service, she could choose the location where they would spend their retirement, and she selected her home state of Wisconsin. She grew up in the small city of Appleton, nestled in the center of the Fox Valley. Doug agreed as promised, but he requested they live outside the major population areas. He had served in many locations across the world where he witnessed governmental collapse firsthand. Places like Yugoslavia, Uzbekistan, Iraq, and even New Orleans after Hurricane Katrina all served as a lesson learned for Doug. As one of the people called upon to help during a crisis, Doug knew what the government's capabilities and limitations actually were. He was concerned the nation was headed for hard times, and having a sustainable homestead for his family was his only demand.

Although her husband would have preferred to live off the grid completely, Penny kept her husband balanced and in check. She told him they could have one foot in the prepper world, but the other foot would remain connected to mainstream society. As always, Doug agreed to her terms as she kept him grounded. They selected a beautiful four-bedroom house that was situated on forty acres of sustainable land. They were just a half-hours drive from her hometown of Appleton. While they were technically within the small town of Rockport, they lived a couple of miles outside the town proper.

Penny knew there was no way her husband would be able to work a nine-to-five job in an office somewhere. She wasn't surprised when he became a Wisconsin state trooper at forty-one years old. The oldest recruit in the academy by over a decade, he still graduated number one in the class. Over the next thirteen years, she would watch him drive off in his dark blue Wisconsin State Patrol car through the same window. It was just four months ago he had decided to hang up his duty belt and retire for the second time. Doug felt times were getting bad in the world, and he wanted to focus on preparing for his family's survival. The fact that they were expecting a grandchild was a big motivator for him to retire. He was determined to ensure she would grow up in a safe environment, as he had seen far too many suffering children in his life.

Penny thought Doug was crazy to join the Rockport Fire Department five years ago at age forty-nine. In an effort to bond with their new son-in-law, who was a full-time firefighter/paramedic in Milwaukee, Doug spent several months going to the fire academy part time on nights and weekends to get his state certification. Most of the cadets in his fire academy were their daughter's age. While Doug was still very fit, he wasn't a young man anymore, and the aches and pains took much longer to heal. She knew serving as a firefighter filled several psychological needs for her husband. It not only filled his need for adventure but also allowed him to continue serving his community. More importantly, it was a place for him to have the comradery that he missed from his time in the military. While Penny was very proud of her husband, she couldn't help but notice the aging warrior with gray hair, fighting to maintain his youth. She believed in Doug's motivations for joining the fire department, but she also felt it was his way of proving to himself that he still had what it takes. She smiled to herself as she thought Peter Pan doesn't want to grow up.

Walking outside onto the deck, Penny let the warmth of the summer sun shine down on her face. Living in northeast Wisconsin, she appreciated the nice weather as it never lasted long enough. Preparing for her daily chores, she slipped on her gardening shoes and picked up the basket she used to collect eggs. As she was about to head to the garden, she paused and looked back at the house. With all the turmoil in the world, Doug had asked her to keep a firearm handy, especially when he was away. While she owned a pistol, she didn't want to wear a holster and gun belt, especially over her cute sundress. She opted for a rifle instead as she could simply lean it against a wall or fence while she worked nearby.

She walked back into the kitchen and retrieved her Henry rifle, which was resting in the corner against the wall. She loved the cowboy-style lever-action rifle, as her favorite movie was *Tombstone*. Doug always got a kick when she said the quote "I'll be your huckleberry" while shooting tin cans down on their range. She would shoot light .38 special ammo while plinking, but Doug had her load hotter .357 magnum hollow-point bullets for home defense. While she gave her husband a hard time about the need for her to have the rifle handy, she was comforted by the ability to defend herself. One of the realities of rural living was self-reliance and a very slow law-enforcement response.

Bringing the rifle with her out onto the property, she leaned it against the decorative red-and-white chicken coop while collecting eggs from their twelve chickens. She enjoyed the self-sufficiency of gardening and raising chickens. She canned many of their vegetables, and Doug pickled many of the eggs harvested. This allowed them to keep a food supply available through the harsh Wisconsin winters.

As an empty nester, she missed having their daughter Maddy living at home. The two had a very close relationship, and she always thought about her while collecting eggs from the coop. Doug bought the chickens as a prepping commodity, but Maddy quickly gave each one a name and made them hers. While Doug could have the eggs, homemade chicken dinners were strictly off the menu. The two would often banter back and forth over the matter, but there was no way Doug would hurt one of her chickens. Like most warriors, Doug had a soft spot where his baby girl was concerned.

Maddy married Mark a few years ago, and they bought a starter home in Rockport. Living nearby, they saw each other several times per week; however, it wasn't the same as living under the same roof. Penny was excited about becoming a grandmother, but she didn't care for the title. She opted for the more progressive term "Nanna" as she felt she was still too young to go by "Grandma." She had already transformed one of the spare bedrooms into a nursery as she offered to babysit each day while Maddy was at work. Penny was determined to provide her daughter all the family support she wasn't afforded while they were serving in the military.

Penny had always worried about Mark working two hours away in the city of Milwaukee. Being the state's largest city, it had an equally large crime rate. Additionally, Mark wasn't content with being a firefighter in a fast-paced department; he had to volunteer for the Special Operations Division. Assigned to Rescue 1, he specialized in technical rescue operations that were beyond the capabilities of regular engine-and-ladder companies. Now that Maddy was expecting, Mark was in the process of transferring to the smaller Appleton Fire Department, which was much closer to home. He had been well into the process of his application when the financial crash placed the department in a hiring freeze.

Over the past few days, the civil unrest in major cities had grown to an epic proportion. The news had been showing clips of burning buildings, shootings, and rampant looting. The mayor had issued an emergency order four days earlier, mandating all Milwaukee emergency personnel remain on duty until the crisis was resolved. Maddy hadn't heard from her husband in the past two days, and now, for some reason, the phones had stopped working. While Penny was very worried about Mark's safety, she was equally afraid her headstrong husband or daughter might attempt to travel to Milwaukee to look for him.

Now that internet access was also out, Penny was starting to believe a government collapse was actually possible. She always enjoyed teasing Doug and his buddies about being crazy preppers, but as with most things, Doug was usually proven right in the end. She was now very thankful he had spent the time and money to prepare them for the bad times that were upon them. She could not think of a safer place to be during uncertain times than with Doug on their forty acres.

CHAPTER 4

The yellow fire line tape was strung across all four sides of where the farmhouse once stood. "That looks pretty good," Doug said to Jessie, the young firefighter assisting him.

"Thanks. Do you really think this was arson?" she asked.

"Yes, I do."

"Why would someone burn down the old couple's home?"

"Well, that will be the main question the investigators will need to determine when they arrive. There are typically six common motivators for arson," explained the old investigator. "Vandalism, profit, revenge, excitement, concealment of a crime, and extremism. There are others, but those are the big six."

Doug's lecture on arson investigation was cut short when the chief called him over his two-way radio.

"Go ahead," said Doug into the microphone clipped to his turnout coat.

"Are you available to come down here to where the farmer's truck is parked?"

"Roger that, Chief. I'm on my way."

Leaving Jessie to keep the fire scene secure, he turned and walked down the lengthy access road to the farmer's truck. He was exhausted from fighting the fire, and the oversize rubber firefighter boots were not designed for lengthy walks on loose gravel. As the truck came into view, he could see the dog sitting on the ground, watching him as he approached. He could also see Brad sitting in the passenger seat and reading something.

"What did you find, Chief?" Doug called out as he approached, hoping it was something that provided insight to the fire.

With a confused look on his face, Brad stepped out of the cab and walked around to the front of the truck as Doug approached. The chief took off his fire helmet and sat it on the hood of the truck next to the wooden box. Doug could tell the chief was trying to mentally piece together the odd situation. The two men had known each other for fourteen years and had developed a personal friendship outside the firehouse. His eyes were glossed over with concern and confusion.

"The dog was inside the cab with the windows partway down. He had food and water in there as well."

"Strange. It's like someone wanted him to be safe from the fire but found by rescuers," replied Doug.

"That's not the strange part. What's strange is the box of personal effects and this note that was left inside with the dog."

"Is it from Farmer Schmidt?"

"Oh yeah, and it's addressed to you personally," he said, looking up from the paper to see Doug's reaction.

"What?" asked Doug in a state of shock. "I knew them, but we certainly weren't close. Elijah was a member of my VFW post, and we would chat at meetings sometimes. Last month he brought Baxter to the meeting, and the dog seemed to take to me, but I have always had a way with dogs. When I was a trooper, I would stop by now and again to check on them, but I did that with a lot of older folks."

Taking off his fire helmet and wiping sweat from his brow, Doug asked, "What did the note say? Did he burn down his own house? Was it a murder-suicide situation?"

With a confused look on his face, Brad replied, "It looks like his wife had been suffering from cancer for several months and passed away this morning. With the medical bills and all the hyperinflation over the past few months, Elijah had exhausted his life savings. He had taken a second mortgage out on the farm but was several months behind. Now, without his wife's social security checks to help make the payments, there was no possible way to keep the bank from foreclosing."

Brad continued, "He goes on to say he was ready to join her in heaven and that he couldn't let the bank take the home his grandfather built."

Doug was surprised by the news, as Elijah had never said anything about his wife being sick or the financial problems.

"There is a P.S.," said Brad as he looked up at Doug. "It's about the dog. He wanted you personally to take care of him. It's hard to make out the writing toward the end. He gets sloppy and doesn't make a lot of sense. I'm guessing he had taken something to overdose on and it was taking effect. But he ended by saying Baxter chose you."

"That's just crazy," said Doug. "Why didn't he say something or reach out to anyone? We are losing so many veterans to suicide."

Folding the paper, Brad asked his friend, "What could anyone have done to help his situation? We are all in the same financial boat nowadays, or not far from it. He just chose to end things on his terms, I guess," he reasoned, struggling to find a reason for such a tragedy. "I expect we will see more of this sort of thing in the coming weeks. Everyone has a breaking point," he added.

"Unfortunately, I think you are right about that," replied Doug. "Folks are getting desperate."

"He left that box of personal effects to you as well. It's some old military medals, photographs, and a country music CD. Sort of an odd combination of stuff. Why do you think he left them to you?"

Shrugging his shoulders, Doug said, "I have no idea. I know they only had one child, a son, who was killed during Operation Desert Storm back in '91. He and I were the same age and we both joined up shortly before that war, but I never met him." He added, "Elijah was a quiet man. Now that I think about it, I guess I don't recall him talking to anyone much other than myself at the monthly meetings."

Glancing down at Baxter, Brad asked, "You going to keep the dog?"

"Yeah, I guess I have to," replied Doug. "He needs a home, and I guess I am partly responsible for his situation."

"What the hell does that mean?" asked Brad.

"That old farmer must have thought I was the closest thing to a friend he had in this life, and I never realized it. I sure as hell didn't see any warning signs," said Doug with a feeling of responsibility for the matter.

"Dude! You need to get that kind of thinking out of your head ASAP! I know you like to keep the burdens of the world bottled up in that head of yours, but this was in no way your fault. If you want to keep the dog, fine, but do it because you like the dog, not out of some perceived guilt!"

Doug knelt down and scratched Baxter on his head and ears. It was obvious Baxter remembered him, and he sat up and placed a paw on Doug's knee while looking at him with his sad eyes. There was something about how expressive his eyes were. It was as though he could see into Doug's soul.

Knowing the note and personal effects could be a valuable piece of evidence during an arson investigation, Doug contacted the dispatch center to see if they had an estimated time of arrival on the state investigator. Additionally, it was out of the ordinary for a county deputy sheriff not to respond to the fire scene. While there were only three to four deputies on duty in the county this time of day, one should have made his way over to Rockport by now.

"Calumet County Dispatch from Rockport firefighter Chapman," he spoke into the radio while holding the transmit button.

"Go ahead, Rockport," replied the dispatcher.

"Just checking to see if we have an ETA for the state arson investigator."

"Negative, Rockport. It's the strangest thing, we haven't been able to reach the state DCI or any of the other Department of Justice offices down in Madison. We have tried all the numbers we have on file, and now both cellular and landlines seem to be down."

"Roger that, Dispatch. We have some evidence up here and a potential crime scene. Is there a deputy available to take control of the scene?"

"Negative, Rockport. There is a missing child up at High Cliff State Park, and all three deputies and the dayshift sergeant are conducting a search-and-rescue operation. Please take whatever actions you can to maintain scene integrity until one of them is able to respond."

"Roger that, Dispatch. Rockport out."

The chief looked at Doug and asked, "Well, what do you want to do?"

As Doug considered all the facts, he sighed out loud while scratching his head. "Well, this is a very unusual set of circumstances. I guess I will take the box and the note with me to maintain chain of custody until it can be turned over to active law enforcement. Let's leave two of the firefighters here for scene security until a deputy can arrive and take charge. If it's more than a couple hours, we can rotate out personnel. I have no idea what's going on down in Madison and why nobody is answering the phones. That can't be good. If we don't hear anything from them in the next few hours, I can investigate the arson scene myself, but that will be your call as the fire chief," replied Doug.

"Well, that sounds like as good a plan as any," said Brad.

As the two of them looked back to the location where the house once stood, they watched about a dozen volunteer firefighters clean up the gear and load the muddy hoses back onto the trucks. All five of the department vehicles eventually made it to the scene as more of the volunteers were able to leave their day jobs and respond. The chief radioed for two firefighters to remain on scene for security in the smaller brush fire truck. It was actually just a Ford F250 pickup with a water tank in the bed. It was capable of going off road to extinguish fires where the larger fire engines couldn't. The chief instructed everyone else to head back to town, top off the fuel tanks, and return to the station to clean hoses.

Doug picked up the wooden box, along with the note and Baxter's dog bowls, while Brad picked up the heavy bag of dog food. Doug whistled for Baxter to follow him, and somehow, he knew he belonged with him. It's amazing how dogs understand things in their own way, Doug thought. Baxter stood up and slowly returned to the farmer's truck and reached his head into the open door, retrieving something from the floorboard. He came out with a tennis ball that appeared to be special to him. The dog seemed to know he was leaving his family home behind him.

CHAPTER 5

Gunfire could be heard echoing in the background as the sound of each shot reverberated between the buildings. Just a few short weeks ago, the sound of random gunfire in Milwaukee would have created a panic and drawn a police response, but with the constant civil unrest over the past month, hearing gunfire had unfortunately become the new normal.

As the exhausted crew of Milwaukee Fire Rescue #1 walked back to their truck, they scanned the area for any hostile threats. After responding to constant calls over the past several days, they were less concerned about being killed in a fire than they were about being assaulted or worse. The last twenty-four hours seemed to be the breaking point for the city. Police officers typically respond to emergency calls and ensure the scene is safe before unarmed firefighters and medics roll in. This practice had slowed over the last few days as law enforcement was simply overwhelmed. The crew of Rescue #1 hadn't even seen a police officer in the last thirty-six hours. Like many of the brave firefighters, they chose to respond to calls without police support under the extreme circumstances.

Mark Cruz was both mentally and physically exhausted after working almost four days straight with minimal sleep. Only taking short naps here and there, his body rarely got into the restorative REM level of sleep, which took ninety minutes to start. Like the remaining members of Milwaukee Fire

Station 23, he was starting to make mistakes due to fatigue. They had been working almost nonstop responding to fires, medical calls, and other emergencies. The city had turned into a war zone days earlier, and the mayor had issued an emergency order mandating all fire and police personnel to stay on duty until the crisis had passed. Mark typically worked a single twenty-four-hour shift at a time and had two full days off to recuperate between shifts. This constant work with minimal down time was simply not sustainable for more than a couple of days. The department was critically short staffed as many firefighters had called in sick, resigned, were injured, or simply did not return from calls. To make matters worse, cell phones and internet access went out citywide, which significantly compounded the crisis. The citizens were in a panic, and store shelves were empty due to the hyperinflation and supply chain breakdown. Even people who still had money in the bank were unable to access it as the banks were closed and the ATMs out of cash. Home break-ins were rampant as people were desperate to feed their families. While some people were willing to kill to get supplies, others were willing to kill to keep them.

Many of the police officers, firefighters, and medical responders were faced with the difficult choice to abandon their post in order to go protect their own families. It was apparent to all that the city government had crossed an imaginary boundary and was no longer operating effectively. Communications were out, and what limited emergency resources were left were like a drop in the ocean. The members of Station 23 were simply exhausted, and all of them worried about their own situations. Mark was no different. He had met the love of his life, Maddy, while serving as an Air Force firefighter stationed in Germany. He was a nineteen-year-old airman, and Maddy had just turned eighteen. They met at the annual Air Force Ball. She had just graduated from the Department of Defense High School on Ramstein Air Base and was the daughter of an OSI special agent. All of his fire buddies teased him and warned him about dating the daughter of a special agent. The OSI was sort of a combination of FBI and CIA that worked directly for the civilian Secretary of the Air Force. While their mission was to conduct felony-level investigations beyond the scope of the military police, they also conducted operations in counterintelligence, counter espionage, and antiterrorism.

They were known as "secret squirrels" who operated in the shadows. They held the highest security clearances, wore civilian clothes, and were often associated with classified activities such as the ominous Area 51. The term "Men in Black" was loosely based on OSI agents who were responsible for Project Bluebook, the nation's investigation into UFOs back in the 1950s and '60s. Although these special agents had a very real and essential mission, the mysterious nature of their existence fed into the many conspiracy theories people loved to gossip about. For a young airman with just a single stripe on his sleeve, dating the teenage daughter of one of these men was intimidating enough, and the constant razzing from the other firefighters about the situation didn't help.

Mark had the best of intentions and treated Maddy like a queen. She was his everything. When Maddy's father retired from the Air Force and moved to a small town in Wisconsin, the two lovebirds stayed in constant communication. While her parents were certain the long-distance relationship would dissolve as she attended the University of Wisconsin–Oshkosh, he would prove them wrong. Three years later, after his Air Force enlistment was complete, Mark relocated to the small town of Rockport to be near her. When she graduated college the following year, the two were married in a simple but elegant ceremony on her parents' property.

While the teenage relationship started off innocent enough, Maddy's dad put the screws to Mark regarding his intention. It was like Robert DeNiro's character in the movie *Meet the Parents* was based on Doug Chapman. But Mark stayed the course and passed all of Doug's tests. He eventually won the old man over and was more than a little shocked when he gave his blessing to marry his daughter. Mark and Doug would become close over the next few years and would spend a lot of time together. They even joined the Rockport Volunteer Fire Department together as a way to bond. Mark and Maddy had a solid marriage and were very content. They spent a lot of time with her parents and their mutual friends from the fire department. The news that they were expecting a child was the next big step in what was a perfect relationship.

When Mark had moved to Rockport a few years earlier, there were no full-time fire departments anywhere in rural Calumet County. This led to Mark accepting a position with the Milwaukee Fire Department, two hours south of where he lived, while Maddy finished college. While the commute was painful, he only worked about nine or ten 24-hour shifts per month. Milwaukee FD was happy to have him, as Air Force firefighters come with numerous advanced certifications and unique experiences. The plan was for Mark to transfer to a smaller department closer to home after Maddy found a job teaching. But as much as Mark loved living in the rural county, he also loved the excitement of working for the fast-paced fire department. Now that Maddy was pregnant, it was time to make the switch. Unfortunately, Mark wasn't so sure there would be a future in government service. From what he had witnessed the past few days, he suspected the government no longer existed.

As Rescue #1 rolled back to the station, Mark looked out the window of the rear jump seat. He was almost catatonic from exhaustion. As he blankly stared off into the distance, he could see several plumes of smoke rising above the urban horizon. The city was in chaos, and the government had simply lost control. Although Mark was dedicated to his duty, he couldn't help but wonder how his family was getting along back in Rockport. Now with no phones or internet access, he couldn't even check in on his pregnant wife. He knew she was a strong person and her parents would look out for her, but he worried just the same. With all that had transpired, Mark finally reached the hard decision to abandon his post and return home to protect his wife and unborn child. This was a decision he had been dreading for the past few weeks as the city fell apart. He knew the time might come, but his sense of duty and honor was incredibly strong. As a military veteran and public servant, he found it difficult to abandon his department, but his department was rapidly abandoning him.

As they approached the fire station, things didn't look right. Station 23 was home to three fire trucks: Engine #23, Rescue #1, and Heavy Urban Rescue #4. The crew of Mark's truck could see that all of the garage doors were open, which was unusual under the circumstances. Engine #23 was absent from its bay for some unknown reason, though it was not on a call.

HUR #4 was parked inside with all of its compartments opened wide. They could see several people running from the building carrying various items from the truck and the station itself. As Rescue #1 pulled into the driveway of the station, it blew its air horn in an attempt to get the looters to scatter. The crew members jumped off the truck and grabbed various hand tools to serve as defensive weapons. Mark grabbed a pick head axe off the side of the truck and made his way inside the station to search for downed firefighters. Several looters ran out past Mark as he entered the kitchen area of the station. Once inside the kitchen, he found two members of HUR #4 lying on the floor in a pool of their own blood. While he knew them by sight, both men were on a different shift rotation. It was apparent that each had been shot multiple times. Mark could smell the burnt gunpowder in the small kitchen and observed several spent 9mm shell casings scattered across the floor. As he checked for signs of life on each man, it was apparent both had expired.

Almost everything of value had been taken from the station and HUR #4. Mark had no idea where the rest of that fire crew was or if they were OK. He additionally had no clue where Engine 23 was and if its crew needed help. As Mark and his crew stood in the kitchen looking down at the two fallen brothers, Lieutenant Allen, the officer in charge of Rescue #1, asked for their attention.

"Guys," the lieutenant said as he pulled off his helmet. "I hate to say this, but I think it's time. Things have taken a turn for the worse, obviously. You have all served the city of Milwaukee valiantly. You are all heroes; please, never forget that. I am confident there is no end in sight, and what little we are trying to do just doesn't make much of a difference at this point. We have now lost all communications; even our radios are out. I can't keep asking you to risk your lives while letting your families go unprotected. I know duty and honor are more than just words to each of you, and I can't overstate how proud I am of that. As the senior officer of the station that is still present, I have written a letter explaining that I am disbanding Station 23. I am releasing you all from duty. I will give each of you a copy of the letter so that, just in case things ever return to normal, they will know you stuck it out to the last possible minute. Thank you all for your service and your friendship."

There was not a dry eye in the station. Everyone was emotionally exhausted from all that they had endured. Watching the city burn and finding the lifeless bodies of their brother firefighters was a breaking point. The next few minutes were somber as the members of Rescue #1 took down the US flag flying above the station. They placed the bodies of the two fallen brothers side by side on the dining room table and draped them both in the flag of their country. It was important to all to recognize that these men died as heroes, protecting their community. There wasn't a lot they could do, but at least it was something. After the impromptu ceremony and a short prayer, the crew of Rescue#1 said their goodbyes to the fallen brothers and to each other.

As he was leaving the station, Mark stopped by Rescue 1 for the last time to take any essential items he thought he might need before it, too, was picked over by looters. He knew that if he made it back to Rockport, he would need the items in his volunteer firefighter capacity. Mark grabbed his large orange paramedic bag and a thermal imager from the rig. He loaded them into his personal Toyota Tacoma and said a short prayer for his family and for a safe trip home.

He had no idea what to expect as the past four days had been a complete blur. He climbed into the driver seat and started up his engine. Reaching under the seat, he pulled out a black hard-sided case. He entered a four-digit code, and the box sprung open. Mark was relieved to find his Glock 19 inside with a spare magazine. He placed the gun in a holster he kept in his glove box and secured it onto his belt. He then did the same with the spare magazine. Looking back at Station 23 one last time, he started his journey home.

CHAPTER 6

It was quiet on board the Rockport fire truck as it headed back to town from the fire at the Schmidt farm. The crew usually talked and joked after a fire call, but this time was different. It was a somber feeling for Doug, sitting in the back of the cab with Baxter at his feet and the box of personal property resting on his lap. Everyone on board was exhausted after battling the fire; additionally, they were all concerned about the uncertainty of their own futures. The global unrest had been the major topic of conversation for the past few months, but more recently, it was affecting each of them on a personal level.

They had all experienced the growing pressures of hyperinflation, supply chain shortages, and a general fear of the unknown, but they wanted to believe the world would correct itself soon and things would gradually return to the way they were. The firsthand experience of the Schmidt farm led to the emotional realization that things were rapidly getting worse than they had wanted to believe. Everyone had a deep respect for Doug, and watching him ride in silence while consoling the dog, who had laid his head on Doug's knee, really hit home.

"That dog seems to like you," said Jessie, sitting across from Doug and Baxter. Her face, like everyone's, was dirty from smoke and soot after fighting the fire.

Not really feeling like talking under the circumstances, he just replied, "Yeah, dogs seem to gravitate toward me."

"It's probably the beef jerky he keeps in his pocket," said Nick, making a corny joke nobody laughed at. Realizing the group wasn't in the joking mood, Nick tried to change the subject. "Jessie, why do you always rush to grab the nozzle before me?"

"Well, someone has to fight the fires in this department," she remarked, using a Wet-Nap to clean the soot off her face.

Jessie wasn't really in a joking mood either. The twenty-two-year-old firefighter was devastated that the bright future she had been working so hard for was about to come to a crashing halt. Coming from a bad family on the outskirts of town, it seemed she was destined to turn out just as everyone expected. With the last name of Wolf, in this part of the county, her family had a reputation for trouble going back at least three generations.

Her mother left when she was little, and her only female role model was an aunt who died of a heroin overdose when Jessie was fifteen years old. After that she started spiraling out of control and getting into trouble with the law. She was convinced that if the world expected her to act like the rest of her family, that's just what they would get.

It was a high school history teacher who made her realize her story hadn't been written yet. That same man got her into sports, intending to teach her discipline and, more specifically, to keep her away from the negative influence and abuse of her family. With him as a mentor, the tough girl from the wrong side of the tracks excelled and graduated high school. That was three years ago. Now she was about to start her senior year at the University of Wisconsin–Green Bay, something nobody had expected of her just a few short years ago.

The day prior, Jessie received notice that the university was closing down for a semester because of the global uncertainty. Not one to complain about things, she typically rolled up her sleeves just to prove she had what it takes. But her hard exterior also disguised a young girl who feared her efforts would be in vain. More importantly, she did not want to let down that high school teacher, who was now sitting in the front of the engine wearing the fire chief's helmet.

Everyone in the fire truck had their own story. The buying power of the dollar was only a fraction of what it had been just weeks ago, and people's 401(k) savings plans had been decimated. Everyone's plans for the future had changed drastically. Even if a person had money, there wasn't much available to purchase. Gas prices had been heavily inflated by the wars overseas, and that cost increase was passed on to the price of goods.

Over the past couple of decades, American consumers had grown more reliant on internet shopping and home delivery services. This led to a huge reduction in brick-and-mortar local stores across the nation. Home delivery was a convenient way of doing things when the system worked, but now that the system was fractured, people were seeing the error of their ways. Deliveries from formerly reliable sources such as Amazon, UPS, and FedEx had mostly stalled over the past few weeks. Gas prices and lack of availability played a huge factor in the crisis, as did the worker shortage. Many employees, especially over-the-road truck drivers, opted to stay home and protect their families rather than leave them for days on end just to earn some money that didn't have much buying power.

Crime and civil unrest in the cities also played a factor in the national supply chain breakdown. Rampant looting and truck hijacking had been an unfortunate reality the past few weeks. Train yards were an early target for theft as the cars full of goods were pilfered in broad daylight. As people fled the urban centers looking for a safe haven, the strain was just transferred to the smaller communities, which were unprepared for the increased population. While Rockport was small and out of the way, the growing pressures of the rest of the world were now being felt there too.

As the fire truck pulled through the chain-link fence surrounding the Rockport maintenance building, it got in line behind the other three fire vehicles waiting to refuel. But something didn't seem right. Through the large windshield of the fire truck, Chief Peterson could see Dale Tucker standing next to the town's fuel tank, arguing with the firefighters from the other trucks. Tucker, as everyone called him, was the town maintenance supervisor and the only full-time employee of the municipality. Working for the town over the past twenty years had given him a sense of entitlement, as he had endured several elected town board administrations over his tenure. The chief stepped down from the officer's seat and walked over to the group, knowing there was often contention between Tucker and, well, everyone.

"What's going on, Tucker?" asked the chief.

Tucker rolled his eyes in annoyance as he watched the chief walk up to him. "I was just telling your guys we are low on fuel so I can only let them fill the trucks to the fifty percent level."

Brad had an annoyed look on his face as he suspected Tucker of pulling another one of his shady operations. "What the hell, Tucker? Why am I just hearing about this now?"

"Due to the increased price of fuel, the village board instructed me not to purchase any more until we got down to 500 gallons on hand. They were expecting the price to drop or maybe the state to assist us financially. That never happened, and now we are down to 500 gallons. I just got the approval from the town board to place an order, but this morning the phones went out."

Angry, but not surprised by this news, Brad asked, "Why was I not informed about this before? As the fire chief, I am responsible for all emergency services."

Tucker gave the chief a cocky grin, exposing his rotten teeth, stained with chewing tobacco. "Well, the board members knew you would bitch about it, so they didn't want you to know. They felt confident the state would bail them out before we got this low."

Brad suspected a portion of that statement was true, but he was sure Tucker had manipulated the situation for his own gain. He was a schemer and a bully, and the elected members of the board often backed down to his abrasive nature.

Looking Tucker in the eye, Brad asked, "Well, who made the decision to limit the fire department to only half a tank of gas?"

With a defiant smile, Tucker said, "Oh, that was me. I was feeling generous. I need most of the remaining fuel for my maintenance vehicles, but I will allow you and your volunteers to have enough to fill your trucks halfway."

Brad let out an annoyed laugh. "What maintenance vehicles? You have a couple of pickup trucks and a riding lawn mower. How does that trump emergency response vehicles?"

Angered by the chief's snarky comment, Tucker allowed the tone of his voice to become more challenging as he replied, "My snowplows and salt truck are emergency vehicles!"

"It's July, Dale!" the chief shot back, elevating his own voice. "There won't be any snow to plow for months, and mowing grass needs to take a back seat to emergency services."

"Well, I see things differently," said Tucker. "As the only full-time employee, I am charged with maintaining this village 24/7. You guys are just a bunch of part-time volunteers who only get called out a few times per month. If you want to get your trucks filled to the fifty percent mark, I will allow it. If not, get your trucks out of my maintenance yard."

The chief reluctantly agreed to fill the trucks to the fifty percent mark, but he would be addressing the matter in short order with the town board. Life safety simply could not take a back seat to mowed grass.

After fueling up to the fifty percent mark, the chief instructed Vic, the driver, to head over to Jenkins's filling station. He wanted to see if he could at least top off the primary response engine and charge it to the town. Jenkins was the only gas station in Rockport and had been in service for as long as any of them could recall. As the big truck turned the corner, they could see a number of cars lined up on the road waiting to pull into the filling station. This was not a normal occurrence in the small town.

The engine pulled over to the side of the road, and Brad jumped out to evaluate the situation firsthand. As he walked up to the station past the waiting cars, he could see a sign out front limiting fuel sales to five gallons per vehicle and requiring cash only. As he got closer, he could see a middle-aged man he didn't recognize standing by an SUV at the pump. The SUV was loaded to the max, and the middle-aged man seemed very agitated as he confronted the station attendant. Brad could hear him shouting profanities at the teenage clerk. Just as he walked up from the stranger's rear, the situation started to escalate.

Brad knew Billy Jenkins, the nineteen-year-old station attendant, because he had just graduated from Rockport High School. The thinly built but scrappy kid had been the kicker for the Rockport Guardians. After graduation, he had no plans to leave town and fell into the family business as everyone expected he would.

From listening to the argument, it was apparent the man was from the Milwaukee area. He had packed up his family and as many of their belongings as could be crammed into the SUV in an attempt to get to their summer cabin up north. Having not been able to find fuel on the interstate during his journey, he was demanding that Billy fill his entire tank. Billy explained to him they were almost out of fuel and didn't expect another delivery. Everyone in line was desperate for whatever fuel they could get; however, the small-town locals were far more civil than the big city traveler.

Once the chief saw the man shove Billy, he knew it was time to intervene. Even when not wearing his firefighting gear, the chief was a man whose physical presence demanded respect. Wearing the bulky gear and the white fire helmet of a chief, his appearance was even more daunting. His confident demeanor, accompanied by his physical presence, was usually enough to resolve most conflicts.

"That's about enough of that," said the chief.

The middle-aged traveler spun around angrily to address who was speaking to him. His aggressive demeanor withdrew when he saw the fire chief. Whether it was his physical size or the official image of the uniform, the man calmed himself and tried to explain that he was just frustrated and needed to get his family to safety.

"I can understand that," said Brad. "But everyone else in this line has a family with needs as well. This young man is doing the best he can dealing with a difficult situation. If he is still willing to sell you five gallons, and that's entirely up to him, I would gladly accept and move on if I were you."

The man's wife was sitting in the truck and yelling at him to just take the five gallons. She was clearly the more responsible half of the marriage. The man reluctantly agreed and apologized to Billy. Brad told the man to step back into his vehicle, and he would pump the gas for him. The man complied, having no other realistic choice in the matter. Once the five gallons had been purchased and pumped, the man left the station for a destination farther north.

"Thanks," said Billy. "It's been a tough morning. People are panicking, and we are just about out of fuel. We kept trying to order more but all of the regional suppliers were out. Now I can't even get them on the phone. We have seen quite a few folks passing through from out of town who are making their way up from Chicago and Milwaukee looking for safety up north. It's kind of odd that they are coming through Rockport since we're well off of Interstate 43."

"That is strange," said Brad.

Interstate 43 runs up the east coast of Wisconsin and follows the Lake Michigan coastline. It connects Milwaukee to Green Bay, and much of the distance between the two cities consist of rural farmland and smaller municipalities. Brad reasoned that as people traveled up north to get out of the cities, they were having trouble finding fuel along the route. They were probably branching out in hopes of finding gas in the smaller communities. Another possibility was that people were avoiding the interstate for some reason.

"If you stay open much longer, you may need to consider some enhanced security measures," suggested Brad.

"Yeah, dad has a revolver inside behind the counter. I guess that doesn't do me much good out here," said Billy.

"I guess not," replied the chief.

As Brad walked back to Engine 41, he dismissed the idea of getting fuel from the gas station. Not only would it be unfair to the customers waiting in line, it could spark arguments and distrust in the local government. Just as the out-of-town customer didn't plan sufficiently and expected to use the resources available to others, the poor planning of the town should not have to take away what was available to the public. One thing was for certain: it was imperative the citizens continue to maintain trust in the local government if they expected to get through the hard times ahead.

As the chief climbed back into the engine, he informed the crew of what happened at the filling station. While the incident was no surprise to the fire crew, it did continue to instill upon each of them that the crisis had finally reached their small piece of the world. As the truck backed into the garage bay at the station, the crew dismounted and hung their turnout gear back in their respective cages. While the other firefighters worked to clean all the mud off of the fire hoses, Doug told Brad he was going to head home and get the dog squared away.

"Sounds good," replied the chief. "Just monitor your radio for when law enforcement can find their way over here and take control of the fire scene."

"Will do," replied Doug.

Baxter sat on the floor of the fire station next to Doug as he shed his gear and placed it back in his designated cage. He placed each piece of his fire ensemble in a specific place and staged so that he could put it on expediently during the next call. He placed his fire helmet in its place at the top of the cage. There were twenty separate cages connected in the row, one for every firefighter. The color of the helmet designated the rank, and the leather front shield identified the individual. A white helmet designated the chief, while a red helmet designated officers in the rank of captain and lieutenant. The remaining seventeen firefighters all wore black helmets. This color system allowed for rapid identification of the fire officer when everyone was dressed the same and operating in a dark and smoky environment.

Once the gear was staged for the next call, Doug was ready to take the new member of the family home. Picking up the wood box and dog bowls, he called for Baxter to follow him. Brad had already loaded the dog food into the back of Doug's truck for him. As the pair walked from the station to the Ram in the front parking lot, Baxter trotted ahead of him as if he knew where he was going. As Doug opened the driver's door, Baxter jumped right in like he belonged there all along. Inside the cab he moved over to the passenger seat, sat down, and placed his ball with care right next to him. Doug placed the box and dog bowls in the back seat. As he climbed into the driver's seat, he made eye contact with Baxter. There was a sense of calm in his eyes that put Doug at ease. He couldn't explain it, but it was a comfort.

CHAPTER 7

As Doug drove back to the house, he wondered if the phone outage was just a temporary inconvenience or a return to the old way of life. If it was the latter, they would need to make a lot of changes in how they communicated, especially regarding emergency calls. Turning on the car radio to see if there was anything on the local news, Doug tuned into the popular country station Y100. His favorite disc jockey team of "Shotgun and Charlie" was on the air. Their typical comedic banter was usually a welcome distraction from daily life, but today their tone was more serious as they were about to give a public service announcement. Before Doug could hear what they were about to announce, the channel went to static. Scanning the rest of the stations, they were all the same.

As he approached the turnoff onto the access road leading to his property, he thought about the security situation and how he could enhance it. He traveled up the winding gravel road for about one hundred yards and came to his open metal gate. The access road to the property was concealed by a thick wooded area, preventing the house and outbuildings from view until a vehicle passed the security gate. The forty-acre plot was wooded on the side that bordered the highway, and the house was a large, two-story brick structure built in the 1990s. It was an attractive four-bedroom home with a finished basement and professional landscaping. But that was not the main reason Doug had purchased it. After a career of working in hostile locations and preparing hard targets and safehouses for special operations use, Doug was very particular as he selected a retirement location for his family. In a word, the property was defendable.

As the truck approached the house, Baxter laid his head down in the seat to retrieve his ball. Doug drove around the house to the rear, near the wooden deck extending off the dining room of the house. The deck was large and stood about three feet high, allowing for use when Wisconsin snow covered the ground. While the front of the house contained the formal entrance, the daily entrance the family used was the sliding glass door off the deck. The parking area offered access to the house as well as the three outbuildings on the property. It also allowed access to a drivable trail that extended around the perimeter of the property.

As Doug pulled the truck to a stop, he put it in park and looked over to the deck. Just as he expected, in one of the patio chairs, his wife Penny sat drinking a glass of iced tea while waiting for her husband to return home. Blake Shelton music played from a speaker inside the house, and she was gently tapping her bare foot to the beat of the music. Doug never tired of seeing his wife waiting for him when he returned home. This had been a common practice over their marriage, whether returning from military missions, patrol duty as a trooper, and now as a volunteer firefighter.

While Penny maintained a distinguished appearance, she did not look near her age of fifty years, nor did she resemble what Doug pictured in his head as a grandmother. Her five-foot-four-inch frame remained fit from regular workouts with Doug in their home gym, in addition to all the chores and maintaining their forty acres.

Doug couldn't help but smile as he saw her rifle propped up in the corner of the deck leaning against the house. Doug knew she gave him a hard time about keeping her rifle at the ready, but he also knew it was a comfort to her, even if she had to be difficult about it. That was just the way their relationship worked. While the couple owned more modern weapons, Penny felt most comfortable with her lever-action cowboy rifle. Doug had bought the Wisconsin-made Henry rifle for himself, but Penny laid claim to it soon after he brought it home. While the western-style rifle did not offer the performance or ammo capacity of Doug's modern AR-15, in the hands of a competent shooter like Penny, it was more than adequate for home defense.

Looking at her husband through the passenger-side window of his truck, Penny was smiling at him with a playful, seductive look on her face. Even after all these years, she still had a way of making him feel special without saying a word. As Penny watched her husband try to return a seductive look of his own, a goofy black-and-white dog head with a ball in his mouth popped up in the passenger window and blocked her view of him. The scene had perfect comedic timing and Baxter stole the show. Penny couldn't help but laugh out loud at the sight. She had always been a huge dog lover, and she had a void in her heart since they had to put down their golden retriever, Max, a few months earlier. They'd decided to hold off on getting another dog for a while to allow them time to travel following Doug's retirement.

Doug reached over and opened the passenger door, allowing Baxter to jump out and run up the deck to where Penny sat. In her excitement over the new dog, she forgot all about Doug for the moment. Stepping up onto the deck, he took a seat in a patio chair next to her. Baxter seemed right at home and soaked up all the attention Penny was giving him. Once the excitement of the greeting was complete, Baxter wandered around the area, exploring all the smells of his new home. Doug poured himself a glass of tea and filled Penny in on all that had happened that day as well as how the dog came to be in their lives.

Penny could tell the death of Farmer Schmidt weighed heavy on her husband's mind. While he never said so directly, she knew he felt the world was on his shoulders, which left him with a cross to bear for any perceived failures. While her husband was successful at everything he attempted, every success contains some measure of failure. His military missions were very successful in terms of the operational achievements, but he lost friends and subordinates in the process—most of them following orders that Doug had given. While the casualties were certainly not his fault, he struggled to make sense of it when he would return to his family while a friend did not.

Penny had mixed feelings about Doug's home office in their finished basement. The room contained a lifetime of memories in the form of photographs, medals, and personal mementos from his career. While Doug viewed the office as his safe space, a sanctuary where he could escape and reflect, she worried that some of the memories brought more pain than comfort to her husband. Penny was psychologically astute, having spent two decades assisting combat veterans and their families. She knew Doug would bear the responsibility for the Schmidt suicide; that was just his way.

"You have to look at things from a different perspective sometimes," said Penny.

Doug knew his wife was correct and that she was about to drop some wisdom on him. She had a unique perspective on things and had a special way of helping people reassess their view of situations. It both served as a mental distraction from the pain and also offered a unique insight most people overlooked.

Turning in her chair, she pulled her sunglasses down just enough to look over the top and make eye contact with him. "Instead of viewing the matter at the farm as a tragedy involving veteran suicide, try viewing it as a beautiful ending of a sixty-year love story. Much of the mental burdens you hold onto, Doug, are formed by your perception of a situation based on your experience. There are many different ways of looking at things."

"I know," said Doug, appreciating his wife's perspective as always. He added, "Is that how you look at it, the ending of a sixty-year love story?"

"It's one way. Without knowing all their circumstances, I will never understand what was in his mind at that point in time. But I can control my perception of what happened. I can choose to look at the beautiful aspect of it." Penny could see her husband was evaluating her words, so she continued, "But I also look at it in a different light than you do, as my personal experiences are different from yours. Based on my limited knowledge of the situation, I guess I prefer to view it through the eyes of that dog over there. I like to think Baxter was there to comfort them in their last days, and now God has put him in our lives for a reason. While I don't know what that reason is, having him here certainly does feel right."

"Well, I can't argue with that logic. There is something about that dog that brings me comfort also."

Doug was always appreciative of his wife's insight into things. He often felt like he did the world a disservice as the reason she chose to be a military wife rather than continue her education and become a psychologist. When they met, she was working on her doctorate and was interested in a career as a criminal profiler. Doug was giving a guest lecture at her university on the topic, as he had recently conducted an investigation on a serial killer. She asked him out for a drink afterward, and the two were married eight weeks later.

Their patio conversation was abruptly interrupted by a transmission from Doug's radio.

"Calumet County to Rockport firefighter Chapman."

Doug picked the hand-held radio off of the table and keyed the microphone. "Go for Rockport firefighter Chapman."

"Chapman, the sheriff is requesting you to come to the courthouse for a special briefing. Are you able to do that?"

"Roger that. It will take me about thirty minutes to get over to the courthouse in Chilton."

"10-4, I will advise Sheriff Decker you are on your way."

CHAPTER 8

After the firefighters washed the hoses, they worked as a team to put them back on the trucks for the next call. Jessie and Nick stood in the hose bed on top of the fire engine while Ryan and Vic lifted the hose up to them one section at a time. The hose needed to be staged in a specific manner so that it could be pulled off expediently.

Other firefighters worked on different tasks, such as refilling oxygen bottles and water tanks, recharging batteries, tightening chain saw blades, and refilling the portable generators. Lieutenant Lou Carter supervised the activity while Chief Peterson completed the incident report in his office.

The department consisted of twenty volunteers: three officer positions and seventeen firefighters. Brad was the fire chief, and Doug's son-in-law, Mark, was the second in command, with the rank of captain. Even though he was younger than many of the firefighters, his nine years of full-time service between the Air Force and the Milwaukee Fire Department made him the most experienced by far. The third in command, with the rank of lieutenant, was Lou Carter. At sixty years old, Lou had been on the department for thirty-nine years, longer than most of the crew had been alive. He had so much local knowledge that he was an invaluable asset to the department. Having served as a lieutenant for the past twenty years, most people in town thought he was called "Lou" as an abbreviation for Lieutenant and were often surprised to learn Lou was also his first name.

Brad was having some difficulty wrapping up the fire report as he still had not heard from the state arson investigator. Now both his cell phone and landlines were out, and he just learned the internet was inaccessible too. That was concerning, and he feared the worst. His buddy Doug had been preparing for a collapse of society since they met years ago. While he made a compelling argument, Brad didn't think he would see it in his lifetime. Nonetheless, as things gradually worsened, Brad started to prep as well, but he had to do it on the down low as his wife didn't approve.

Hearing a knock on the office door, he looked up as Lou walked in and took a seat in the empty chair across from his desk.

"The guys are done, so I dismissed them."

Doug nodded his head and said, "Nice work today."

"How much longer do you think the county radio will continue to work?" asked Lou.

"I have no idea."

"How are people going to be able to call for assistance if the phones are out?"

"No idea about that either. I guess we will wait a day or two and see if they come back on. If not, we will need to figure something out."

Lou thought about the situation as he brushed his fingers over the bushy, oversize mustache that completed his stereotypical firefighter look. "What are you going to do about Tucker and the gas?"

The frustrated look reappeared on the chief's face. "I guess I need to go talk to the town board."

"Good luck with that," Lou said with a smirk.

When Brad left the firehouse, he decided to run home and take a fast shower before trying to speak to the board members. He wanted to present a more professional image than Tucker had. As he drove the Suburban down the county highway toward his home, he passed the access road to Doug's house. Now that the collapse seemed to be imminent, he wished he had listened to his friend and started preparing years earlier. Brad's property was the next one down the highway, but it was designed to entertain and hold social gatherings, not survive an apocalypse.

Pulling into his driveway leading up a small hill to his upscale house, Brad remembered when they had it built. Kimberly's grandfather had passed away and left a sizable amount of money to her in his will. While they were not rich, the amount was equivalent to about ten years of his salary as a local high school teacher. That could have bought a very comfortable home in Rockport and still left a couple hundred thousand dollars in reserve, but Kimberly opted to go big. After upgrading the countertops and opting for the high-end doors and fixtures, they still needed to take out a small mortgage on the house. Brad didn't say anything as the money was a gift to her, however, in hindsight, he wished his home was concealed in the trees and defendable like Doug's.

As he walked into his house, he could hear the television in the living room. Walking in from the entryway, he saw Kimberly sitting on the floor doing a Pilates workout, following along with a DVD. Wearing yoga pants and a tank top, his 45-year-old wife seemed even more attractive to him than the day he met her.

Smiling at his wife, he asked, "Not using your Peloton bike today?"

"No, the internet is out so I couldn't log on. The phones are out too."

Brad sat down on the sofa while his wife continued her workout.

"Yeah, they are out all over the place. I'm starting to think the collapse is happening."

Kimberly rolled her eyes and said, "The sky is not falling, Chicken Little. I'm sure the phones will be back on any time now."

"I'm not so sure about that."

"I know there is a lot going on right now, but I'm sure it will all blow over soon enough. I don't need you going all Doug on me."

Not knowing how to respond to his wife, he opted to avoid the conversation as he usually did.

"I'm going to take a fast shower then head back into town. I need to have a chat with the town board."

"OK. Can you bring home something for dinner?"

"Kimberly, I told you two days ago, all the food places are closed."

"Still?" she asked.

Brad just walked upstairs, not answering his wife. He took a fast shower and put on clean clothes. He then entered a large walk-in closet, reached up to a top shelf, and pulled down a silver pistol safe. Opening it, he pulled out a Springfield 1911 pistol and two spare magazines loaded with .45 ACP. Ensuring the pistol was loaded, he secured it in an inside-the-waistband holster and pulled his shirt over it, concealing it from view. Although his wife was in denial, Brad knew things would be getting far worse, even in the little quiet town of Rockport.

CHAPTER 9

Doug was growing more concerned by the minute. With the phones out and the county dispatch not being able to get ahold of anyone at the Department of Justice, things were starting to seem dire. It was highly unusual for Doug to be requested via radio to go to the courthouse and meet with the sheriff, but the two were old friends. Sheriff Wes Decker had served with Doug as a state trooper, and both were members of the SWAT team. Wes retired from the state patrol the year prior to Doug when he was elected as the sheriff of Calumet County. Doug didn't know what Wes wanted to speak with him about, but he was sure it wasn't going to be good news.

As Doug prepared for the drive to Chilton, he didn't plan on taking any chances. Pulling up the right side of his untucked flannel shirt, he drew the Glock 9mm pistol that was concealed underneath. Grasping the top of the slide with his left hand, he pulled the slide back just enough to verify that a round was chambered and it was prepared to fire if needed. Doug had performed this "press check" prior to every shift for thirty years. He re-holstered the weapon and felt his left hip to ensure his spare magazine was secure in its pouch, also concealed under his shirt. Doug had carried a pistol daily during his service and had no intention of stopping after retirement. As somebody with the status of qualified retired law enforcement officer (QRLEO), Doug was issued retired credentials that allowed him to carry his pistol nationwide. While the QRLEO credentials and his retired badge authorized him to carry his weapon concealed, it did not bestow any active law enforcement authority.

Due to the uncertainty of the situation, Doug decided to bring a little more firepower for the road trip just in case. He walked through the large master bedroom and into the closet. Inside was a biometric gun safe with an electronic fingerprint identification lock. While Doug kept the majority of his firearms unloaded in the basement safe, the guns he kept ready and loaded for emergencies were in the smaller closet safe for fast access. The closet safe held four long guns and two handguns. The safe could be rapidly accessed by a fingerprint by all four members of his family. After entering his fingerprint and opening the steel door to the safe, Doug looked inside. He observed two empty spaces that normally stored the Glock that was in his holster and Penny's trusty rifle. Still inside the safe was Penny's Glock 19 as well as the AR-15 he had built specifically for her. He was still amused that she opted for the lever-action over the semi-automatic rifle. The safe also contained Doug's AR-15 and a Benelli M1 tactical shotgun.

He reached inside the safe and pulled out his AR-15. The rifle was a custom built by Bravo Company USA in Hartland, Wisconsin. The carbine had a tactical light mounted on the foregrip and was topped off with a Vortex 1-6 power scope. This allowed Doug to engage targets at very close range on 1 power as well as distances well past 400 yards on 6 power. Doug and his son-in-law had the exact same rifle setup and often trained together on the range they'd built on the property. Doug picked up the rifle and removed the magazine to verify it was loaded. After ensuring it was, he reinserted it and chambered a live round. He placed the weapon on safe and slung the rifle across his body. The weapon now hung hands-free in front of his torso, ready for rapid access.

Doug closed and locked the safe, then reached down and picked up a set of body armor from the floor of the closet. The black tactical vest contained two ceramic plates located inside the front and back panels. The level III+ plates were capable of stopping rifle ammunition up to the powerful .30-06 caliber. The front of the vest additionally contained two ammo pouches that held spare AR-15 magazines, an individual first aid kit (IFAK), and a radio pouch. The upper chest and back portions of the vest were covered in Velcro, and affixed to it were large patches with the words "STATE TROOPER" in white letters. Now that he was retired, Doug pulled the Velcro Trooper patches off the vest and placed them on top of the safe.

As Doug walked through the house with the rifle slung and the body armor in his hand, he said goodbye to Penny and Baxter, who were sitting on the floor playing. While most wives might have found this situation some-what alarming, to Penny it was just business as usual. After thirty years of this lifestyle, she knew what threats existed. The rifle and body armor were just tools of the trade that helped keep her husband safe. To her they were just PPE—personal protective equipment—for his profession, the same as turnout gear for a firefighter or a surgical mask for a doctor.

"Love you," said Penny. She always said that rather than "be careful." It was her way of letting him know how she felt rather than warn him of poten-tial danger that he obviously knew existed.

"Love you too," he said to Penny as he bent down to give Baxter a fast pat on the head. Baxter then rolled onto his back, indicating he also wanted his belly scratched.

"No time for that, boy. I need to go." Penny was happy to take over the responsibility of scratching Baxter's belly while Doug stood up and adjusted his gear.

"Doug, on the way back can you please stop in and check on Maddy?" asked Penny. "Maybe see if you can get her to come home to stay until Mark gets back, especially now that the phones are out."

"I already planned to," replied Doug. "It will certainly be better having us all in one place until things settle down. I'm going to close and lock the gate to our access road on my way out. Be sure and keep your rifle handy."

"I will," she replied with an exaggerated eye roll and a fake tone of annoyance.

Doug climbed into the Ram and placed the body armor and rifle on the floorboard of the passenger seat. He pulled the truck around to the side of one of the outbuildings next to an aboveground fuel tank that held 550 gallons. In foresight of a collapse, he had it installed two years earlier. While Penny complained about the expense at the time, now that the price of fuel had quadrupled, she recalled the wise purchase being her idea. As he topped off the fuel tank, he conducted a walk-around to check the tires before leaving on his journey. Once the vehicle and gear were ready for the trip, he started it back up and drove down the winding driveway through the gate to his property. He got out of his truck at that point and closed the heavy metal swinging gate behind him. After locking it, he pulled onto the county highway and drove toward Chilton to see what the sheriff had in store for him.

The route Doug took was mostly through back country roads and farmland. He passed more than one abandoned vehicle along the side of the road, presumably out of gas. Just outside the small town of Stockbridge, Doug came upon a farmer and his son standing next to a tractor on the side of the road. Doug recognized the farmer as a member of the Stockbridge volunteer fire department. What was unusual about the situation was that the farmer had a hunting rifle slung over his shoulder, and his son had a shotgun resting against the parked tractor. They gave Doug a friendly wave, so he pulled up alongside them.

"Morning, Tom. What are you hunting this time of year?"

"Good morning, Trooper Chapman," said the farmer, faking a serious tone. "We aren't hunting nothing, just thought it was a good idea to have some security these days, that's all."

"I figured," replied Doug. "I was just kidding about the hunting. And I retired from the state patrol a few months back."

"You still with the Rockport Fire Department?"

"Yeah, I'm still doing that. What crop are you harvesting?"

"Green beans. But I'm not sure what I am going to do with them all. The vendor I usually sell to just went belly up. Now I can't even call any other place because the phones are out."

"Well, I'm sure you will find plenty of hungry folks around these parts pretty soon. You may want to start finding something to barter for with your neighbors."

"I was thinking the same thing. It's just bad luck, I guess," he said.

"My wife would tell you that's just a matter of perspective. Your biggest problem is about to be having too much food on your hands. I imagine most folks will be having the opposite problem before too much longer."

"Well, when you put it that way, maybe it isn't all that bad after all."

"Maybe not," said Doug as he drove off, continuing on his way to see the sheriff.

As the town of Chilton came into view, things felt odd there as well. For a nice summer day, there was almost no one outside. The city of Chilton, with a population of four thousand, was almost four times the size of Rockport, yet it was still a relatively small town. Interestingly, the first resident of Chilton was a formerly enslaved African American named Moses Stanton and his Native American wife in 1845. The city was formed around a sawmill and originally named Stantonville. When it became the county seat in 1853, the name was changed to Chilington. Unfortunately, the notation documenting the change was mistakenly missing the "ing," and it was recorded officially as Chilton.

Doug drove through the town toward the brick courthouse that was connected to the jail and sheriff's department. Doug parked his Ram in the parking lot and walked into the reception area, where the front-desk clerk sat behind bulletproof glass. As he greeted the young receptionist, it was apparent she had been crying and seemed disheveled. Recognizing him from his former trooper days, she stated the sheriff was waiting for him and buzzed the door, allowing him to enter the secure portion of the department.

"The sheriff is in his office," she said, trying not to make eye contact in a futile attempt to hide her tears.

As Doug walked down the hall toward Wes's office, he could hear a different woman crying in a cubical off to the side. Having made death notifications several times over his career, Doug feared the worst. He came to the sheriff's office at the end of the hall and stood in the open doorway of his friend and former SWAT partner. As the two made eye contact, the look in Wes's eyes conveyed to Doug that his friend had lost someone under his command. Wes, sitting behind his desk, looked like he had been through a ringer. He appeared completely fatigued and his uniform was wrinkled and disheveled, not a common trait from a former state trooper.

"What happened, and what can I do to help?" asked Doug.

The sheriff sighed. "I'm not even sure I know where to begin. I certainly don't have all the answers or fully understand what's going on myself. Fear and panic have taken over, and crime is spiking like I have never seen. With the damn phones and internet going out today, people are even more scared than before."

Doug knew there were issues with the phones, but this was the first he had heard about the internet. He had been busy at the fire all day and hadn't tried to go online since earlier that morning. The loss of both phone service and internet access caused Doug to fear involvement from a powerful nation-state adversary such as Russia or China. He wondered if it was some sort of cyberattack, electromagnetic pulse, or maybe even an attack on US satellites. Perhaps it was reprisal for the United States entering into the wars overseas.

The sheriff continued, "This morning I had four deputies and a corrections officer killed. Another corrections officer was badly wounded. While we are still trying to figure it all out, this is what I think happened. Since all the civil unrest down south, the outlaw motorcycle gangs in Milwaukee have been having turf wars. A smaller gang, the Dark Arrows MC, was forced out, and they relocated up in the village of Harrison in the northern part of the county. They have spent the past few days intimidating folks in the area and shaking them down for their possessions. Last night my deputies were able to take the gang's leader, Ty Wilcox, into custody for a series of violations—robbery, assault, resisting arrest, felon in possession of a firearm, parole violation, and so on. The other members of the gang were not too happy about that."

"I bet not," replied Doug.

After a pause, the sheriff continued, "This morning we got a report of a missing, diabetic five-year-old girl at High Cliff State Park, in the far northern part of the county between Rockport and Harrison. My deputies went up to conduct a search-and-rescue operation. When they met up at the cliff where she was last seen, they got out of their squads and started reviewing a map to establish search patterns. At that point they were ambushed by multiple gunmen from concealed locations. They never had a chance."

"How many deputies?

"Four," replied Wes. "Three deputies and the day watch sergeant."

"Which ones?" asked Doug. He had worked and socialized with many of the deputies as a trooper.

"Miller, Olsen, Wagner, and Sergeant Weber."

Doug let out a long breath as he tried to picture each of the brave lawmen.

"Wasn't Olsen expecting a child soon?"

"Yeah, his wife Sarah is about eight months pregnant."

"You notify her yet?" asked Doug.

"Yeah," replied Wes, as he looked down, breaking eye contact.

Doug could see the pain in his eyes and knew firsthand what he was going through. He wished he possessed some of the skills Penny had so he would know what to say at times such as this. He opted to do what most men do and just nodded in understanding.

"What happened to the Corrections Officers?" asked Doug.

Wes took in a deep breath then exhaled. "I think the ambush was a diversion to split our resources. The gang leader was being arraigned in court this morning at the exact same time as the ambush. During the proceedings, several heavily armed gang members broke him out of the courtroom, and Corrections Officer Bob Drexel was shot and killed. Corrections Officer Cindy Doyle was shot in the stomach and arm."

"What's her condition?" asked Doug with a look of great concern.

"Do you know Cindy?"

"Yeah, she's a friend of my daughter, Maddy. They went to the university together.

"I didn't know that. Her injuries were significant. She was shot with an AK-47, and one round shattered the bone in her left upper arm. I'm not sure if the brachial artery was severed or not, but it was bleeding profusely. I put the tourniquet on her myself. The other round penetrated the soft body armor she was wearing under her uniform shirt. While it was designed to stop handgun ammunition, the high-velocity rifle round easily punched through it. God only knows what damage that bullet did inside."

Wes paused, then continued. "We got her to the small hospital here in town, where they stabilized her. After that they sent her up to Appleton by ambulance for surgery. With the phones out, I haven't been able to get an update on her status. I sure don't want to lose another one of my team today."

Doug could see Wes start to get emotional, so he changed the subject. "What makes you think the ambush in the state park was a diversion? Just the timing?"

"No. We got at least one lucky break today. There were at least five gunmen who ambushed my boys. The attackers rode motorcycles and wore the gangs' cuts on their leather vests. After they killed my deputies, they came out of their concealed locations to loot the dead. But the gang didn't anticipate a Wisconsin DNR conservation warden to also respond to the search-and-rescue call," explained Wes, referring to the Department of Natural Resources. "The warden drove in on a back trail and didn't enter the ambush zone the gang set up. He arrived moments after the ambush and got the jump on the gang after they exposed themselves. He was pretty handy with his patrol rifle, killed two and likely wounded a third. The survivors fled on their bikes and didn't get any of my officer's gear."

"Who was the game warden?" asked Doug, using the common name for the DNR conservation warden.

"It's a new kid, just graduated from the DNR academy a couple weeks back. I think his name is Scott Connelly. Can't be more than twenty-three or twenty-four years old." Wes changed subjects. "Now here is the situation I need your help with. As sheriff of the county, I am responsible for the safety of over fifty-two thousand citizens spanning 324 square miles. When fully staffed, I have twenty-six deputies. With the losses from today, the preexisting vacancies, and a number of unplanned retirements and resignations, I only have ten deputies left for the entire county. I have very limited fuel for them to patrol with, and most people can't even call us for help without operational phones."

"What about state resources?" asked Doug.

"Well, the governor issued an emergency order directing the vast majority of state resources down to the bigger cities of Madison and Milwaukee about a week ago. The civil unrest was out of hand, and the local law enforcement agencies were overwhelmed. The state patrol, DNR, and University of Wisconsin police departments sent most of their officers down south to help out in the urban areas. The Department of Justice was providing all the sheriffs an intelligence update every morning over the last week. It was like a war zone down there. Two days ago, I stopped getting intel briefings. Now I can't even call or email them.

"Doug, I need to deputize you. I need you to serve as the regional deputy sheriff for Rockport and the nearby areas. You have the expertise, experience, and character to succeed. I will grant you the full authority to keep the peace any way you see fit. Things as we have known them are changing rapidly. You will need to be creative and find the best way to serve and protect your community. While I'm sure you have plenty of questions, I don't have any answers for you. We are taking this one day at a time, and I sure as hell hope I can count on you."

"You know I can't say no under these circumstances," said Doug.

"I was hoping you would see it that way," replied the sheriff.

"What are you going to do with your jail inmates?"

"Well, I just don't have the staff to watch them now, and even if I did, I don't have the means to feed them much longer. Later today I plan on releasing all but the most dangerous prisoners. I know that will make your job in the field all that much harder, but I have no other choice. There are about seven or eight prisoners I will need to keep locked up. I can't house any more than that."

"What about that motorcycle gang?"

"It kills me not to go after them, but that's just not the responsible thing to do right now. If it were the old west, I would form a posse and we would go hunt them down. Give them justice at the end of a rope. If you come across them, do what you think is right. I fully trust your judgment. You understand the intent of the law better than any man I know. But, as you well know, many of the modern-day criminal statutes are completely reliant on modern-day technologies and capabilities. You may have to find a way to police your region like it was two hundred years ago. Be creative, and be just."

"I will need support. Can I form a posse for my area?" asked Doug,

"Sure, but just make sure they work under your direction. I am giving you my full authority to oversee all law enforcement matters in your region. You will serve as the Calumet County representative for Rockport."

"Do you have any extra resources available for me to take back?" asked Doug.

"What do you need?"

"Well, I plan on making the volunteer fire department my posse. That way we can work as a public safety department and provide fire, law enforcement, and emergency medical response to the community. I could use a way to identify them as law enforcement. Do you have any extra badges, raid jackets, or Velcro sheriff patches? That sort of thing," asked Doug.

"That's a great idea, Doug! Let me see what I have," said the sheriff as he stood up and walked out of the room.

While Wes was out of the room gathering supplies, Doug stood and looked at the wall in his office. In a matted frame on the wall was the Wisconsin State Patrol Meritorious Service Medal with a green, white, and blue ribbon. Doug remembered when Wes was presented the award as well as when he earned it. They were working a SWAT assignment assisting DCI special agents with a high-risk warrant, hoping to rescue a kidnapped six-year-old girl. When the tactical entry team breached the front door, they were fired upon immediately by the kidnapper. Wes was on point and took a grazing round to the helmet, leaving a nasty gash in the Kevlar. Unfazed by the blow to the head, Wes returned lethal fire, killing the suspect instantly. While Wes was taking out the shooter, Doug was clearing the basement and recovered the lifeless body of the small child. Her innocent life had been taken just a few hours earlier. The hell she no doubt experienced prior to her slow death would stay in Doug's memory for the rest of his life. He had seen firsthand the kind of evil that exists in the world, and he knew, as civilization collapsed around him, the worst was yet to come.

Wes walked back into the office and saw Doug looking at the medal on the wall. He knew exactly what Doug was reliving in his mind. Not knowing what to say, he redirected Doug's attention to the three boxes of supplies sitting on the red dolly just outside his office.

"This is what I can spare. It's not a lot, but at least it will give you a start."

Wes then placed a silver, seven-pointed star on the desk. The center of the badge had the Wisconsin state seal. Above the seal had the words "Deputy Sheriff," and below had "Calumet County." "I don't have a bunch of these, so I will give this one to you as my regional deputy." He then sat an old cardboard box on the desk and opened it up, revealing a pile of obsolete badges. "These have been sitting in the filing cabinet for probably thirty years or more. These were the previous badges worn by the deputies before we switched to the star badge, probably sometime in the 1970s or '80s, I suspect. The old badges were a silver shield with an eagle on top and very much resembled the typical Wisconsin firefighter badges most departments used. I think these will suffice for your posse members."

"These will work just fine," said Doug.

Doug picked up the star badge and looked down at it resting in his hand. After thirty years, he thought his lawman days were behind him. The future would be hard enough trying to take care of his own family. Having to look after another thirteen hundred residents of Rockport in these uncertain times would be far more challenging.

Doug left the sheriff alone so he could deal with the burdens of leadership. He had a grieving team that needed to be consoled. Moreover, he had the insurmountable task of keeping the peace across the entire county. While Doug wasn't sure how he would manage the task before him, he did know one thing. He was glad he was not the sheriff of Calumet County.

CHAPTER 10

As gunshots rang out in the distance, Mark wanted to get out of Milwaukee as soon as possible. Putting his Tacoma into drive, he pulled out of Milwaukee Fire Station 23 for the very last time. He turned east onto West Greenfield Avenue and drove in the direction of Interstate 43, which would take him north, out of the city. As part of his prepper mindset, he always filled up his fuel tank when he arrived in Milwaukee so he would not need to stop for gas if he had to make the two-hour commute home during an emergency. As he approached the on-ramp to the interstate, he observed several abandoned cars along the side of the ramp. This was concerning; however, he was already committed as he accelerated up the on-ramp, so he did not stop. As he neared the top of the ramp, he could now see around the blind corner. Blocking the path was a black-and-white Milwaukee police car, parked perpendicular to the road in a hasty checkpoint. Being a firefighter for almost a decade, Mark had a fundamental understanding of how police conduct traffic control, especially on highways, and this vehicle placement was highly suspicious. The police never blocked a road perpendicular to the lane of travel, and they certainly would not block an on-ramp at the top around a blind corner. The fact that the red-and-blue emergency lights were not activated was an additional clue that something was out of the ordinary. In fact, something was very wrong.

As the Tacoma closed the distance to the squad car, Mark could see that the rear window of the police car had been broken out. He slowed the truck in preparation to reverse back down the on-ramp. As he decelerated before getting too close to the squad car, two armed men popped up from a concealed area behind one of the abandoned cars on the shoulder of the on-ramp. The men, who were obviously not police officers, pointed weapons at Mark while running toward his truck.

The ruse with the police car was intended to bring travelers to a stop, where they could be ambushed for a carjacking or robbery. The fact that Mark didn't pull all the way into the ambush zone caught the men off guard, and they ran down the on-ramp toward him in an attempt to prevent their target from escaping.

Rather than stop the truck to reverse out, Mark used the forward momentum of the slowing vehicle to his advantage and accelerated again. This caught the men off guard once more as they had not anticipated that response. As the would-be robbers separated from each other, Mark kept the front of his truck pointed at the man closest to the parked squad car. Ducking down in the seat as much as possible when the men started shooting, he wanted to get his body behind the engine block for cover. Mark felt the truck impact what had to be one of the men just as he heard his passenger side windows explode, showering him with broken glass. He immediately looked up and directed his truck to ram the rear quarter panel of the police car blocking his path.

Mark had previously discussed this sort of tactic with his father-in-law. Doug had conducted antiterrorism operations all over the world, and vehicle operation in a high-threat area was a trained tactic. His advice when ramming a fake checkpoint was to aim the front of your vehicle at the rear quarter panel of the car that was blocking the path. This was because the trunk compartment was typically far lighter in weight than the engine compartment. The lighter trunk area would be much easier to move. By ramming the rear of the car at an angle, the glancing blow often made the rear tires break contact with the ground, which allowed the blocking car to be spun out of the way. Doug said it was important to keep accelerating through the vehicle strike.

As Mark's truck made impact with the rear quarter panel of the stolen squad car, it spun out of the way just as Doug said it would.

The next thing Mark noticed was the impact of being struck in the face just before his truck veered left and hit the retaining wall head on. Not sure what happened, Mark looked over his left shoulder through the driver's side window. He could see one of the men lying in the road and the second man advancing on him, shooting wildly. Mark could hear and feel the rounds impacting the side of his truck. From the stationary Tacoma, Mark drew the Glock 19 from its holster and aimed at the existing threat. As he squeezed off several rounds from inside the truck cab, the concussion from the pistol blast was surprising. His bullets shattered his driver's side window as they passed through it before striking the assailant, who was now only a few yards away. With his ears ringing from the concussion of his shots, Mark opened his door and attempted to exit the truck, but his seat belt had tightened due to the accident. Mark reached across his body with his left hand and released the belt mechanism while keeping his weapon pointed at the threat. As he exited the truck, he kept his weapon trained on the men, both of them now on the ground. He made sure to move at a tactical angle to keep his eyes on the downed men.

While it appeared that both of the men had been incapacitated, Mark felt it was not in his best interest under the circumstances to approach them. He returned to his vehicle to see if it was still operational. It was at this point that he noticed his front airbag had deployed when he rammed the police car. That's what struck him in the face and caused him to veer into the retaining wall. After seeing this, Mark recalled Doug warning him about airbag deployments and told him to turn his head to the side when ramming another vehicle. Glancing under the truck to look for leaking fluids, he didn't see any; however, he did notice several drops of blood hitting the ground at his feet. He then conducted a rapid medical assessment on himself to check for injuries. Not finding any obvious bullet wounds, the only injury seemed to be a swollen and bloody nose from the air bag. Rather than get some bandages out of the medical kit, he felt it was wiser to get back on the road and put some distance between himself and the ambush scene.

The front of the truck didn't look as bad as he'd anticipated. After hitting the police car, it probably slowed to just a few miles per hour before making impact with the wall. Mark pulled a Benchmade knife from his left pocket and snapped the blade open. He cut the deflated airbag out of his steering column and tossed it onto the ground so he could continue with the journey. Securing the knife back in his pocket, he then pulled the Glock from its holster. Leaving the bullet in the chamber, he removed his magazine and replaced it with his fully loaded spare. He then re-holstered his pistol and placed the partially loaded mag back in its pouch, this time facing rearward as an indication it was no longer fully loaded.

As Mark reentered his truck, he said a fast prayer that it would start. He then placed the vehicle in park as it was still in drive from before the accident. He was both surprised and thankful when it started right up. Backing the truck up, he turned the wheel, directing his vehicle back up the highway, and continued his journey.

Mark wanted to get off of the highway as soon as possible, but until he was out of urban Milwaukee, he felt the highway was his best option. It was eerie that there was no traffic on the road since just a few days earlier, the I-43 north was deadlocked with cars as people fought to get out of the city. But today, it appeared that everyone who could get out had done so, and rest were apparently sheltering in place.

Mark had to slow his truck to a crawl at many points to avoid random cars abandoned on the highway. It was difficult to differentiate if the cars were part of a potential ambush, had run out of gas, or had simply crashed. Some of the vehicles had been completely burned out, while others contained the corpses of the occupants. Along the route, he saw dead bodies lying on the pavement. It was hard to believe the images he was seeing were on a highway in the Midwest United States.

After two hours, Mark had finally made his way through the heavily urban area. He was having a hard time deciding if he should continue on the interstate or transition to surface streets. Now that he was out of the city, surface streets would be safer but a far less direct route. It would add hours to his trip, and he was completely exhausted and without food and water.

Glancing at his iPhone, Mark realized he could not access his GPS. That made the decision easier, and he chose to stay on the interstate until he got closer to home and was more familiar with the local geography.

CHAPTER 11

As Doug walked out of the sheriff's office, his mind was spinning. His thoughts had been preoccupied for weeks on how to provide for his family along with serving his community as a volunteer firefighter. Now he had to figure out how to provide law enforcement as well in a time of unprecedented danger. How would people contact him for assistance without phones or internet? How would he patrol his region and respond to matters with limited fuel? It was like he was a sheriff back in the old west, except he didn't have a horse.

With the system collapsing, what would he do with a person that he had to arrest? With the limited court system, who would decide on matters of law? All of these challenges seemed insurmountable and would require much thought.

Doug pushed the dolly holding the three boxes of supplies out to his truck and opened the door to the back seat. Inside was the wood box from the Schmidt Farm. He had intended to turn it over to the sheriff or state arson investigator for a proper investigation. That seemed like a lesser priority now, with all that was happening in the world. Regardless, as the new law enforcement officer for Rockport, it would now fall to him to investigate anyway. When time would allow, he would look into the arson just to close the book on the case. It was important to Doug that the human remains be recovered from the fire scene. They deserved a dignified burial and Mr. Schmidt was a veteran who had served his country. He was deserving of a few words for that alone.

As he drove out of Chilton, he took a different route back to Rockport to refresh himself with the various farms and properties in the area. He wanted to assess which citizens may need more assistance and which ones may be in a position to help their neighbors. At a time like this, responsibility would fall back to individuals to provide for themselves and each other. Families, neighbors, and churches would once again serve a primary role in a stable community. Over the past few decades, Americans seemed to have abandoned these principles in favor of a government-provided security blanket. Now that the system was collapsing, it would be challenging to revert back to the "good neighbor" philosophy.

Doug switched his thoughts to his daughter Maddy. She was strong, independent, and much like him in many ways. The quick-witted high school teacher could certainly handle herself, but times were not normal, and everyone needed support from those around them. While Doug had routinely checked in on his daughter, his concern grew more dire as Mark was working in Milwaukee. Now that communications were out, Doug knew it was time for her to move back home until things settled down. One of his worries was that his pregnant daughter might try to travel down to Milwaukee to check on her husband. While she was scrappy and could handle herself, Doug knew her confidence level far exceeded her actual abilities. His other concern was that Maddy, like her mother, was stubborn beyond reason. He was worried that he might not be able to convince her to move back home with him. If he couldn't convince her, it was just as likely his wife Penny would take her rifle and go stay with Maddy until Mark returned.

As Doug traveled the back farm roads, he saw very little vehicle traffic. He assumed people were staying home to conserve fuel. He thought about all the differences between urban living and rural life. Rural people were far more self-sufficient and better prepared for a situation such as this. They knew how to use hand tools, farm the land, hunt and fish for food. They were used to planning ahead for the harsh Wisconsin winters, but most of all, they were resilient. Doug hoped that small-town America would be able to pull through the bad times ahead. He knew he would play a key role in helping his town to survive.

As Doug drove through the center of Rockport, he stopped at the stop sign near the fire station. He saw Brad walking out of the building and toward his Suburban in the parking lot. Doug pulled into the lot, and Brad walked up to his open driver's side window. Doug could see the annoyed look on the chief's face as he approached. He assumed Brad had been dealing with the town board about Tucker and the fuel situation.

"So, what did the good sheriff want with you?" asked Brad.

Doug filled him in on the details of what he learned in Chilton and the plan he formulated while driving back. While Brad was overwhelmed with all the news, he couldn't argue with the logic of Doug's plan. They would need to get the town board's cooperation, or at least push them in the right direction. Once they got that, they would need to talk with the firefighters. Both men were confident the majority would agree to serve on the sheriff's posse.

"So, how soon can we meet with the board?" asked Doug.

"I had a very hard time trying to communicate with all five board members individually without the use of a phone or email, so I set up an in-person meeting for tomorrow at 11 a.m. It will be at the town hall to discuss how to move forward as a community. You can present your plan at that time."

"That sounds good. Can you also contact the guys and set up a meeting with all the firefighters later in the day, say 3 p.m. at the station?"

"Yeah, that's a good idea," replied Brad.

"Good. Also, you can bring the guys pulling scene security at the Schmidt Farm back. I will get to that when I have a chance, but there is no reason to leave them out there. We have bigger things to worry about."

"Roger that," replied Brad.

"Sounds good. See you tomorrow."

As Doug drove away from the fire station toward Maddy's house, he tried to formulate a plan to talk her into returning home. As he turned onto her street, he expected to see her Jeep Wrangler parked in the driveway, but it was not there. Doug pulled into the empty drive and walked up to the front door. Taped to the door, inside the screen, was a piece of folded paper. Opening the note, he saw that it was a letter from Maddy to Mark in case he came home. It said she had gone to stay at her parents' place and to meet her there.

Well, that was easier than expected, thought Doug with a smirk. Maybe now that she was pregnant, she was starting to view things through the eyes of a parent. Regardless, Doug was relieved that she came to the most logical conclusion on her own and didn't allow her stubborn nature to drive her actions.

As Doug left town to return to his property, he once again took mental stock of the things he would need to do around the property. They were already in a good position as Doug had selected the property with this very scenario in mind. The property was off the beaten path and not visible from the roadway. There were only two access points: the main drive from the county highway and a small dirt road leading from the back of the forty-acre plot onto a network of unnamed farm trails between neighboring properties. The land had a freshwater well, a large chicken coop, several outbuildings, some solar panels, a pond, fruit trees, and several acres that could be used for gardening.

Doug was able to anticipate that things were reaching a breaking point weeks earlier than most, so he had started stocking up necessary supplies. After cashing in his retirement investments, he and Penny made several trips up to the Costco in Appleton to buy items such as food, batteries, and hygiene goods. Expecting a baby, they also stocked up on a supply of diapers, wipes, and formula. One of the outbuildings was filled with shelving units and held all the supplies. Doug had two large propane tanks installed on the property to provide fuel for heating and cooking. All in all, the family was ready to survive for several months, if not indefinitely.

As Doug turned off the highway onto the access road leading through the woods to his gate, he took a moment to reevaluate the entry-control setup. At present there was a heavy metal gate that swung out, blocking the roadway. There was a sign on the gate indicating private property. Only five people had a key to the lock: the four members of the family and Brad. About fifteen yards outside the gate sat an electric eye sensor that would ring a buzzer inside the home, letting the occupants know someone was entering the property. If the gate was closed, the buzzer would alert them that someone was at the gate. Doug felt the security measures would suffice for now, but he made mental notes as to how he could enhance security if the situation escalated.

After unlocking the padlock and pulling his truck through, he secured the gate behind him. He followed the path around the blind corner concealed by trees, and his house came into view. He was relieved to see Maddy's Wrangler parked outside. Parking alongside the Jeep, he retrieved his rifle from the seat next to him and got out. Walking up the deck and entering the house, he found his girls relaxing in the living room. Penny was on the couch while Maddy sat on the floor playing with Baxter. This warmed Doug's heart as his mind was taken back to an earlier time when his daughter was little. He was also amazed at how easily Baxter just fit into his family. It was like he always belonged, even though he had only been in their lives a few short hours.

Doug leaned his rifle against the wall near his recliner and sat down facing the family. He couldn't help but notice Penny's rifle resting in the opposite corner, next to an AR-15 with pink accents. Doug and Mark built that AR for Maddy a few years earlier so she could participate in the three-gun competitions they held on the property with some of the firefighters. Doug was pleased to see that his daughter recognized the need for personal defense and took it upon herself to arm. He feared she would think he was overreacting, just as daughters have perceived their overprotective fathers for generations. Maddy made eye contact with her father as he looked at her rifle resting against the wall. She was waiting for him to make a comment and, as always, had a witty response ready to go. When Doug made eye contact with her, he knew she was waiting for him to say something. Not giving her the satisfaction, he just smiled and nodded. Maddy smiled back. The two were very close and could communicate just as well with their eyes and facial expressions as they could with words.

Doug switched gears and started to fill them in on what he had learned from the sheriff. As he told them about the four deputies who were killed at

High Cliff State Park, he could see the emotion in their eyes. While for many people, hearing about the death of cops was just a statistic on the news, to a police family it was a personal tragedy. He then told them about the jailbreak and the dead and wounded correction officers.

He could see the concern on his daughter's face about her college friend who worked in the jail.

"Was Cindy there when it happened?"

"Yes, she was badly injured. They took her to Appleton for surgery, but without phone communications, I wasn't able to find out her condition. As soon as I hear something more, I will let you know."

Doug paused while his daughter processed the information.

Seeing that her daughter was getting emotional from the news, Penny redirected the conversation and asked, "So, Wes had you drive to Chilton just to give you a status report for old times' sake?"

"Well, not exactly," said Doug.

Giving her husband a look that he knew all too well, she asked, "Do you have another badge somewhere on your person?"

Not knowing how to respond to her, Doug reached into the pocket of his flannel shirt and pulled out the seven-pointed silver star.

Not surprised at all, Penny asked, "And how much does this new position pay?"

Smiling at her, he said, "The love and admiration of my wife and daughter is all the compensation I need."

"And you are going to do this all by yourself?

"Not exactly."

"Well, you didn't involve Mark and Brad in your shenanigans, did you?"

"Of course not!" said Doug.

Smiling nervously at his wife, he continued, "But if they volunteer to be on my posse, I would certainly give it some serious thought."

Rolling her eyes, she reminded her husband he had already retired from law enforcement twice before. But she knew it was a calling for him, which was part of what attracted her to him in the first place.

CHAPTER 12

The conversation was interrupted by the sound of a buzzer at the front of the house, indicating a vehicle was at the gate. All three of them stood and walked to the front window to view the road leading to the gate. If it were the chief or Mark, they would see a vehicle coming around the bend soon. If not, Doug would walk through the thick trees to investigate. As they waited, Baxter moved in front of them and jumped up, resting his front paws on the windowsill to see what they were all looking at.

Moments later they were all relieved to see Mark's Tacoma come into view. The truck appeared as if it had been through a war. The front end had a lot of damage, and the side windows had been broken out. As the truck turned to drive around to the back of the house, they were shocked to see what appeared to be multiple bullet holes in the passenger side. The three of them, with Baxter close behind, turned to go through the house to the back deck where he would park his truck.

Maddy ran down the steps of the deck and hugged Mark tight as he crawled out of the damaged truck. After their embrace, she stepped back to look at him and make sure he was OK. Mark looked like a wreck after four days of nonstop work in Milwaukee. He hadn't bathed or shaved in that time, and the dried blood on his face and shirt from his nose only added to the horrific look. He stated he was not injured but was completely exhausted.

"Well, you are safe now," said Penny from up on the deck. "Let's get you cleaned up, and you can tell us about what's going on in Milwaukee."

Dazed from lack of sleep, Mark walked upstairs and into the bathroom. He peeled off his dark blue Milwaukee Fire Department T-shirt and dropped it on the floor. He had been wearing the shirt for days, and it was soiled with blood, not all of it his. After removing his blue uniform cargo pants, he let them fall to the floor with a clunk. They were much heavier than normal with the added weight of the pistol. He then stripped off his underwear and socks and climbed into the hot shower. His mind was swimming with all the events of the past few days. He had witnessed so much tragedy followed by the events on the trip home and taking two human lives. As a career firefighter and Iraq War veteran, he had seen tragedy before, but this was an entirely new level for him. So much horror in such a short period of time coupled with his lack of sleep led him into a dull, zombie-like state. A hot shower was the first step in the healing process.

He wasn't sure how much time had passed, but the water hitting his body was getting cold. He heard someone calling his name from some distant location, but it wasn't registering in his brain. Finally, he felt a hand grabbing his arm. It was his wife.

CHAPTER 13

As Mark wiped the sleep from his eyes, he tried to focus on where he was. The ceiling fan, spinning above his head, was unfamiliar. As he lifted his head to look around the room, he was surprised to see the happy face of a border collie sitting on the bed staring back at him. This confused him further as he had no idea whose dog it was. Looking under the sheets, he realized he was also naked. Rubbing his eyes once more, trying to get them to focus, he was interrupted as the dog started licking his face as if to say, *Time to get up, friend.*

"OK, OK, I'm getting up," said Mark. As he sat up and looked around the room, he finally recognized it as one of the guest bedrooms at his in-laws' house. Mark wasn't exactly sure how he got there as the past few days were a blur. The memory of the ambush was coming back to him, but he could not recall the rest of the journey home, or how he had gotten to Doug and Penny's place. He had absolutely no idea whose dog was licking his face.

Sitting up, he saw fresh clothes sitting in the chair next to the bed. His wife must have had the foresight to bring them to her parents' house. Maddy was always thinking two steps ahead, a strategy instilled in her at a very young age from playing chess with her father.

After putting on the fresh clothes following a good night's sleep, Mark was feeling refreshed. Rubbing his shoulder where the seat belt had constricted him during the accident, he was interrupted by a single bark from the dog. Looking over his shoulder, he saw the dog sitting in the hallway just outside the guest room. He seemed to be calling Mark to follow. As Mark followed the dog down the hallway, Baxter kept looking back to make sure he was coming.

As the two came down the stairs, he could smell the aroma of fresh bacon. It was just now he realized how famished he was. Entering the kitchen, he was greeted by his awaiting family. Maddy got up and gave him a tight hug, followed by Penny. Doug, standing in the kitchen drinking a cup of coffee, said, "So how was the trip home?" Mark assumed Doug had already inspected the damage to his Tacoma.

While eating the huge breakfast Penny prepared for him, Mark filled them all in on what happened in Milwaukee as well as on his journey.

"Milwaukee collapsed over the past week. While we all saw it coming, nobody could stop it. The hyperinflation hit harder and faster than expected. Everyone's money was basically worthless, not that there was much available to buy anyway. The government kept telling people not to panic as things would normalize. They were just trying to stall and put off the inevitable.

"When the people ran out of money, the real problems started. People were breaking into homes all over the city looking to take food and supplies from their neighbors. That left a lot of people with gunshot and knife wounds. I lost count of how many calls we got for such wounds over the past few days. The police were completely overwhelmed and couldn't make it to calls with us. We started violating our own protocol and responding before the police could make the scene safe. That turned out to be a bad call as a lot of our fire crews were injured or killed trying to help. Our supplies ran low, and the hospitals were so full they couldn't take any more patients. After a couple days the coroner stopped responding to calls, and we were just leaving bodies where they lay so we could respond to the next call."

The family listened intently while he continued.

"A lot of the police and fire personnel saw this coming and fled the city to protect their own families. This compounded the problem as it immediately slashed our emergency resources. Then the phones and internet went out, and nobody knew why. People were guessing some sort of military strike from Russia or China as the US was entering the wars. The city became a complete war zone overnight. In the end, even our radio communications went out, and we never learned why. The last straw was that our station was looted, and they killed two firefighters. I have no idea what happened to the rest of the Station 23 personnel. The engine company was just gone, and the rest of the Heavy Urban Rescue crew was nowhere to be found. My lieutenant made the hard call and dismissed the station. With no direction, communication, or supplies, there was nothing we could do to help. It was like fighting a four-alarm fire with a garden hose." Mark shook his head. "Then on my trip home, a couple guys tried to ambush me at a fake police checkpoint."

Maddy squeezed his hand tight as he told the story. He explained how he took them out and rammed through the police car just as Doug had instructed. Mark made eye contact with Doug in a nonverbal thanks.

"Air bag?" asked Doug, pointing to his nose.

"Yup, I forgot to turn my head," said Mark. "Everything just happened so fast."

"They always do," replied Doug, with a knowing tone from personal experience.

Once Mark finished his story, Baxter walked over and placed his big head on Mark's lap with his soulful eyes looking up at him.

Mark petted the head of the dog who was trying to console him. "So, when did we get a dog?" he asked.

Doug filled him in on what he had missed the past few days and how Baxter had come to join their family. Additionally, he wanted Mark to accompany him to the town board meeting and share his Milwaukee experience. He needed the board members to completely understand the situation they were all facing.

"We need to leave for the meeting in about forty-five minutes," said Doug.

"I'll be ready in twenty. I want to stop by my house first and grab some things," replied Mark.

"I figured as much," said Doug, knowing Mark would want his rifle and body armor.

Mark and Maddy went upstairs to spend a few minutes alone before he had to leave. Of course, Baxter followed them just like he was another one of the kids. The three of them lay on the bed chatting about what the future may look like after the baby came. While they both were worried, they knew they were far better off than most people because of all their preparations.

As the two conversed, Baxter crawled in between them to try to be part of the group. It was funny yet sweet.

"You know, that dog sat on the bed next to you for hours just waiting for you to wake up," said Maddy. The herding instinct was strong in the breed, and it was clear he wanted the family to be all together. It was clear after just one night that Baxter had adopted them as his pack.

CHAPTER 14

Doug pulled the Ram into the driveway of Mark's house and then turned off the engine. "Need any help?" he asked Mark.

"No, just grabbing my rifle and kit for now. I will need to make a few trips later on to collect what we need to bring out to your place," replied Mark.

While he waited, Doug sat in the truck and tried to find a radio station. Satellite radio was completely offline, along with all of the local stations. He wondered how much longer the power would stay on, knowing things would get bad fast once it went out. The initial concern would be water. The people who lived in town would still have water for a day or two until the municipal water tower ran dry. Electrical power was required for the pumps to refill the tower. The people outside of town who used well water could use a generator to pump water, while they had fuel to do so. Doug had purchased a Lehman's Well Bucket as an emergency backup. The skinny bucket could fit down inside the four-inch well pipe so water could be retrieved with a rope as in the old days.

Mark returned to the truck a couple minutes later with a rifle matching Doug's and a similarly set up tactical vest. Putting the heavy vest in the back seat next to Doug's, he brought the rifle with him into the front seat.

As they left Mark's place and headed the four blocks over to the town hall, they could tell they were the last two to arrive. The chief's Suburban was already there, as were the cars belonging to the board members. The town board consisted of five members elected for a two-year term. They typically had no experience or education in government as most were retired farmers or local businessmen. They would likely not be prepared to lead a community during a crisis of this nature. They typically only met once per month and earned a nominal salary of just $75 per meeting.

As Doug and Mark entered the modest town hall, they were greeted by a well-dressed lady in her early seventies. Mrs. Valarie Barnes, the town board chairwoman, was well known for her gardening abilities, and her flowers had won several awards at the county fair. Her late husband had been an influential man in his day, owning one of the largest dairy farms in the area. After his passing, her children ran the farm into the ground and squandered much of the fortune. Mrs. Barnes sold what was left of the farm and bought a nice house near the town center. She was a very proud woman and enjoyed her position as the town chair, which she believed gave her the social status she felt she had lost. She viewed the position as largely that of social coordinator or festival planner rather than a leader during a crisis. It was clear to Doug that she didn't fully grasp the gravity of the situation they were in.

Mrs. Barnes directed them to a table where the chief sat on one side opposite the board members. Doug and Mark took their seats next to the chief as the meeting began. Doug thanked them all for coming and started off by asking Mark to share his experience in Milwaukee. As he did, they were all shocked and in disbelief. Once the situation was in perspective, Doug filled them in on his meeting with the sheriff. It was apparent that the board members were in way over their heads.

"What exactly are you asking of us?" asked Mrs. Barnes.

"Leadership," replied Doug.

"We need to take action to pull the people together or else we will end up like Milwaukee. We need to start planning how our municipality will function going forward. We need plans for food, security, health care, education, and so on. Tomorrow we will need to do the same basic things that we did yesterday, but we will need to do them in a completely different environment. Our ancestors were able to survive and even thrive without all the modern conveniences we have grown dependent on. We can do it again if we stick together. But one thing the town needs is a leader. Someone to inspire us all to work together."

"And who did you have in mind?" asked Mrs. Barnes, assuming she would be the natural person in the social hierarchy of her own mind.

"I would recommend Chief Brad Peterson for the position of town supervisor," said Doug. "While the board would still serve as the governing body, the chief would bear the burden of being available 24/7 to resolve the many tedious issues that will certainly come up."

Doug's experience in counterterrorism had made him a polished negotiator and politician. On more than one occasion he had sat on the floor of an Afghan village convincing tribal elders to support the coalition forces rather than the Taliban. He was an expert at leading people to the logical conclusion while simultaneously allowing them to save face and believe the idea was theirs to start with.

It was clear that Mrs. Barnes was a bit put off by the notion, but she also realized she did not want to be available to the public twenty-four hours per day.

"Here is what I propose," said Doug. "First, the town board will meet daily at 9 a.m. until we get things figured out. Without modern communications, it is essential to meet frequently. Second, the town board will create working groups to address the pressing issues at hand. These will be things such as public safety, health care, education, communications, commerce, et cetera. Each board member will lead a committee and recruit subject matter experts to assist.

"Third, we will convert the Volunteer Fire Department into a combined Public Safety Department. We will handle all law-enforcement, fire, and medical calls. The chief will serve as the head of the fire and EMS, but I will serve as the top law-enforcement officer since I have been deputized to do so by the elected sheriff. The firefighters will become members of my posse and work under my authority. The village will need to select a person to serve as a justice of the peace to hear minor issues and disputes. For major crimes, we will need to transport suspects to Chilton for a judge trial.

"Fourth, we need to come up with some sort of communication process. I suggest starting up the old local newspaper again. A simple daily paper could be used to distribute a lot of information to the masses in short order. It is also important for folks to remember they are all part of a larger community so they don't start feeling alone and abandoned. I suggest we designate key locations around the village to post information. This will give each area a sense of community and allow us to get our message out to all.

"Fifth, the town will need a doctor's office. We already have a veter-inarian and at least two doctors who live here. We need to see if we can utilize their expertise and if they will volunteer their time for the good of the community. Obviously, we can't force anyone to help out or donate their time. That would be communism. But we do need to establish an environ-ment of 'help thy neighbor' if we hope to get through the hard times ahead.

"Sixth, commerce. While money is of little value going forward, people still possess goods and services to trade. The committee needs to come up with a way to facilitate bartering among the community members. While some farmers have a surplus of goods, other people possess necessary skills, including manpower. I suggest some form of farmers market or swap meet where people can get together and resolve their own issues.

"Anyway, that's just a start. As each of these working groups puts their heads together, many more issues will certainly come up," Doug concluded. "So, what do you all think?"

The board members were simply overwhelmed with the informa-tion overload. They were so focused on their personal lives that they hadn't considered all that went into governing a community during a crisis. When the system breaks down, every aspect of governance needs to be reevaluated. Most of the board members were regretting taking public office for the social reasons. After suggesting a short list of initial tasks ahead of them, they were all motivated to name Brad as the town supervisor, while Doug would serve as the Calumet County representative and law enforcement officer.

After a unanimous vote, Brad reluctantly accepted the position. While he was certainly not seeking individual glory, he knew he was in the best position to help the community survive. "I do have one thing to address," said the chief. "The town fuel supply. Tucker said you allowed it to get dangerously low, and now he is rationing what is left to the emergency vehicles while keeping his maintenance vehicles fueled."

Town board member Bill Rogers, a meek retired accountant, raised his hand to explain.

"Tucker did approach me about a week ago regarding ordering fuel, but the prices were shooting through the roof. I had asked him to wait a few days to see if the price would drop, but it didn't. After that I told him to order what we needed. It didn't seem like a critical matter as we had plenty of fuel on hand."

"How much fuel did we have at that time?" asked Doug.

Looking in a folder containing the town's financial documents, he replied, "Well, the diesel tank was down to around sixteen hundred, and the gas tank around twelve hundred. That should have been enough for three or four months under normal circumstances."

"How did it get all the way down to five hundred gallons in less than a week?" asked the chief.

While nobody in the room wanted to accuse Tucker of stealing the fuel, it was the first thing on all of their minds. Tucker had always been a shady character who tried to bully his way through life.

Doug was the first one to break the silence. "I propose we start off with an immediate inventory of everything the town owns. We need to know exactly what resources we possess in order to establish a plan to best serve the people."

The board members all agreed; however, they feared the confrontation with Tucker they knew would result. They were glad they now had a town supervisor to take the lead.

After they all were in agreement, they clarified some of the details and adjourned until the next meeting. Everyone seemed more confident now that they had a plan of action in place. Following the meeting, Mr. Rogers would accompany Brad over to the maintenance yard to inventory everything there.

CHAPTER 15

Back inside the Ram, still parked at the town hall, Mark asked what was next on the agenda. Doug thought for a moment as he watched Brad and Mr. Rogers drive away to go inventory the maintenance yard and confront Tucker.

"We need to head over to the station so I can prepare for our meeting with the guys," replied Doug.

After thinking a bit longer, he couldn't resist the urge and said, "But first let's go over to the maintenance yard and watch Tucker's reaction when Brad asks him about the fuel." While he didn't exactly think the chief would need backup, he knew that looking into the inventory would uncover some shady activity, and Tucker was not one to easily comply.

At the yard, Doug recognized the only other vehicle there besides the chief's Suburban. It belonged to Randy, a young seasonal maintenance employee. Besides Tucker, the town employed two additional maintenance crew members on a part-time basis. They would do the bulk of the manual labor under Tucker's watch.

Randy was a decent enough young man, although he wasn't exactly the ambitious sort. At twenty-three, he was perfectly content working part time with no benefits. He lived with his brother in the small trailer park on Blackburn Street, and as long as they had beer money, he was content.

Doug waited a few minutes before he walked into the shop as he didn't want to interrupt the chief's momentum. As he and Mark slipped inside, they could hear Randy trying to justify something, but Brad wasn't buying it. From the conversation, it was obvious that over the past few weeks they had been taking items from the maintenance shop out to Tucker's place north of town. While Randy argued it was just for safekeeping, he was unable to make a convincing argument.

When Brad spotted Doug standing by the door, he informed Randy that Doug was the new deputy sheriff in town.

"Deputy Chapman," called the chief. "We have a young man here who would like to report the theft of a lot of village equipment, to include several hundred gallons of fuel. He was ordered by a town employee to relocate the items but has just now realized he was inadvertently involved in the theft. As a witness to the crime, rather than an accomplice, I think he would like to make a statement."

Randy looked uneasy, especially in front of Doug and the fire chief, both of whom had a reputation as no-nonsense individuals. He stuttered and said, "I-I'm not sure if I actually saw anything or not."

"That's too bad," said Doug. "It would be a lot easier if you were a good witness—you know, duped into the theft—rather than an accessory to taking the town property. Especially during a crisis such as this. If we were to find stolen property in your trailer, it wouldn't look very good. But if you were to turn over the items that were given by your boss that you hadn't known were stolen, well, that would be a whole different ball game. So, Randy, are you a witness or an accessory?" asked Doug.

While Randy didn't do well in school, he was street smart. As he pondered his options, he didn't see much benefit in covering for Tucker. And he knew if the tables were turned, Tucker would throw him under the bus without a thought.

"OK, I'm a witness," said Randy. "What do you want to know?"

Doug took notes as Randy listed all the property they had taken, and it was a lengthy list. It included things such as power tools, a generator, and all sorts of shop items. They had been filling several cans of fuel each night for the past three weeks and taking them out to Tucker's place. Tucker would dump them into his aboveground fuel tanks and bring the empty gas cans back the next day to do it again.

Randy also said something else of interest. Tucker had an old friend he'd rode motorcycles with down in Milwaukee years ago. That guy and his biker friends were out at Tucker's place one night when he dropped some gas off. "They weren't too friendly, so I left pretty fast," said Randy.

"Thanks for the assistance," said Doug. "I'm sure you will keep out of trouble from here on out. And keep this conversation between us." Randy nodded his head as Doug, Brad, and Mark walked out of the door.

Doug walked out to the truck and used his radio to attempt to contact the county dispatch center. He wasn't sure how much longer the radios would be operational considering Mark had told him they were out of order in Milwaukee.

"Rockport Deputy Chapman to Calumet County Dispatch."

"Go ahead, Chapman," replied the dispatcher.

"Dispatch, have you been advised of my new law enforcement standing by the sheriff?"

"Affirmative."

"Good. I need to obtain a verbal search warrant. Can you get a radio to one of the judges?"

"I think so. I just saw Judge Tarny in the building. Please stand by while we track her down."

Doug knew Judge Tarny well. He had appeared in her court many times as a state trooper. The previous protocol to obtain a search warrant required a written affidavit and proper paperwork. Doug was hoping that under the circumstances, he could get a verbal warrant approved.

"Deputy Chapman from Calumet County," the microphone barked.

"Go for Chapman."

"We have Judge Tarny here. She said to proceed with your verbal affidavit."

Doug provided a fast briefing, identifying all the pertinent information required by the law. He identified the place to be searched and the items to be searched for, and he explained the probable cause elements leading him to believe the items would be found there.

"I approve the verbal warrant, Doug, but it must be served within the five-day standard."

"Roger that, your honor. I will follow up with the documentation as soon as practical after it is served."

"Understood. Judge Tarny out."

Doug looked over at Mark in the passenger seat and said, "We have a green light." As the chief walked up to Doug's open window, Doug gave him a thumbs-up.

"I got the warrant, but we might need some help serving it. I figure we may need to make several pickup loads to collect all the items unless you can get your hands on something like a U-Haul."

"I can get a truck," said Brad. "I'm much more concerned about the fuel and how we can get that back. It would take forever to ferry several hundred gallons back in five-gallon jerry cans."

"Well, it may make for a long night then," said Doug. "Once we serve the warrant, we need to take all the evidence while we hold the scene, or we can't go back. We may need to post a public safety officer there while we ferry the fuel."

"Will do. I will go get a truck and meet you back at the fire station to brief the guys. After that, we can serve the warrant."

"Sounds good," replied Doug. "One more thing: it may be a good time for you to start packing a pistol. You are a law enforcement officer now, and things may get ugly."

Brad grinned and pulled up his shirt to show him the pistol he was concealing. He carried the large pistol inside his waistband in an appendix carry holster.

"I figured as much," said Doug. "Once we fill the guys in on the news, they will need to start packing also."

With a grin, Brad said, "I suspect a good many of them have been packing for a while now."

"I figured that too," said Doug. "See you back at the station."

CHAPTER 16

Inside the fire station, Doug and Mark were setting up for the meeting with the guys. It wouldn't be long until the bulk of the firefighters would arrive, undoubtedly anxious for any news. Mark had pulled two of the fire trucks out of the building and parked them in the driveway to make room for the gathering. While he did that, Doug set up seventeen folding chairs facing a fold-out table with three additional chairs on the other side. Doug, Mark, and Brad would sit at the table facing the firefighters.

Doug wanted to see what supplies were in the boxes he got from the sheriff before everyone arrived. As he itemized the contents, Mark took down the inventory on his clipboard:

- Twenty-one obsolete Calumet County Sheriff badges to identify posse members

- Three large boxes of disposable "flexicuffs" hand restraints

- Ten sets of metal handcuffs and keys from the jail

- Three sets of leg shackles from the jail

- Four sets of used body armor

- Eight car door magnets that read "Sheriff"

- Eight sets of Velcro "Sheriff" patches for the body armor

- Two Taser stun guns with eight cartridges

- Four complete sets of police duty belts with Glock pistols

- Five canisters of OC Pepper spray

- Ten wooden police batons

- Two sets of Stop Stick tire deflation devices

"That should be a pretty good start," said Doug.

The firefighters were starting to arrive, anxious to find out what was going on. They didn't know much other than what they heard over the fire radio. They knew that sheriff deputies and state agents had not been able to make it out to the Schmidt fire, then Doug was called out to Chilton by the sheriff. That, coupled with the loss of phone and internet access, made all of them nervous.

The time for the meeting came, and only fourteen of the firefighters had arrived. Brad had told Doug that three of the members were not interested in continuing to volunteer as they wanted to focus on their own families. Doug hoped they would have changed their minds, but apparently, they hadn't.

Brad, sitting at the center of the folding table facing the firefighters, said, "OK, let's call this meeting to order. I know you all have a lot of questions, but unfortunately, I don't have a lot of answers. That said, Captain Cruz can fill you all in on what has happened in Milwaukee over the past few days."

Mark stood up from behind the table to address the group. During the next twenty minutes, while describing his experience, you could have heard a pin drop in the fire station. All the firefighters could visualize the story as he was telling it. When he was done, they all were worried about their own situations. They knew now that their fears were valid and their future uncertain.

After Mark sat back down, the chief called Doug up to address what he learned at the sheriff's office. Doug stood up from the table as well while he briefed the department. They all had a great respect for Doug due to his military and law enforcement experience. As he explained the situation in their county, including the shortage of deputies and lack of resources, they now understood why no law enforcement had responded to the fire the day before. They took the deaths of the deputies especially hard as they were familiar with each of them on a personal level.

Doug could see varied emotions in the audience ranging from fear to shock to anger. He gave them a moment to digest the information and then stated, "Now that you all have an idea of the situation we are facing, I have a proposal for you all to consider. I propose changing the Rockport Volunteer Fire Department to the Rockport Public Safety Department. In this regard, we would add law enforcement to our current fire and medical missions. I believe this is necessary in order to protect our community. As the only regional sheriff's deputy, there is no way I can do it alone. I have been given the authority to raise a posse to assist me, and I can think of no better team of men and woman that I would rather serve with." Doug thanked them all for listening to his proposal, then returned to his seat.

Once Doug sat back down, the chief stood up to address the group. "OK, guys. I know that's a lot to take in, but we need a decision from you. I propose a vote on switching to a public safety department and adding law enforcement responsibilities. If it is not us, then nobody will be protecting our families and community. Those of you who do not wish to be a sheriff's posse member can remain in the same capacity that you are now, fire and EMS only. Now let's vote. Raise your hand if you are in favor of changing the department mission to include law enforcement response." Brad noted that sixteen hands were raised.

"All opposed?" Brad noted that one hand went up. "Does anyone who is opposed want to discuss?" asked the chief.

Walter Skinner stood up to speak. "I volunteer to serve my community as a firefighter, not as a cop. I have no interest in sticking my nose into to other people's business."

Doug nodded his head and stated, "That's fine Walter. Any firefighter who chooses to serve on the posse under my direction will do so on a voluntary basis. If someone would like to just do the traditional fire and EMS stuff, I totally understand. I will only grant posse status to those volunteers who choose to do it."

Walter sat back down but still had a sour look on his face. It was common knowledge he was not a fan of law enforcement. A few years earlier, the local school had suspected him of hitting his teenage son, and the school liaison officer investigated. While he was exonerated by the deputy, he felt it had been none of their business to start with.

"Anyone else wish to comment?" asked the chief. After a moment, he continued, "Hearing nothing, the vote is sixteen to one in favor of transitioning to a Public Safety Department. So be it. Doug, the floor is yours."

"Thanks, Chief," said Doug as he stood back up. "OK, like I said, this is a voluntary position in addition to firefighting duties. Those who wish to become part of the Calumet County Sheriff's Posse and help protect the residents of our community, please stand up and raise your right hand."

Fifteen members stood to take the oath administered by Doug. Walter remained seated.

Standing in front of the United States flag, Doug turned to face the others and raised his right hand. "Please repeat after me. On my honor, I will never betray my badge, my integrity, my character, or the public trust. I will always have the courage to hold myself and others accountable for our actions. I will always uphold the Constitution, and will remain loyal to my community and the Calumet County Sheriff's Department."

Everyone who was standing raised their right hand and repeated the oath after Doug. After the oath, Doug thanked them personally and presented each member an obsolete Calumet County Sheriff badge to identify them as a posse member operating under his deputized authority. Doug now wore the seven-pointed deputy star badge on his old state trooper duty belt that he had pulled out of retirement.

Once everyone had been congratulated and thanked for stepping up once again to serve their community, Doug had to give his first command. "OK, we have a valid search warrant for Dale Tucker's property." This didn't seem to surprise anyone in the room. "I need six of you to come with me and Chief to serve it and bring back stolen items from the village. We will likely need to make several trips hauling gas. Captain Cruz, I need you to stay here with the rest and come up with an operating plan moving forward. Now that communication is out, I recommend designing a shift to ensure we have three or four public safety officers on duty at all times to respond."

"Will do," said Mark, seeing the need in his assignment but wishing he could go along to serve the warrant.

Twenty minutes later, Brad rode with Doug to Dale Tucker's property. Six newly sworn public safety officers followed in a U-Haul and a second pickup. All three vehicles had magnetic Calumet County Sheriff decals on the doors, and every officer was armed with at least a handgun. The vehicles rolled into Tucker's personal compound, which was reminiscent of a junkyard. The property was two acres in size and contained an old farmhouse and two outbuildings. There were several broken-down cars on the property, and nothing seemed to be maintained well. Tall grass, weeds, and debris covered most of the property. While Tucker had never married, nobody knew if anyone else lived at the property.

The Ram pulled up near the farmhouse, and the other two vehicles waited back near the road as instructed. As Doug and Brad walked up to the house, Tucker opened a beat-up screen door that was barely hanging on the hinges. He stormed down the steps demanding to know what they were doing on his property. Doug pointed to the badge on his belt and informed him he was now the regional deputy for this section of the county.

"So what? What are you doing on my property?" shouted Tucker.

Doug took an angled position with his gun side positioned slightly away from him. This was called the interview stance in the police world, and it allowed the officer to appear relaxed but actually placed them in a reactionary position. He kept Tucker at an arm's distance so he could view his entire body and watch for aggressive posturing. He scanned his clothing for bulges that could conceal a weapon. Dressed in filthy jeans and an even dirtier black T-shirt, Tucker didn't appear to have any obvious weapons, but a gun could easily be concealed under the untucked shirt, especially behind his back.

"Well, Tucker, I have reason to believe you may have stolen Rockport property in your possession."

"Screw you! Get the hell off of my property!" shouted Tucker.

Keeping a calm voice and maintaining his trooper-like composure, Doug asked, "May I have permission to search your property for said items?"

"I said get off my property." Tucker's face started to turn red from anger.

As Doug observed his behavior, he made note of his physical responses. Tucker was taking an aggressive posture, raising his voice, balling up his fists, and getting more animated in his gestures. Based on Doug's training and experience, he recognized these cues as pre-assault indicators.

Doug had prior knowledge that Tucker was a bully and not afraid to start a fight. His reputation for overreacting in an emotional state was well known. "Dale, I have a warrant to search your property, and I am here to serve it," advised Doug.

"The hell you are!" shouted Dale, making a furtive move with his right hand toward the back of his waistband.

Doug had spent a career as a police officer watching people's hands. He was taught as a young recruit that "the eyes are the window to the soul, but it's the hands that will kill you." As Tucker made the move toward the rear of his waistband while shouting aggressive threats, Doug reacted.

With Doug's hands held at chest level during their conversation, they looked innocent enough, but in reality, they were ready to strike. When Tucker made his move, the palm of Doug's left hand struck Tucker in the center of his chest, knocking him off balance and onto the ground. At the same time, Doug created a reactionary gap and drew his Glock, aiming it at Tucker.

"Show me your hands!" shouted Doug.

Brad was caught completely off guard by Doug's actions, as he had not been trained to observe a suspect's physical cues. To him it looked like Doug just hit him in the chest and drew his gun. It all happened very fast, and he wasn't sure what was going on.

"Watch the house," Doug said to the chief in a surprisingly calm manner. "Watch the windows and doors. We don't know who else is in there." Brad drew his pistol and kept it at the ready while Doug dealt with Tucker.

Lying on the ground, Tucker found himself in a state of shock and experiencing pain in his lower back. He had fallen flat on his back, and his concealed pistol was poorly placed in the center of his waistband. When he hit the ground hard this sent excruciating pain through his lumbar spine. This was the very reason police officers never place gear over their spine on their duty belts.

"Keep your hands out to your side," commanded Doug in a confident voice.

In pain and confusion, Tucker complied.

"Roll over onto your stomach!"

Tucker rolled over onto his stomach as he looked down the barrel of a Glock.

Once on his stomach, Doug commanded him to place his hands on top of his head and interlace his fingers. Tucker complied with the command.

Doug knelt down, placing his knee on Tucker's shoulder to prevent him from getting up. Using his left hand, he grasped Tucker's interlaced fingers as well as some hair on his head and locked them together with a gentle squeeze. Holstering his Glock with his right hand, he then pulled up Tucker's shirt to remove the hidden revolver from his waistband. After securing the weapon in his own waistband, Doug placed a set of handcuffs on Dale and searched the rest of his body for additional weapons.

Brad was amazed that Doug was able to recognize Tucker was armed and react so fluidly. It was only after Doug pulled the gun from his waistband that Brad realized he had been just seconds from a gunfight. It was at this moment the reality of being a cop began to set in.

Doug rolled Tucker over and helped him into a sitting position. "OK, Tucker, let's start over. As the appointed deputy sheriff for this region, I am going to search your property under a warrant issued by Judge Tarny. Are there any other people on the property?"

"I got nothing to say!" he shouted, with grass still in his hair from rolling on the ground.

"That's your right," said Doug. He then motioned for the waiting public safety officers to approach his position.

The posse members walked to where Doug and Brad were standing. The tough firefighters were still in awe regarding how fast the situation went down. They were just now starting to understand the heavy weight of the new badge they were all wearing. While they were up to the challenge, they would certainly take more precaution than before.

"Listen up," said Doug.

"Jessie, you stay with Tucker here. If he tries to get up or go anywhere, put him in the dirt. Brad and I are going to search the house. I want the rest of you to search the property for people. Our first priority is our safety, and we need to secure everyone on the property. We will search for evidence once that task is accomplished."

The public safety officers all accepted their assignments, but now with a bit more insight about the potential danger of their new job.

Doug once again drew his Glock from its holster and said to Brad, "Let's clear the house. I will take the lead and you cover me while I search. When I go into rooms to search, you stay in the hallway and keep your eyes on the unsearched rooms."

"Got it," replied Brad.

As the two entered the house, Doug shouted, "Sheriff's department. We have a search warrant. If you are inside the house, call out now!" He waited a few seconds for a response; however, none came.

As they entered the home, Brad remained posted just inside the front door and kept his gun trained on the uncleared stairway and kitchen area while Doug searched the living room and bathroom. As Doug moved to search the kitchen, Brad instinctively lowered his gun for a moment while Doug passed so as not to point it at him.

The house was filthier on the inside than it was outside. Brad had known Tucker in his capacity as the town maintenance supervisor for nearly twenty years and never imagined he lived like this. Brad also noticed his heart was beating rapidly. This surprised him, as he had battled fires inside houses similar to this on many occasions. It was just now that he really started to understand the differences between police and fire tactics. A burning house was a known threat, while searching a house for bad guys was an unknown threat. As a fire chief, he was an expert on reading smoke signals and fire flow patterns and could foresee how the fire would develop. But in his present situation, the threat was unknown and could pop out from a door or from behind a piece of furniture without warning. The not knowing was nerve racking. When he fought fires, he was covered in protective gear. Now he just had a used bullet-resistant vest protecting only his torso. Brad slowly breathed in through his nose and exhaled through his mouth to lower his heart rate.

As Doug cleared the first floor, he got close to Brad and whispered, "OK, let's move upstairs. I will walk up the right side of the stairs facing backward and point my gun up at the hidden landing above in case there is someone waiting for us. You will walk forward next to me on the left side of the stairs and point your gun up the stairwell. We will move together as a unit."

"Roger," replied Brad.

As the two of them moved as a team up the narrow stairwell, there wasn't much room to move. As Doug took each new step up while facing backward, he could see a little bit more of the concealed landing that looked down on them from the second floor. Stairwells were always a challenge to clear as it placed them in what is called a "fatal funnel." As they got to the top of the stairs, they both turned to face the same direction. Brad maintained cover on the hallway while Doug searched the first two bedrooms. As Doug returned to the hallway, he signaled for them to move toward the final room. As they moved, Brad pointed to a cardboard box on the floor. The box was filled with bloody gauze and bandages.

As the two made their way to the final doorway, Doug peered in at a tactical angle, only exposing enough of his body to see around the doorjamb. Inside the room on the bed was a man lying on his left side. Blood-soaked bandages covered his right side, and he appeared to be unconscious. As the two men entered the room, Doug observed the man's clothes resting on the floor. The pile of filthy clothes consisted of motorcycle boots, jeans, T-shirt, and leather vest with the Dark Arrows MC logo on the back and a 1% patch on the front.

As Doug lifted the dirty, blood-soaked vest up, he examined the chest portion to reveal a small hole on the front and rear of the right side. Looking over at the man on the bed, he saw that the wound lined up with the hole in the vest. He said to Brad, "This is one of the bikers that ambushed and killed the deputies at High Cliff State Park."

"You sure?" asked Brad.

"Pretty sure," he replied. "This was the same gang that was terrorizing the village of Harrison, just a few miles from here. Just after the gang ambushed and killed the deputies, a DNR game warden got the jump on them unexpectedly. The warden engaged them with his AR-15 patrol rifle. He killed two and wounded a third. This must be the third man he shot, who was able to get away. The hole in the vest was small, like a .22 caliber, but it had the velocity to completely penetrate both sides of the heavy leather vest as well as the suspect. That would be consistent with the game warden's .223 bullet."

Doug further explained the meaning of the 1% patch to Brad. "The 1% is commonly used to describe an outlaw motorcycle gang. The term was coined in response to the 1947 Hollister riot, in California. The American Motorcycle Association made a public statement that 99% of motorcycle riders were law-abiding citizens. In response, the outlaw clubs—gangs—started wearing the 1% patch."

After pulling a latex glove from his pocket and putting it on his hand, Brad checked the man's carotid pulse and found none. "He's dead," said the chief.

Doug was an experienced homicide investigator while in the OSI. He said to the chief, "He has been dead for about twenty-four hours. That also lines up with the timeline of the ambush."

"How did you estimate the time of death? Rigor mortis?" asked Brad.

"Well, when determining the time of death, there are several postmortem indicators that help us forensically. The first thing to observe is corneal clouding of the eyes. This occurs minutes after death. The next to set in is livor mortis. This happens when the arteries stop pumping blood and it pools in the lowest areas of the body due to gravity. This accounts for the red/purple discoloration of the skin on the left side of his body resting against the bed. It starts around thirty minutes after death and becomes permanent eight to twelve hours later. Rigor mortis is the stiffening of the muscles after death. It sets in about four hours after death and lasts for twelve to thirty-six hours."

Brad was always amazed at the knowledge his friend had of so many different topics. "Interesting," said the chief. "So, because the pooling of the blood is fixed in place at the low areas of the body, he has been dead at least twelve hours. But because his muscles are still stiff from rigor, he has been dead less than thirty-six hours?" asked Brad.

"Exactly. But know we have two things to investigate. We need to complete our search warrant for the stolen items from Rockport, but more importantly, we now have a lead to the bastards that killed the deputies in cold blood."

As the two men returned outside to see what Tucker had to say for himself, they overheard him cussing out Jessie as she held him down with her knee in his chest. It was obvious he had attempted to get away and she wasn't having any of it. They overheard him say to her, "Your uncle is going to skin your hide when he hears about this."

Although neither of the men had known that Jessie's uncle was an associate of Tucker's, it stood to reason as both shared the same moral compass. Had he known, Doug would not have assigned her to watch over him.

As Doug approached, he told Jessie she could let him up. Assisting Tucker back into a sitting position, he knelt down in front of him.

"Tucker, I am placing you under arrest in connection with the murder of four Calumet County deputies. If and when I find stolen property, I will also charge you with that. I am about to read you your Miranda rights. Don't answer any questions yet, but think long and hard about whether you want to cooperate or not.

"You have the right to remain silent. Anything you say can be used against you in a court of law. You have the right to have an attorney present during questioning. If you cannot afford a lawyer, one will be appointed free of charge. Do you understand these rights?"

"I didn't murder anyone!" shouted Tucker.

"Glad to hear it, but I can't discuss that matter with you until you confirm that you understand your Miranda rights."

"Yes! I understand!" he shouted.

"Great! Are you willing to make a statement without a lawyer present?" asked Doug.

"I didn't murder any cops!" he again shouted.

"I will take that as a yes, you are willing to speak with me without an attorney present," said Doug in a surprisingly calm and collected tone. Looking up at the chief, Doug said, "Brad, please have the posse members pull back into a defensive position while we get this sorted out. Have them keep watch outside the compound as we don't want to get ambushed by any bikers who may show up. Also, grab my rifle out of the truck so you have some long-range cover capabilities."

It was at that moment Brad truly realized the danger they were in. If the gang was able to get the drop on four experienced deputies, his firefighters wouldn't stand a chance. "Roger that," he replied with a lump in his throat.

"Now, Tucker," said Doug, returning his attention to the handcuffed man on the ground covered in grass. "Just how did you come to be in possession of a dead biker?"

"I had nothing to do with that!"

"Have you heard of the term felony murder?" asked Doug. "That's when a murder occurs during the commission of a felony, and all participants are then charged with the murder, even if they didn't pull the trigger. An example would be a getaway driver during a bank robbery. If the bank robber kills a bank clerk, the getaway driver is also charged with the murder. Now I'm not a lawyer, Dale, but I would imagine the district attorney might wonder about your involvement, given the dead guy in your bedroom."

"I didn't know they planned to kill those cops. The leader of the club, Ty Wilcox, is an old friend of mine. We rode together years ago. When things got bad in Milwaukee last week, they came up north and stayed someplace around Harrison. I guess the cops started harassing them and took Ty in on some trumped-up charge. The next day the gang's second in command brought this wounded guy here and dropped him off. Told me to keep him alive or else. I am no doctor, but I tried to stop the bleeding. I put him on his left side because I thought the bullet must have collapsed his right lung. Anyway, he died just after they rode off," said Tucker.

"Well, you are right about one thing Tucker, you are not a doctor," said Brad.

"How many bikers were there?" asked Doug.

"I only saw five or six of them, but I know there are a few more."

"Where are they staying now?"

"I don't know. Some place up near Harrison, I suspect. They may be on the run if they shot it out with the cops," replied Tucker.

"Who is this second in command that brought him here?"

"He's a big guy and goes by the name Tank. Maybe six foot three, solid build, late thirties, thick black beard."

After Doug was through interrogating Tucker, he instructed the public safety officers to complete the search for stolen items. He had two of them stand watch while the rest of them collected the stolen items and loaded them into the U-Haul truck. Doug took evidentiary photos with his cell phone of all the items seized and the dead body. Even though he could not send them electronically, he could show them to the district attorney and judge so they could decide how they wanted to proceed.

When all the evidence was loaded into the truck, Doug instructed them to collect all the firearms from the property and load them as well. He intended to hold the guns for safekeeping and to prevent the gang from getting them. Next, he instructed the officers to collect as much fuel as they could from Tucker's fuel tanks. While they were only able to scrounge up fourteen five-gallon fuel cans back in town, that would have to suffice for now. They collected seventy gallons and loaded the cans into one of the pickups. If this had been a normal search warrant, Doug would leave an officer at the scene while they ferried the fuel back to town in several trips. However, with the new threat of the biker gang, Doug didn't feel it warranted the risk of leaving a man behind.

"So, what's going to happen to me?" asked Tucker.

Doug scratched his head while he thought about it. "That's a good question," Doug said out loud. He thought to himself that if it were a normal day, he would simply transport him to the county jail and book him in. But now that the sheriff was letting out all but the most dangerous inmates, he likely would not hold him.

"Well," said Doug, "one option is to take you down to Chilton and let you sit in the Calumet County Jail. But, as you know, those deputies are not too happy about losing a bunch of their buddies—the same buddies that you would likely be charged with helping murder. That might not be too comfortable for you, if you know what I mean."

The look on Tucker's face made it obvious he was piecing together just what a predicament he was in. "What's the other option?" he asked in a quiet and deflated voice.

"I could leave you here, but the bikers may return. I'm guessing they would not be too happy that you let their buddy die, or that you let the sheriff take his body."

Realizing his desperate situation, Tucker said, "Well you might as well just put a bullet in my head now then."

"That time has passed, Dale. If you had been a little faster on the draw when I got here, that's how your story would have ended," said Doug very matter-of-factly. "Now, I have to make some choices. Since I believe you were not directly involved with the murder of the deputies, I am inclined to not book you into jail at the moment. But as I am going to declare this property a crime scene because of the dead body, you can't stay here. I am guessing the town board will terminate your employment at the next meeting. And I would not be surprised if the new town supervisor didn't suspend your employment until that time." Doug paused and looked up at Brad.

Realizing this was his cue to speak, Brad said, "As the appointed town supervisor, I am suspending you from any and all duty with the town of Rockport until the board votes."

With that said, Doug continued. "So, do you have any family around here where you could go and keep out of trouble?"

"I have a sister over in Manitowoc. I guess I can go stay there."

"I think I can accept that, Tucker. But here are my rules, and they are firm. You stay out of Rockport altogether. I will allow you to pack up your truck and go to Manitowoc to stay with your sister. You will not be in possession of a firearm until the court decides your fate. You will not return to this property until you get written permission from the district attorney. Do you agree to these conditions?"

"Yes, I do," he said reluctantly, not wishing to face the bikers or the vengeful deputies. "But things are getting crazy. Can I have a gun to protect myself?" he asked.

Doug was a strong advocate of the Second Amendment and could understand his request. But under the circumstances, and given the fact that Tucker just tried to shoot him, he chose the safer route. "Sorry, Tucker, I just don't trust you. If I were to let you take a gun and you ended up killing an innocent person, it would be on me. You are a jail inmate who I am releasing on his own recognizance. I did see a compound bow inside your home. I will allow you to take that for hunting and close-range personal defense. That's the best I can do."

Tucker nodded in agreement. Doug helped him to his feet and removed the handcuffs. He instructed two of the public safety officers to escort him while he loaded his truck and left the property.

"You sure that was the right option?" asked Brad.

"Nope, it will probably bite me in the ass," said Doug as he looked off into the distance. "But under the circumstances, I think it was the best of the bad choices. If this were a hundred and fifty years ago, the posse would have just strung him up from that tree over there and been done with it. But we have become too civilized over the years. Unfortunately, that may bite us in the ass as well."

CHAPTER 17

As the two walked around the large garden on the property, Maddy asked, "How many tomato plants do you have, Mom?"

"Not exactly sure, maybe thirty or so. They have a long shelf life when canned, so I planted a bunch of them this year. I also planted a lot more kail, lettuce, cucumbers, peppers, and carrots this year too."

"We have a pretty good food supply going, but the key is sustainable foods," said Penny as the two walked around the garden.

"How long do you think we can last on what we have?"

Penny looked up as she tried to do some math calculations in her head. "If it's just us four plus a baby and a dog, maybe three years, just on what we have stored."

Penny was in charge of food supplies, and she had a pretty good handle on things. The stage one foods were what they would eat first. These were store-bought foods kept in their pantry and the refrigerator. The stage two foods were long-term storage foods that could last up to twenty years. This would be the bulk dry goods sealed in mylar bags with oxygen absorbers. They had about 50 five-gallon buckets of various items such as rice, beans, and oats, along with some staples such as flour, sugar, and honey. Stage three foods were the sustainable foods that they could produce themselves. This included foods grown in the garden, eggs from their chickens, and any fish or meat they could harvest.

Penny had been very hesitant when Doug suggested cashing in his 401(k) investments a month earlier, but now she was very glad he had. It had lost almost 40 percent of its value, and all the financial advisers said it was stupid to cash out while they were down so low. They advised the couple to ride it out as the market always comes back eventually. But Doug said, "You can't eat money; you can only eat what it can buy." The two prayed on it for several days and decided to take the money out and pay the tax penalty. The cash allowed them to make several key purchases just in the nick of time— fuel tanks, solar power, a generator, and necessary items they would need to work the land. Penny wasn't sure about the off-road utility vehicle or the farm tractor with the backhoe, but Doug convinced her, as always.

"I'm nervous to have a baby with all that's going on, but I feel this is the best place we could possibly be," said Maddy.

"I think so too. Your dad put a lot of thought into this over the years, and I feel like God has a plan for us. Did you know your dad bought a bunch of various size diapers and baby formula at Costco a couple weeks ago?" asked Penny.

"He did? Well, that will certainly be useful," said Maddy, thinking about all the things the baby would need but would be hard to get—things like immunizations and medicine. Even though Mark was a paramedic and her dad was an EMT, their expertise was more focused on emergency medicine, not pediatrics.

"Your dad has been adding a lot of books to his survival library. He even added some pediatric books for the medical section."

"Really? I was just thinking about that very thing."

As the two walked back to the house, Maddy said, "I wonder when the boys will get back. They have been gone all day. I thought they just had to go to a town board meeting."

"You know your father; I'm sure he found a dragon that needed slaying somewhere along the line," she said with a sarcastic tone of experience.

As they got closer to the house, they called out for Baxter to join them. He had made it his mission to be in charge of the chicken coop and enjoyed watching them through the wire fence. He came running after them, and they all entered the house.

Just as Penny was starting to make dinner, they heard the buzzer indicating a vehicle was at the gate. Both girls went to the window along with Baxter to wait for their husbands to drive around the bend. After several minutes they still didn't see the Ram pull through the trees.

I wonder what's taking so long, thought Penny.

Maddy saw some movement in the tree line between the gate and the house.

"Is that dad?" she asked, spying a man moving around back in the trees.

"I'm not sure," said Penny. "He is too far back in the trees." Both women squinted as they looked out the window at the tree line one hundred yards away.

"Where are the binoculars?" asked Penny, not being able to find the set that Doug kept by the window.

"They are on the kitchen table; I was watching a deer out back earlier. I'll get them," said Maddy as she ran to the other room.

Maddy returned with the Steiner binoculars her dad always said to put back in their proper place for just such a reason. She focused the lenses to see clearly into the woods and said, "That's not daddy."

"Is it Brad?"

"No, I don't know who it is. I don't recognize him at all. Wait, now there is another guy. He is looking at the house with binoculars," said Maddy, and the two women ducked behind the wall to hide themselves.

"Where is your gun?" asked Penny with a sense of panic in her voice as she remembered that she left her rifle outside resting against the outbuilding by the garden.

"Oh no! I left it next to yours," Maddy said with a deflated voice. She then ran toward the back of the house to go retrieve the guns. Baxter followed her playfully, not yet sure what was going on. When she got to the back of the house, before she exited the sliding door onto the deck, she saw movement out the window. Maddy instinctively dropped to the floor in a sense of panic. Baxter, now noticing something was wrong, looked at her, trying to understand the situation. Maddy raised her head slightly to see through the window and spotted a man with a rifle slung over his shoulder looking inside her jeep. The man was talking into a walkie talkie, probably to the men in the tree line by the gate.

As Maddy crawled back to the front room, Baxter started barking at the man through the window, sensing his presence was frightening the girls.

"There is a man with a gun outside by the cars," she said in a panicked whisper.

It was at this point Penny remembered Doug kept extra guns in the bedroom closet. The two ran to the master bedroom and into the closet while Baxter barked loudly at the back window. Penny placed her finger on the keypad, and the safe opened. She reached in and picked up the AR-15 and handed it to Maddy, as she was more familiar with that type of rifle. Penny then reached in and grabbed her Glock and verified it was loaded.

Baxter stopped barking, and a minute later they heard the buzzer again. They wondered if Baxter had scared the intruders off and the buzzer was signaling their vehicle leaving the property. The girls moved back to the living room and watched the tree line with the binoculars for the next thirty minutes without seeing any sign of them.

After an hour of waiting, they felt pretty comfortable the men had left. They must have been scouting for things worth stealing, and what they found on the property was the motherload. They certainly saw the huge garden, chicken coop, and outbuildings. They may have even seen the fuel tanks before Baxter started barking. They would certainly be back at some point.

Feeling a little safer, Penny walked out to retrieve their rifles from the garden as Maddy covered her with the AR-15 from the house. When she returned, they closed and locked the door behind them. The realization started to hit home they had no way of calling for help and were responsible for defending themselves. Even if they could have called for help, their husbands were the ones who would need to respond.

"So, do you think we should tell the guys we left our rifles outside?" asked Maddy.

"Nope," said Penny. "We survived and learned our lesson. I think it best we take that little bit of trivia to our graves."

Maddy giggled. "Yeah, that would be a pretty big 'I told you so' from the old man."

CHAPTER 18

The public safety crew returned to town from Tucker's property, and the three vehicles pulled up to the town maintenance yard. Doug had already documented everything for his report, so he instructed the team to unload the truck and then bring the weapons back to the station for safekeeping. "Bring that fuel in the gas cans back as well. We might as well use it for the public safety vehicles since it's already in cans."

"What about the body?" one of the guys asked.

Doug pointed over to the John Deere backhoe sitting in the back of the maintenance yard. "Take that and dig a grave in the field behind the yard. Find a way to mark it somehow."

As the team returned the stolen property back to the yard and disposed of the body, Doug and Brad returned to the station to check in with Mark.

The fire station was a flurry of action. All the guys were moving about, each carrying out the tasks assigned to them. Some were swapping gear from one truck to another, while others were working in small groups. Mark saw the two enter the station, and without words the three of them walked over to the chief's office. Once inside, the chief sat behind his desk while Mark and Doug sat in the two chairs positioned in front of it.

"What a day," said Brad. "We got more accomplished in one day than the town board has in, well, ever."

Doug filled Mark in on what transpired with Tucker.

"Do you think we will see him again?" asked Mark.

"The best thing for everybody would be if we never saw that guy again. But I doubt we will be that lucky," said Doug. "So, it looks like you have been busy back here. What did you come up with?"

"Things are really coming together," said Mark. "The guys are motivated about their new role as public safety. While everyone was scared of the unknown, having a plan to be the solution rather than a problem has got them all motivated."

"Even Walter?" asked the chief.

"Well, no, not Walter," Mark replied with an eye roll. "Anyway, here is our response plan, pending the approval of both of you.

"First, since the community is without phones, we will staff a three-man crew on twenty-four-hour shifts that can respond to calls if and when people come to the station for help.

"Second, the three-man crew will staff the wildland fire pickup truck as the primary response vehicle. That way they have a small water tank and hose in the bed for limited firefighting, medical bags for EMS response, and police gear for law enforcement calls. That will be far more mobile than the big Engine 41 as it has off-road capabilities and uses a lot less fuel.

"Third, we will recruit a few volunteer administrative assistants to staff the office around the clock in shifts. That way we can receive citizens and coordinate things behind the scenes while the guys are out on calls. They can work sort of as a local dispatcher for Rockport.

"Fourth, as long as radio communications are up, the on-duty crew can call for backup if needed from the off-duty officers.

"Fifth, while I expect radio communications to go down eventually, we have a backup plan in place. If the on-duty crew responds to a big call and needs more resources, the admin volunteer will go across the street to the church tower and ring the bell. Just like the old days, it can be a call for assistance to the officers close enough to hear it.

"Also, for communications, the on-duty crew will leave a running log of what transpired on their shift. That way the next crews will be informed of any situations they may inherit.

"So, what do you think?" concluded Mark.

Both men nodded in approval. "I like it," they said at the same time.

"When will the first shift be up and running?" asked Brad.

"They are already on duty. Lou, Ryan, and Vic are the first shift. They will work from now until tomorrow afternoon. The shifts will change out each day at 2 p.m. I kept both of you off the shift rotation so you can respond independently across all the shifts."

Doug thought through the process. "My concern is the guys are not trained in law enforcement yet and will need guidance at times. Obviously, we will do some training, and I will make some standing protocols on how to handle common situations for when I am not around. I'm concerned about how they will be able to ask for my guidance when we eventually lose radio communications."

"I thought of that also," said Mark. "You know firefighter Joe Tanner has that big ham radio setup at his house?"

"Yeah, that could come in very handy when we lose the county radio system."

"Well, Joe has a bunch of older equipment, and he has enough for two other radio sets. He will put one here at the station and one out at Doug's place. He also has a few cheap Chinese hand-held radios that can operate on ham frequencies. He called them Baofeng, I think. With those, the on-duty guys can at least communicate with Doug for police guidance."

"That's a great idea," said Doug.

"I have another thought also," said Mark. "There is safety in numbers and plenty of room out at our place. If Brad and his wife were to stay with us, it would be easier for communication so both of you, in your respective roles, could be near the ham radio. Also, it would be more hands to work the land and provide security."

Doug looked at Brad and said, "I think that's a great idea, and you would be more than welcome. It makes perfect sense, and I like the idea of another gun around, especially for times when Mark and I are away."

Brad thought about it and said, "Yeah, it's a great idea, but I'm not sure I can get Kimberly to leave our house now that she finally got it decorated the way she likes it. She is still in denial that things are getting so bad. But I don't like having her home alone with all that's going on. I will need to talk with her."

"OK," said Doug. "You talk with her and let her know you are not only welcome, but it would be helping us out. It's times like this we all need to pull together. Your house is perfect for entertaining, but it's not set up well at all for defensive capabilities. Those huge windows may look nice, but they are a vulnerability at a time like this."

"I know," said Brad. "I will see if I can talk her into it."

"Sounds good. Now I think Mark and I had better get home to the girls. I told them we were just going to the town board meeting, and now it is almost dark. And I still need to write my report and complete the search warrant return."

"Roger that. See you tomorrow."

As Doug and Mark drove back to the property, Doug felt it was time to check on how Mark was dealing with killing the two men in Milwaukee. Over his career he had a lot of experience in post-traumatic stress and the importance of a post-incident stress debriefing. Typically, it was done after the person had two complete rest cycles to allow the brain sufficient time to process all the information properly.

"So how are you doing with all the stuff you experienced in Milwaukee?"

"Fine, I guess," said Mark, knowing what Doug was trying to do and anticipating the chat. "A lot of it is still a blur, and I have been so busy since then I haven't really had a moment to think about it. I saw so many horrible things over the past few days that the ambush didn't have a huge impact on me. I certainly have no regrets; it was them or me."

Doug sat quiet and just listened as Mark talked. He felt that was the most therapeutic thing he could do at that point. Once it was clear that Mark was done talking, he said, "I expect you will have a lot of different feelings and emotions over the next few weeks. It's important not to bottle them up."

"I know, and thanks," said Mark, with a silent understanding that he knew Doug was there for him and understood what he was going through.

As they pulled up to the gate, Mark got out of the truck to unlock the heavy padlock. While he was doing so, Doug saw him bend down and pick something off the ground and look at it. He then opened the gate for Doug to drive through and secured it behind him.

Mark walked up to the driver's side of the truck as Doug lowered his window.

"What you got?" asked Doug.

Mark held up the cigarette butt that he'd picked up from the ground next to the gate. "Any idea who might have left this at the gate?" he asked.

Doug looked at the butt with concern. "Pull the card from the trail camera," he instructed as he handed Mark a key he kept in his truck.

Taking the key, Mark walked about fifteen feet into the tree line near the gate. Bolted to a tree was a camouflage trail camera that was motion activated. While it was designed for hunters to view deer, it also worked to capture vehicles at the gate. Mark used the key to unlock the protective case and removed the memory card from the camera. They would view the photographs on the computer back at the house.

Mark got back into the truck. Held up the memory card and said, "Let's go see who paid us a visit."

CHAPTER 19

By the time the six public safety officers finished putting back all the stolen equipment, it was starting to get dark. "Well, I guess it's time to go dig a hole," said Nick as he climbed up onto the backhoe and started it up. Being a farmer his entire life, he was very familiar with the machinery and made short work of digging a hole several feet deep.

Jessie stood over the body of the dead biker while Nick and the others worked on the grave. She reached into the right cargo pocket of her uniform pants and pulled out a package of cigarettes. She knew it was a bad habit, one she had been working hard to quit. She started smoking when she was eleven years old, as it was common in her family as well as the company they kept. She had a rough childhood, and looking down at the dead biker, she couldn't help but think he could have easily been one of her brothers or cousins. If the chief had not taken her under his wing and showed her what life could offer, she imagined she would be running around with some guy just like this and probably meet the same fate. She didn't know where she would end up in life, but she didn't want her dead body to be dumped in a ditch behind the maintenance yard, mourned by no one.

She took a cigarette out of the pack and lit it. Jessie hated the fact she could not kick the habit as she prided herself on being able to achieve anything if she put her mind to it. Embarrassed that she couldn't stop, she told the others that she wasn't trying to. But she never smoked in front of the chief. She wasn't sure if it was out of respect for him or because she wanted his approval as some sort of a father figure. When he was her high school coach, he rode her pretty hard about it. Brad was her idea of what a father could be, not the poor examples from within her own family. She joined the fire department not only to follow in his footsteps but, mostly, to keep him in her life after high school.

Stepping to the side as the backhoe pulled up to the body, she put out her cigarette. They all picked up the body and placed it on the loader for the short ride to the open grave. Once there, they dropped the body into the hole and covered it with dirt. Not sure what to say, they all remained silent.

Jessie held the biker's driver's license in her hand. She didn't share the information with the others, and she wasn't sure why. For some reason it was personal to her. His name was Oscar Redding, and he was twenty-six years old and from Milwaukee. Oddly enough, he was an organ doner. He was somebody's son. He might even have had a little sister somewhere in the world. Although he certainly got what was coming to him, she couldn't help but wonder about the family he left behind. And also, the family she left behind.

They returned to the station with the fuel cans and about a dozen guns well after the sun went down. As they entered the bay, the chief motioned for Jessie to come to his office. While she rolled her eyes as if she was annoyed, inside she desperately wanted to speak with him as she felt alone and isolated. Her university closing down during the last semester before graduation caused her to fear all of her accomplishments were for not.

"What's up, Chief?" she asked, walking into the office.

"Have a seat," he said pointing to one of the empty chairs. He could smell the cigarette smoke on her uniform as she walked in, but with all that was going on, he felt it best not to say anything. Brad and his wife had not had children, and Kimberly wasn't interested in adopting. Motherhood was not on her social agenda. Brad thought of Jessie like a daughter, and he wanted the best for her. He knew her tough exterior was hiding the little girl who longed for someone to care about her.

"So, what do you think about all that's going on in the world?" asked Brad.

"I'm surprised it took this long; the wheels have been coming off this bus for a long time."

"That they have," replied Brad. With a smirk, he asked her what her plans were as a way of trying to get her to open up to him.

"Well, I just learned the university will be closing down just when I only have one semester to go, so that's happening." She was afraid Brad would be disappointed, as he was the only one pushing for her to go to college.

"You already have the education; they can't take that from you. And now I wouldn't worry too much about repaying those student loans," he said with a grin.

"I guess that's one way of looking at it, but I was doing it all for that stupid piece of paper that I will never get," she said in a tone of defeat.

"That piece of paper didn't mean all that much last week, and it means far less now. The actual education is what's important. The fact of the matter is you have three and a half years of college education. I suspect most kids soon won't even be going to high school. Additionally, you have a trade that is still essential, unlike many folks. As a firefighter, EMT, and now a police officer, you have invaluable skill sets. You are young and healthy; a lot of folks aren't, and with the collapse of medical facilities and pharmacies, they will be bad off pretty fast. And you have a lot of good friends here at the firehouse to support you. I would say you are far better off than most of the folks I know."

After hearing that perspective from the chief, she started to view her future as not so gloomy after all. Her story wasn't ending because of all this; it was just starting.

"Thanks, Chief. That helped a lot."

As Jessie was walking out of the office, Brad said in a low voice behind her, "And on the bright side, the absence of cigarettes will make it all the easier for people to quit smoking."

Jessie walked out of the office pretending not to hear him. Once around the corner she turned her head to the side and sniffed her shoulder to see if she could smell the cigarettes on her clothes.

CHAPTER 20

As Doug and Mark pulled into the parking area next to the other cars, Baxter ran down from the deck to greet them. The girls were sitting in the dark out on the deck because it was a nice night and they wanted their eyes adjusted to the low light in case their visitors came back. They didn't want a light on inside the house because that made it easier to see in and harder to see out.

As Doug walked up onto the deck, he could see that Penny was wearing her Glock in a holster on her right side. Between that and the lights, he figured something must have spooked her.

As the girls filled them in on the incident from a few hours earlier, Doug was very concerned. He was confident the men were looking for a target of opportunity, and they were a big one. The concealed location of the property behind the trees prevented most folks from knowing they were back there. The fact that these guys were searching for homes said a lot. The fact that they were using binoculars and two-way radios said even more.

Doug took the memory card down to his office while everyone, including Baxter, followed. After he started his computer up, he entered the memory card and brought up the images. He toggled through the various photos of each of them coming and going and finally got to a vehicle he didn't recognize. It appeared to be a white Ford extended-cab pickup with a lift kit. It looked like a model from the late 1990s. The truck had a rather unique set of black mag wheels that would make it fairly easy to identify in an area full of farm trucks. While the photos were not ideal, they could make out four people, two riding in the cab and two in the bed. At least two of them carried slung rifles, and at least one had an exposed pistol in a holster. One stood by the truck and smoked a cigarette while the others walked into the tree line, apparently trying to see where the blocked road led.

"I'm pretty sure they will be back at some point. We'd better keep a watch around the clock until we get things figured out. I will stay up and take the first shift since I need to write my report anyway. Mark, you get some sleep and relieve me at 2 a.m.," said Doug.

"Roger that."

"Dad," said Maddy, "I want to carry a pistol also, but the gun belt you gave me doesn't fit over my baby bump any more. Do you have a bigger one?"

"I think I have something that will work for you." Doug got up and walked across the basement to a set of decorative barn doors. These were a must-have when they finished the basement as Penny was addicted to watching home designer Joanna Gaines on HGTV, and Joanna was famous for her remodeled barn doors. As Doug pulled open the door, he entered the unfinished area of the basement. This was the area where he kept his larger gun safe and shelves full of supplies that needed to be temperature regulated.

He came back out with a black Bianchi shoulder holster. He was adjusting the straps so they would fit her much-smaller frame. Maddy recognized it from her childhood as the one her dad wore when he dressed in a suit for work.

Doug handed the holster to Maddy and said, "Try this on." A shoulder holster was common for pregnant law enforcement officers and military personnel as it did not require the use of a belt. The holster held a pistol under the left arm and two spare magazines under the right arm.

"Can I put a Glock in this?" asked Maddy.

"No, it's made for an M11." The Sig Sauer M11 was a military pistol issued to people who needed a more compact gun than the standard Beretta

M9 for concealment. Air Force Office of Special Investigations and Naval Criminal Investigative Service special agents typically carried this pistol, along with a few other special groups.

"Do we have one of those?" asked Penny.

"Pretty much," said Doug. The civilian version of the M11 was the model 228. Doug had one in a shadow box on the wall in his office. His team had given it to him upon his retirement. It was laser engraved with his OSI badge, name, and dates of service.

Doug pulled the framed gun off the wall and sat it on his desk. Opening the glass, he removed the pistol and pulled back the slide to verify it was unloaded. Once verified, he handed it to his daughter.

"I can't take this one. It's special," she said.

"It was going to get passed down to you eventually, and at least now I can see you use it before my funeral," he said with a sarcastic tone. Once he said it, he noticed his wife giving him a stern look, letting him know his comment wasn't funny under the circumstances. "Anyway," he went on, "I will get you some magazines and a few boxes of 9mm for it. Tomorrow, you can take it to the range and get familiar with it."

Doug had built a shooting range on the back side of the property soon after they purchased it. Over the years it became more elaborate as he added metal reactionary targets at various distances. He would often host shooting competitions on weekends for his family and friends. Most of the guys on the fire department competed in three-gun competitions at his place and had acquired some pretty impressive skills. Doug was confident Maddy would have no issue transitioning to the new pistol; she just needed a few magazines to get comfortable with it.

CHAPTER 21

It took Doug almost two hours to complete his report and the search warrant return document. He would need to get them to Chilton within the next four days to be in compliance with the judge's order. He typed the report on his laptop outside on the deck so he would be able to hear a vehicle or person approach. Now that the paperwork was done, he still had about four hours of his security shift before he would be relieved. Estimating that burglars would wait until most people were asleep before they snuck in, he wanted to be positioned out in the woods before 11 p.m.

Selecting the best location for his folding camp chair out by the gate required some thought. He wanted to be concealed in the dark and in a location where headlights would not inadvertently illuminate him. He wanted to be near a thick tree that could be used as cover and sweep away the leaves and twigs on the ground so he could move with stealth in the dark. Once he found the best location, he set up his chair and ensured it was well concealed about fifteen yards from the gravel road.

Sitting in the dark shadows and concealed by the trees, he wore dark clothing, his gun belt, and body armor. The Velcro area now bore a "Sheriff" patch rather than "Trooper." Resting across his lap was his Benelli M2 tactical semi-automatic shotgun. It held eight 12-gauge shells. The shotgun had a surefire flashlight mounted on it so Doug could verify the threat before shooting in low light condition. He had it loaded with heavy 00 buckshot rounds, which would expel a blast of nine lead balls with every pull of the trigger. While Doug's AR-15 was a far more versatile weapon, the shotgun was the better choice for this particular situation. Doug could only see about twenty yards in the dark woods, and at that range the 12-gauge was the reigning champ.

It was about midnight when he heard the sound of a truck engine slowly pulling up the gravel road from the county highway. He couldn't see any headlights shining through the trees, which meant they were intentionally trying to go undetected. The truck stopped about fifty yards short of the gate.

Doug radioed the on-call public safety officers and advised them of the situation. It would only take them a few minutes to respond to his location. Mark also signaled he heard the transmission from inside the house and would only take a couple minutes to get dressed and respond.

As the four men from the truck walked the rest of the way up the access road to Doug's concealed location, Doug used a thick tree for cover as he prepared to confront the would-be thieves. He waited until they were ten yards away to make his move.

The incredibly bright light on the shotgun illuminated the men with 1,000 lumens, simultaneously taking away their night vision while also disorienting them.

"Sheriff's department! Show me your hands!" shouted Doug.

The men froze for a brief second like deer in the headlights of an oncoming car. Three of them turned to run, bumping into one another and falling in the process as their pupils had immediately constricted, rendering them night blind for the next few minutes. The fourth man, also night blind, chose to draw his pistol and start firing in the direction of the light. He chose poorly as he was met with a single blast from Doug's shotgun.

At the range of ten yards, all nine lead balls from the 12-gauge penetrated his chest, destroying both lungs and heart. He collapsed to the ground, dropping his weapon in the process. Moments later, Doug heard the truck engine start up and the vehicle reverse rapidly down the gravel road. He next heard a crash and the crunching of metal. To Doug it sounded like the driver had backed into a tree due to his night blindness. Once the vehicle finally made it to the main road, Doug saw the headlights come on as it traveled down the highway, moving away from town.

Doug got on the radio to the county dispatch, not sure if they were monitoring any longer.

"Rockport Deputy to Calumet County Dispatch."

After a minute Doug heard a reply from another deputy elsewhere in the county.

"Deputy Chapman from Charlie-7, we no longer have a dispatcher after hours."

"Roger that, Charlie-7. I wasn't sure. I have shots fired up in Rockport and a suspect down. Is there any sort of officer-involved shooting protocol any longer?" asked Doug.

"Negative, Chapman. You are the law in your region. Handle it as you see fit, and get a report to the sheriff when you can. We have had several officer-involved shootings across the county the past couple of days. Stay safe and watch your back."

"Will do. Just in case you are in a position to intercept, I have three suspects headed east on County Highway KR in a white Ford pickup."

"Sorry, Chapman, I am nowhere near your neck of the woods."

"Roger that. Chapman out."

About a minute later, Mark called out from the dark, "Approaching from your six," to alert Doug he was coming up behind him and to avoid friendly fire.

"Approach," called out Doug.

As Doug and Mark moved up to the body on the ground, they held him at gunpoint. Once they got closer, they could tell he was no longer alive. Due to the massive nature of the wound, they did not attempt to provide medical attention. It would only have been a waste of valuable resources.

"Rockport Lieutenant to Deputy Chapman," said Lou over the radio. "We are approaching your location; do you have instructions for us?"

"Check the road for a few miles to look for that white Ford truck, occupied three times. If you don't find it, return to my location. Use caution, they are armed."

"Roger that," replied Lou.

Doug searched the body but could find no identification. The man was probably around thirty years old and had the look of a methamphetamine user—very thin, rotting teeth, sores on his skin. He had several amateurish tattoos on his body, most likely jailhouse ink.

As the two stood over the body, the Rockport fire department wildfire truck pulled up and turned on the overhead white lights, illuminating the entire area. Lou, Vic, and Ryan got out of the truck as the on-duty team, and Jessie accompanied them. All were armed and wearing their new badges.

"Looks like he chose poorly," said Lou.

"Yup," said Doug. "Let me take some photos for my report, then you can haul him back to town. Bury him out behind the maintenance yard."

"He doesn't have any identification on him," said Mark.

"His name is Merl Hill," said Jessie matter-of-factly.

"You know him?" asked Doug.

"Used to, back in the day. He ran with my oldest brother, Rosco. I haven't seen either one of them for a few years. Last I heard they were in the county jail serving time for meth."

"You OK?" asked Lou, concerned about Jessie losing an acquaintance.

"He ain't nothing to me! Sounds like he got what was coming to him," she said.

"You know anyone with a late 1990s white Ford truck with a lift kit and custom black mag wheels?" asked Doug.

Jessie thought about it. "I haven't seen him in seven or eight years, but I think one of my uncles used to have a truck like that. Tommy was his name; I think he lived at a junkyard about ten miles east of town. I have no idea where he stays now."

"Well, let's keep our eyes open for that truck. I suspect we may see them again."

While the guys were concerned about Jessie's emotional state, she was worried the guys would judge her for knowing Merl.

CHAPTER 22

Morning came far too early for Doug as his cell phone alarm beeped on the nightstand next to his bed. He wished for a few more hours of sleep, but he needed to be up for the town board meeting starting in just an hour. Deciding that fifteen minutes was all he could spare, he rolled over to hit the snooze button. As he rolled over to reach for his phone, he came nose to nose with Baxter, who was sitting next to the bed waiting for him to get up. Knowing that hitting the snooze was no longer an option, he reluctantly turned off the alarm and sat up.

After getting dressed, he picked up his gun belt and secured it around his waist. Out of habit, he drew his Glock and performed a press check, ensuring it was loaded and prepared for duty. Now that he was active law enforcement once again, there was no longer any point in concealing his firearm. He re-holstered the weapon and went downstairs to the kitchen. Although he could use a good breakfast, there wasn't enough time. After filling his travel mug with some coffee, he grabbed two protein bars and placed one in the cargo pocket of his pants for later. One of the preps Doug had neglected was to stock up on his favorite coffee. He had been drinking Fire Department Coffee (FDC) for a long time as it was veteran owned and operated by active firefighters. It was his favorite, and he dreaded the day when he drank his last cup.

He wanted to stop by the fire station to get a morning briefing before the 9 a.m. board meeting. As he walked out onto the deck, he saw Penny preparing to tend the garden. She was also covering the security shift, having relieved Mark about an hour earlier.

"You get enough sleep?" she asked.

"No, but I need to get going."

"Do you think those guys will come back?" she asked, obviously concerned after her husband killed a man on their property last night.

"Not likely," said Doug, trying to put her at ease. "I think they got more than they bargained for last night." Doug hoped he was right but feared he wasn't. "Just as a precaution, I think we should have at least one person awake at all hours for security."

The night before, he told his wife about the invitation for Brad and Kimberly to stay at the house. Under the circumstances, she welcomed more people at the house to share with the chores and security. She was very fond of Brad, and he would be extremely useful at times like this. But while she and Kimberly were friends, she was best in small doses. Living under the same roof with her for an extended period could put a strain on the relationship.

Doug gave Penny a kiss goodbye and Baxter a pat on the head. "Make sure Mark is up by one thirty, because his shift at the station starts at two."

"I know," said Penny. "I love you."

"Love you too." He climbed into his truck and placed his rifle and body armor in the front passenger seat.

As he drove off the property, he was sure to lock the gate behind him, and he placed a fresh memory card in the trail camera. Driving a few yards further down the gravel road, he could see blood on the ground where the man he'd shot eight hours earlier died. As he pulled further around the curve, he could see damage on a tree consistent with a pickup truck backing into it. There was some paint transfer on the tree bark, and on the ground at the base there were pieces of a broken taillight. *I guess that truck will now be that much easier to identify*, he thought.

Turning onto the county highway, Doug drove the short distance into town for a fast briefing at the fire station. As he walked into the building, he saw Lou making a fresh pot of coffee in the kitchen. Always looking to top off his mug, he joined him at the coffee pot. Doug could see the fatigue on Lou's face as he added a little more coffee ground to the filter to make it a stronger pot.

"Long night?" he asked, all too familiar with the look.

Nodding his head, Lou replied, "Oh yeah. After we left your place and dumped that body back at the maintenance yard, we came back to the station. There were three teenagers waiting for us, two girls and a boy. The boy was pretty beat up, broken nose and a couple teeth missing. One of the girls had way too much to drink, and a couple of guys at the party were taking advantage of her. The boy came to her rescue and caught a beating for his chivalry. The other girl tried to call the police, but the phones were out. The next best thing she could think of was to bring them here for help."

"Where did it happen?" asked Doug.

"That big fancy house on Lake Winnebago. The one owned by the paper mill executive, Roger Griffith. I guess Mr. and Mrs. Griffith have been stuck in Atlanta because of the civil unrest for the past couple weeks. Now with the collapse, it's doubtful they will ever return. Their obnoxious college boy, Stuart, is all alone in there with a complete bar full of alcohol. He was hosting a bunch of local kids at what he was calling an End of the World Party. Apparently, he believed there were no more consequences in life. There must have been forty kids partying like there was no tomorrow. Most of them were under eighteen and several so intoxicated they could barely stand. One girl overdosed on heroin; we brought her back with a couple doses of Narcan. If this was at a normal time, we would have transported several of them to the hospital as medical emergencies."

"What did you do with the overdose kid?" asked Doug.

"My options were pretty limited. I had Vic and Ryan take her to Doc Shelby's house in the fire truck while Jessie and I stayed at the mansion to look after the rest of them."

"You took her to the veterinarian?" asked Doug.

"It was the only option we had. And we learned last night that without the contract ambulance service we used to have, we now need to transport patients ourselves. Leaving firemen behind and using the engine to transport is not a great option. I am having the guys take apart the old ambulance—the one that we converted to a heavy rescue unit—back into a medical transport."

"Good idea," said Doug. "What actions did you take from the law enforcement perspective?"

Lou looked up at him with a completely exhausted look on his face. "Wasn't too much we could do. There were way too many of them for just Jessie and me. We couldn't call their parents, couldn't write them tickets or arrest anyone. They knew we couldn't do much, and some were not cooperating, especially Stuart. Finally, I made the call to dump out the rest of the alcohol, to which Stuart objected. At one point he took a swing at Jessie, which didn't end too well for him. The two of us finally got him under control, but we all got a lot of lumps in the process. We handcuffed him to a heavy piece of furniture for the rest of the time we were there. We collected all the car keys we could to keep the kids from driving drunk. Then we brought the most highly intoxicated kids into one room so we could monitor them while they sobered up. We found one girl in a bedroom passed out and partially undressed. She was sixteen years old, and one of the other girls told us Stuart took naked photos of her while she was passed out. Jessie took his cell phone as evidence."

The coffee now ready, Lou poured a cup, then set the fresh pot down in front of Doug so he could top off his travel mug. Lou continued, "We stayed for about four hours until we were sure the highly intoxicated kids would be OK and made sure any vulnerable kids got a ride home. We took the girl we found undressed home and let her mother know what happened since she was only sixteen. I left all the car keys we collected on the chief's desk along with Stuart's cell phone. I imagine some parents will be by later to collect them."

Doug was more than impressed. "It sounds like you guys handled a bad situation better than I would have expected," said Doug. "What did you do with Stuart?"

"He stayed handcuffed the rest of the time we were there. He spent about an hour screaming his head off that he was going to sue us for everything we had. After that he just got quiet and gave me the stink eye the rest of the time. Once Vic and Ryan returned with the truck and we were ready to clear the scene, the four of us unhandcuffed him and let him know you would likely be by to chat with him at some point."

"I look forward to it," said Doug, as he put the lid back on his travel mug. "I never liked that kid or his old man. I arrested his dad a few years back for drunk driving and possession of cocaine. He crashed his Escalade into a parked car, and just like his boy, he had a big mouth. He hired a high-powered attorney from Madison, and somehow, they got the DA to dismiss the charges. Never even made it to court."

"Amazing," said Lou. "Well, we just got back to the station about half an hour ago, so I haven't written my report yet. Everything will be in there, including the girl we returned to her mother."

"Thanks, and great job last night!" said Doug as he took his coffee and headed over to the town board meeting.

CHAPTER 23

Doug walked into the board meeting with a couple minutes to spare, but the eager members and the chief had started without him. It seemed they all had taken on their new responsibilities with vigor and were making solid progress. Doug filled them in on all that had transpired since yesterday's meeting, the incident at Tucker's place, the shooting at his house, and the party at Stuart's. They were surprised at how quickly things were falling apart.

"Well, we have actually made some good progress here," replied Mrs. Barnes. She then slid a copy of a document across the table for Doug to view. As he looked around the table, he could see everyone else was looking over the same document.

Medical Committee: Three medical providers have agreed to see patients. Dr. Shelby, a veterinarian; Dr. Hanson, a cardiologist; and Nurse Practitioner Ransom, an OB/GYN. They will each see human walk-in patients two days per week out at Shelby Veterinary Clinic. The Public Safety-Paramedics and EMTs can see emergency patients who show up at the fire station after hours.

Commerce Committee: We will use the high school gymnasium for a swap meet, daily between 9:00 a.m. and 3:00 p.m. This will give the people a chance to get together and trade for goods and services. As money no longer has value, people will barter for goods and services.

Public Safety Committee: The Rockport Volunteer Fire Department will transition to a Public Safety Department and provide police, fire, and emergency medical services.

Communications Committee: The town board will hold a Town Hall open forum in the high school gymnasium every Wednesday evening at 4:00 p.m. Additionally, we will print a daily information bulletin and post it at key locations around the town.

Education Committee: In addition to traditional K-12 education, we will establish an adult educational program to teach essential skills like gardening, hunting, fishing, water purification, first aid, etc. We will establish a list of teachers and people who possess critical skills to bring it all together.

"I'm impressed!" said the chief after putting down the document. "You all hit the ground running and got a lot accomplished."

"Yeah," echoed Doug. "I think we have a very good start for sure."

Mrs. Barnes smiled with a sense of pride. Doug thought to himself that maybe there was more to the woman than he realized. Maybe she just needed a real challenge in front of her to make her shine as a leader.

"I only have one suggestion," said Brad. "I know we have a couple social workers in town. Maybe we could get them to see patients a day or two as well. I think as we move forward, a lot of folks will need some counseling. People are already experiencing social anxiety from losing their social media community, and pretty soon all the people with mental health conditions will run out of their medication. This could be anything from depression all the way to schizophrenia."

They all thought about the prospect of mental health emergencies and what they would do with a person who needed to be committed. Nobody had a good answer, but they all recognized that a rapidly growing need would soon develop.

"What is going on with the retirement home out on fourth street?" asked Doug.

Mrs. Barnes got an angry look on her face and said, "It's just terrible. They can't operate any longer, so they asked the people to come take their family members home. While many have done so, there are about a dozen patients still there whose families won't take them. Some of the staff are great people and won't simply abandon their duties, but they have their own families to take care of as well. I'm trying to work on that issue, but it's just so frustrating."

Satisfied that the town board was now moving forward, Doug and Brad left to tackle the new issues of the day.

"What do you have going on today?" asked Doug.

"I need to see if I can find a gurney for that old ambulance so we can get back into the patient transport business. I also want to see if I can get some of the officers who are off duty today to run back to Tucker's and bring back some more of our fuel."

Doug pondered all the things on his to-do list and said, "I want to run out to Chilton and hand over the search warrant return and my reports on Tucker and the guy I shot last night. I would like to be back to the house before Mark goes on duty at two o'clock this afternoon. Penny is pretty freaked out, and I'm concerned the other three guys may try to return."

"Think they are stupid enough to try to come back?" asked Brad.

"I stopped underestimating people's ability to be stupid a long time ago," he said, taking a sip of his coffee. "Speaking of stupid, I need to run out and have a chat with Stuart Griffith. Want to run over there with me?"

"Sure, someone's got to keep you out of trouble," he said in a joking tone. "I will follow you in my truck so you can head out to Chilton from there."

As the Ram and Suburban pulled up in front of the 6,500-square-foot home, Doug thought to himself that he may have made the wrong career choices in life. Then he pondered his situation compared to Stuart's, and he knew his choices in life were just fine. Even with all the money the Griffiths had, they were poorly prepared for the current situation.

As the two men walked up to the front door, they observed several cars parked haphazardly on the front lawn. Brad looked over at Doug with a quizzical look on his face.

Doug chuckled and said, "Yeah, Lou took the keys so the kids wouldn't drive drunk. They are sitting on your desk for the parents to come collect."

Brad smiled while nodding in approval. "Pretty creative, I will give him that."

"Yeah, the old guy is an out-of-the-box thinker, that's for sure. That's just what we need these days. I'm pretty sure I would have responded like a twenty-first-century police officer before the collapse. That system just doesn't exist anymore. While I thought I would have to teach Lou how to be a cop, maybe I need to be the student for a while," said Doug. "Before we go in there, did you talk to Kimberly yet about moving out to our place?"

"Yeah, she was pretty set with staying at our house. She thinks I'm overreacting and that things will get back to normal eventually. I think when she learns that you shot a guy last night while she was home alone just a few hundred yards away, that may be enough to change her mind."

"Good luck. I think the sooner you both get out to our place, the better off we will all be." Turning back to the business at hand, Doug knocked on the door.

After he knocked, they heard a voice from within the house yell to come in. Doug opened the door and peered inside slowly, just in case someone was waiting inside to get the jump on them. As the two men walked into the multimillion-dollar home, it was clear Stuart did not have much respect for his parents' property. The place was trashed, and several high-dollar bottles of wine sat empty all over the living room and kitchen.

Stuart sat at the expensive dining room table with a couple of his lacrosse buddies. It looked like he may have gotten a broken nose during the scuffle with Jessie and Lou last night. It was swollen, and he was holding an ice pack against it. Apparently, they had been expecting someone else when they yelled to come in, based on their reaction seeing the two men.

When Stuart realized the two men standing in his living room were wearing gun belts and police badges, he stood up and shouted for them to get out while charging at them aggressively. As Stuart attempted to shove Doug in the chest with both hands, Doug simply turned his body to the side and delivered a lightning-fast jab directly to Stuart's already broken nose. This sent Stuart crashing to the floor, holding his nose as it bled.

"What did you think was going to happen?" asked Doug in a surprised voice. "Didn't you get dealt with last night by a girl and an old man? Did you think we would be easier?" he asked, looking over at the massive size of the fire chief.

Doug looked over at the two preppy boys sitting at the table with shocked looks on their faces. One of the boys then realized that a white line of powder was laid out on the table in front of him. He nonchalantly attempted to swipe the powder off the table with his arm but was only successful in spreading it around.

The situation was rather comical, and Doug couldn't help but laugh out loud at the sight. "Do you two live here?" he asked.

They both shook their heads no.

"Then scram!" he said, pointing his thumb over his shoulder toward the door behind him.

Brad was both amazed and amused at how fast Stuart's buddies abandoned him during his time of need.

Doug walked over and picked up one of the fancy dining room chairs and brought it over to where Stuart was sitting on the floor holding his nose. Placing the chair directly in front of Stuart, Doug sat down on it. As Stuart placed the palm of his hand on the floor to push himself up to his feet, Doug put the heel of his boot on the back of his hand, preventing him from doing so.

"Please keep your seat Stuart, we need to have a chat."

Stuart reluctantly sat back on the floor looking up at Doug. He wasn't as defiant as he had been moments earlier as there was nobody left for him to try to impress.

"How old are you now, Stuart?" asked Doug.

"I just turned twenty-two."

"Did you know that most of the kids you provided alcohol to were under twenty-one? Hell, the majority of them were under eighteen," said Doug with a calm voice as he maintained pressure on the back of Stuart's hand with his boot.

"I didn't provide anything. If they drank my dad's liquor, that's on them."

"Where are all the drugs, Stuart?"

"What drugs?" he asked defiantly.

"For starters, the drugs the girl overdosed on here last night. Then we can talk about that white powder over on your table. You do know that if that girl dies, you will be charged with her murder?"

"I want my attorney," he said smugly.

"That is your right," said Doug. "You want to give him a call? I'll wait." There was an awkward pause as the two looked at each other in silence for about thirty seconds.

Stuart didn't look quite so smug when he realized there was no phone to call his father's attorney down in Madison. He then started to piece together his actual dilemma. His father's attorney may not be working anymore after the collapse. How would he pay for an attorney without his fathers' money? He couldn't even call his father's business partners for help.

"Here is the deal, Stuart. I am placing you under arrest," Doug advised, just in case the young man wasn't sure.

"For what?" Stuart asked, as if he was surprised by the fact.

"Well, let me see. I guess we will start off with two counts of battery to a police officer, followed by possession of narcotics and contributing to the delinquency of minors for the alcohol. Then I suppose I'd better add on the sexual assault of a child."

"What child?" asked Stuart defiantly.

"She is sixteen, Stuart. You are twenty-two."

Stuart looked down in a deflated manner.

"And I suppose we will round off the charges with child pornography for the cell phone photos."

"Can we work something out?" asked Stuart with a tone of desperation.

"What did you have in mind?" inquired Doug.

"How about my dad's Corvette?

"And now we can add bribery to the list of charges," said Doug.

Pulling Stuart up to his feet, Doug turned him around and handcuffed him behind his back. Knowing he didn't have a police cage in his personal truck, Doug cuffed his right hand, then ran the other cuff behind Stuart's belt before he cuffed the left hand. This would prevent Stuart from trying to slip the cuffs down over his legs as the cuffs were held in place by his own belt.

"Can I at least get my shoes?" asked Stuart.

"They will give you a set of slippers at the county jail," said Doug as they walked him out of the house in his socks.

At the Ram, Doug opened the front passenger door and moved his rifle and armor into the back seat. He then put Stuart in the front passenger seat and belted him in place. He took a disposable set of flexicuffs, which were basically an oversized plastic zip tie, and secured his ankles together. As he closed the passenger door, Doug turned to speak with Brad.

"You think the jail will hold him under the current circumstances?" asked Brad.

"No chance," said Doug with a chuckle. "But I'm headed there anyway, so I will drop him off at the jail and let them turn him loose. He can think about the consequences of his actions while he walks back."

"Well, that should keep him out of our hair for three or four hours," chuckled Brad.

Doug smiled. "Longer if he's not wearing shoes."

Just as the two were about to leave Stuart's place, they were interrupted by the sound of loud music blaring from a car driving down the street. The car was an early 1990s Chevy Camaro, with badly faded blue paint and a differently colored driver's side quarter panel. The car slowed and turned into the large circular driveway of Stuart's house.

"You want to bet that's who Stuart thought was at his door when he told us to come in?" asked Brad with a laugh.

The car pulled in directly behind Brad's Suburban. The two teenagers inside obviously had not seen the large "Sheriff" magnets affixed to the doors when they pulled up. The way they were dressed and the car they drove made them seem very out of place at the affluent residence. Doug highly doubted they were university buddies of Stuart's. As they got out of the car and walked around the Suburban, they came face to face with Brad and Doug. The teenagers stopped in their tracks and looked down at their gun belts with exposed police badges.

"Morning, boys. You all lost?" asked Doug.

The two kids didn't know what to say and just stood there with their mouths open. It was clear they were panicking while trying to look nonchalant. The boy who drove was maybe sixteen years old, and the passenger was even younger.

Pointing to the green school backpack that was hanging off of the driver's shoulder, Doug asked, "Does that bag belong to you, or did you just find it someplace and want to turn it into the police as lost and found property?"

Still in a state of shock, they looked at one another again then back at Doug.

"Found it," said the driver, nervously holding it out to Doug.

"You can put it in the back of my truck. I'm sure I can find the owner," said Doug.

The teenager slowly put the bag in the bed of Doug's truck, careful to keep his hands exposed at all times and not make any sudden moves.

"Thanks, guys. You have yourselves a good day now," said Doug while resting his hand on his pistol, trying to send a strong message. It was clear by their faces the message was received.

"You too," the younger one said. They got back in their car and drove away.

Brad and Doug looked at one another and let out a laugh.

"Is being a cop that much fun all the time?" asked the fire chief.

"Well, it does have its moments," said Doug.

Doug opened the backpack and, just as expected, found what appeared to be methamphetamines inside.

"I guess old Stuart used up the last of dad's cocaine and had to settle for this." He pulled out five plastic bags he estimated weighed an ounce each.

"What's all that worth?" asked Brad.

"Well, last month it would have cost around eight hundred dollars per ounce. With the hyperinflation today it would cost, well, dad's Corvette, probably," said Doug with a laugh. "I better get this kid to Chilton so I can get home before Mark has to report for duty."

"Roger that! See you later," said Brad.

Brad grinned as he watched Doug climb into the cab of his truck with the green backpack in hand. He laughed to himself as he overheard Doug talking to Stuart before closing his door. "Good news, Stuey. Those nice boys found your backpack."

CHAPTER 24

"How much farther?" asked Ty Wilcox, the leader of the Dark Arrows Motorcycle Club.

"Just a couple miles," replied Tank, his second in command, as their pickup traveled down the dirt road.

The gang had taken refuge in an old run-down motel near Lake Winnebago, between High Cliff State Park and the Town of Rockport. The old motel was well off the beaten path and only occupied by a few meth addicts, whom the gang had run off the day before.

"You think it's wise to stay this close to town after breaking me out and shooting the corrections officers?" asked Ty.

Tank shook his head no and said, "It's just for a couple days. We ran into some problems and had to regroup."

"What problems?"

"We had to create a diversion to draw the deputies away so we could do the jailbreak. We set up an ambush in the state park that worked out well enough. We killed four of them."

The gang leader didn't look very pleased at the news. "Killing cops brings a whole lot of unnecessary attention, Tank," he said in a chastising tone.

"Times have changed, boss," said Tank.

"Was that the problem you were talking about, or is there something else?"

Hesitating to answer, Tank said, "Well, the ambush went well enough, but afterward there was another shooter who attacked us from a different ridge. He killed Jimmy and Dave and wounded Oscar."

"Did my little brother get hit?"

"No. He didn't get hit, but I don't think he is doing great mentally. He thinks he is still overseas fighting the war half the time."

"My brother will be fine. He just needs some more time. How bad off is Oscar?"

"Not too good. He took a rifle round through the chest. We dropped him off at your buddy Tucker's place and told him to tend to his wounds."

"Tucker's place? What the hell does he know about first aid?" asked the gang leader.

"I didn't have a lot of options, boss."

"Well, we can't stay in that motel for long. Every lawman in the state will be gunning for us now."

"I don't think there are too many lawmen left these days," smirked Tank. "We should only be there a couple of days, then we can move on to wherever you say. Your pal Tucker is brokering a drug deal with a guy named Tommy Wolf. As soon as we get the batch of meth he is cooking, we can be on our way."

"OK, but I want to get moving soon. I don't need a bunch of pissed-off cops looking for revenge. What do we have for security?"

"The place is pretty desolate and off the main road. There is only a single roadway leading to the motel. I have a man posted in a pickup at all hours watching over the rooms and the bikes. I think we will be fine for a couple days."

"I hope you are right," said Ty. "Killing cops is never good business."

CHAPTER 25

It was a warm summer day, and the heat of the sun was beating down on his position. As he lay motionless in the tall grass, concealed perfectly in his environment, Conservation Warden Scott Connelly adjusted the focal piece of his spotting scope until the image became clear. He watched as a large, bearded man wearing a leather vest over his bare skin walked out of the front door of the old eight-room motel. The man was smoking a cigarette while standing in the parking lot next to thirteen parked Harley Davidson motorcycles.

Taking meticulous notes as he observed the position, he documented everything he saw, including people, facilities, weapons, and activities. Scott's full-time job less than a year earlier was as a cavalry scout for the US military. Known as the "eyes and ears" of the Army, cavalry scouts are specially trained to obtain, distribute, and share vital combat and battlefield intelligence on the enemy and combat circumstances. The mission he was performing now as a Wisconsin conservation warden was no different.

For a high school graduate in the far northern Ashland County, there wasn't much to offer a young man. Scott joined the Army and served his four-year tour before returning to Wisconsin and starting his dream job as a game warden. In this position he would be able to spend much of his time in the wilderness, which was his passion.

He graduated from the Wisconsin Conservation Warden Academy, which was co-located with the State Patrol Academy on Fort McCoy, and spent the next twelve months traveling around the state working with different regional wardens to complete the field training. His first field assignment was in Calumet County, working under Warden Justin Markson. He had only been assigned to the area a few days when the governor issued an emergency order calling most state law enforcement officers down to the cities of Madison and Milwaukee to assist with the civil unrest.

As a game warden, Scott felt very out of place working in urban Milwaukee, responding to city police calls as the government collapsed. Within a few days, his training officer had been killed and the joint law enforcement effort they supported had fully collapsed. When phones, internet, and radio communications in Milwaukee stopped working altogether, Scott had no direction or leadership support. He felt the best course of action was to return to his designated region in Calumet County until he could get a new assignment. Just as he returned to his area, he was surprised to hear a radio call from the Calumet County Dispatch sending deputies to High Cliff State Park for the search and rescue of a small girl. Apparently, Calumet County still had radio communications. As he was on the back side of the state park, he responded to the call to offer assistance from the back trail system.

As he approached the rally location for the search and rescue, he heard multiple rifles firing dozens of rounds. Dismounting his truck and grabbing his patrol rifle, he closed in on the sound of the shots through the dense terrain. When he reached the ridge, he could observe the bodies of four deputy sheriffs who had just been killed in an ambush about two hundred yards away on the next ridge. Several men wearing biker vests were approaching the bodies with rifles in hand. One of the deputies must have still been alive, because a gang member shot him as he lay on the ground defenseless.

Scott rapidly dropped down into the prone position to steady his rifle and make himself a smaller target. Centering his sights on the chest of the first man, he squeezed the trigger a single time. Watching his first target fall, he systematically moved onto the next target and did the same. By the time he moved onto the third target, the gang members were firing back and running for cover. Controlling his breathing to steady the shot, he aimed at the running target and pulled the trigger a third time. The third target fell briefly but was able to crawl to a location out of Scott's field of vision.

Scott reported the situation to the Calumet County Dispatch, but they were at the same time dealing with a jailbreak at the courthouse. Over the next two days, Scott tracked the bikers to the rural motel, where all eight rooms as well as the front office were now under their control. In addition to the motorcycles, they had three pickup trucks in their fleet. They were using one of the trucks as a security post at the far end of the parking lot. They had a folding camp chair and a beer cooler set up in the bed. A guard was always posted in the bed of the truck, watching over the motel, the vehicles, and the only road leading in.

Scott, concealed in the tall grass, had completed his intelligence-collecting mission. He had observed all angles of the motel compound over the past day. He had made a detailed sketch and noted all of the pertinent details. It was now time to go get some reinforcements from the sheriff's department.

After low-crawling back to his patrol truck, concealed hundreds of yards away on the other side of the wood line, he pulled off the camouflage ghillie suit that made him blend into the environment. Now dressed in his warden uniform, consisting of black cargo pants and a gray police uniform shirt, he climbed into his state-issued police pickup. He started it up and followed back trails and farm roads until he was well on the other side of the motel, then proceeded on to the sheriff's department.

As Scott approached Chilton, he saw a young man walking toward him traveling northbound on State Street. The man looked out of place as he was not wearing shoes and had a bloody nose. As Scott pulled over in his marked law enforcement vehicle, he asked the man if he needed any assistance. The man looked annoyed and said in a sarcastic tone, "I was told to walk home and think about the consequences of my actions."

Scott was a bit confused about the man's reply but thought he must have his reasons. He then continued on his way to the sheriff's department. Once in the parking lot, he parked his truck next to a gray Dodge Ram with a magnetic sheriff's decal on the door. As he entered the door to the sheriff's department, he found no one staffing the front desk to greet him. He rang the call bell and waited a couple minutes until Sheriff Decker himself appeared behind the bulletproof glass to greet the customer.

The sheriff looked exhausted but seemed very pleased to see the young game warden standing in his lobby. Scott met the sheriff two days earlier under the worst possible circumstances, as they looked over the bodies of his slain deputies. As horrible as it was, the sheriff was thankful Scott was there and inflicted a measure of justice on some of the killers. Opening the door to the secure area, the sheriff welcomed him inside and extended his hand.

"Warden Connelly, very glad to see you have stayed with our profession! What can we do for you?"

Scott grasped the sheriff's hand and gave it a shake. "Thank you, sir. Please call me Scott," the twenty-three-year-old rookie lawman said to the sheriff of the entire county. "I know where the biker gang is holed up," he said, getting right to the point.

Scott could see the look in the sheriff's eyes shift from one of welcome to vengeance.

"Let's go in the conference room and talk," he said in a serious tone as he secured the lobby door behind them. Entering the conference room, Scott saw a stern-looking man sitting at the table with some papers spread out in front of him. The man was around fifty years old and fit, and his short gray hair was worn in a military style, high and tight. The man looked familiar to Scott, but he just couldn't place him.

The sheriff introduced the man as Doug Chapman, a retired state trooper who just became the regional deputy for the town of Rockport. Doug stood and extended his hand to greet the young warden. Scott shook his hand as he recalled where he knew him from.

"Trooper Chapman, I recognize you from the academy at Fort McCoy. You came up to teach a seminar on counterterrorism operations based on your military experiences. It was impressive."

"Thanks. Please call me Doug," he said as they all had a seat. "So, I hear you are the man who got three of the gang," said Doug with a tone of gratitude.

"Yeah, I guess. I know I got two, but I may have winged a third," he said. The sheriff updated him that Doug found the third guy, and he had in fact died from his wound.

"So, you said you know where the gang is holed up?" inquired the sheriff, wanting to have the conversation in front of Doug so he did not have to repeat it. This got Doug's attention, and he directed his focus to the young man.

Scott took a breath in and let it out before he started his briefing. As a rookie lawman, this was by far the biggest thing he had experienced, and he was about to brief the county high sheriff and another lawman he aspired to be like. He cleared his throat and gave his brief, providing sketches and notes of the target.

"Impressive!" said Doug as he examined the familiar format of a combat reconnaissance sketch and detailed information. Looking up at Scott, he said, "You have military training."

"Yes, sir. I just got out before attending the academy. I was a 19 Delta."

"A cavalry scout," said Doug, translating the military specialty code into a term the sheriff would be more familiar with. "It looks like that scout training has already paid off big for us."

Scott was very proud of the compliment but fought to maintain the serious demeanor on his face.

As the three men viewed a large area map, they identified the motel as the former Sunrise Inn near the east shore of Lake Winnebago. The lake was the largest in Wisconsin, measuring thirty miles long and ten miles wide. Calumet County spanned the east half of the lake. The Sunrise Inn was a popular place in the 1950s and '60s for people coming up from the cities to experience summer waterskiing and winter ice fishing. It was located between the town of Rockport and the village of Harrison. In the 1970s, new roads were developed that left the motel off the main path. By the 1990s it functioned more as a low-income housing unit where the guests stayed for long periods of time.

"Well, Doug, being that I don't currently have a deputy covering the village of Harrison, this will be your operation. I can personally assist and can bring three or four deputies with me, but that won't be enough. Do you have any operator types in your Public Safety Department?" asked the sheriff.

"No," said Doug. "A lot of them are pretty good with firearms as we shoot competition out at my place. Five have prior military experience, but mostly in jobs like firefighter or communications—no direct-action type guys. I'm sure we could pull it off, but it would need some solid planning and a few practice runs."

The sheriff thought about it and said, "We need to do something. It's not just revenge for our guys; this gang will continue to terrorize the community until they have taken everything."

"Agreed," said Doug. "Give me two days to plan and train my guys. If all goes well, we will hit them at sunrise the day after tomorrow. We will stage out at my place. Wes, I will plan on you along with at least two others to show up no later than noon tomorrow for briefing and run-through."

"Sounds good," said the sheriff and former SWAT operator. He had complete faith in Doug's skills, and knowing he was in a better spot to evaluate his men, he allowed him to take the lead.

"What do you want me to do?" asked Scott.

"Glad you asked. You are the star of the show," said Doug. "I would like you to come back with me to my place and help plan the operation, if you are able."

"I don't have any direction from my leadership, and everything I own is in an army duffle in the back of my truck. I guess I work for you now until I hear something from the state DNR."

"Sounds good," said Doug.

While Doug looked over the sketch, he said, "In a perfect world, we would end up taking them all into custody without a fight. Then your problem would be how to keep them incarcerated for life and how to feed them."

The sheriff looked back at his friend and said, "This isn't a perfect world. It won't be as long as they are still breathing."

This was a bit concerning to Doug. He knew his friend was not in his right frame of mind, operating with high emotion and an extreme lack of sleep. Doug wanted payback as well, but they needed to do it with a measure of justice. It would be easy to set the motel on fire and shoot them as they ran out. That would be safer for his friends as well. While that was one of the contingency plans, they must first attempt to take them into custody and let a jury of their peers decide their fate. But he also had to balance the risk of his men with the threat. And there lay the challenge.

Doug gave Wes his police reports and the search warrant return before walking out to the parking lot with Scott. "If you want to follow me back to the Rockport Fire Station, I can introduce you to the guys and let them know you will be helping us. Then we can head out to my place and get started."

"Sounds good."

"How are you set up for food?" asked Doug.

Scott shook his head and said, "Getting pretty low. I have one MRE and two cans of chili left. I need to find a resupply pretty soon."

"Save your food; dinner is on me," said Doug as he crawled into his truck.

Scott followed Doug on his way back to Rockport. About five miles outside Chilton they passed that same guy walking up the road without shoes on. Scott thought it was odd when Doug honked at him and waved as he passed.

When they arrived at the Rockport Fire Station, both trucks pulled into the parking lot. As they stood in the lot, Doug explained how the firefighters had become posse members just the day before. "They are a solid bunch of guys and good shooters, but they have had little to no tactical training. Most of them hunt and will be of some use to us, but we simply can't put them in a position to fail. We need to stack the deck in our favor as much as possible or it's a nonstarter."

They entered the station, and Doug introduced Scott to the firefighters there. Mark had just arrived to serve as the officer in charge of the next shift starting at 2 p.m. He had the crew all working to modify the rescue truck back into its original service as an ambulance. As they greeted the young game warden, Jessie jumped down out of the back of the ambulance holding the automated external defibrillator (AED) they used to shock cardiac patients. The attractive female firefighter caught Scott's attention as he tried to maintain his conversation with the guys. He tried to hide the fact that his gaze looked past Mark toward the young woman.

Jessie was wearing a pair of blue 5.11 brand uniform pants, black boots, and a Rockport Fire Department T-shirt. Although there was nothing special about the clothing, it did highlight her athletic female figure. It seemed out of place for a firefighter to be wearing a police duty belt with a Glock 19 on her hip, but that was a sign of the times. Her brown hair was pulled back into a ponytail that extended through the opening in the back of her fire department ball cap. It was hard for Scott to take his eyes off of her.

At the same time, Jessie was looking at the game warden standing with Doug and Mark. It wasn't until a few moments later she realized he was looking back at her while she stared at him with a stupid look on her face. Embarrassed, she quickly turned to the side in an attempt to pretend she was working on the taillight of the ambulance. As she did this, Vic walked past her carrying a fire hose and said, "If you are trying to jump-start the truck, the engine is in the front."

Jessie closed her eyes and lowered her head down, embarrassed that she was acting like a schoolgirl, but worse that she was busted by Vic in the process.

Doug brought Scott and Mark into the chief's office for a briefing. After explaining the situation, he gave Mark his instructions.

"I will need you home to help plan for the operation. Find someone to cover the rest of your shift and get back in time to get a good night's sleep. I also need you to notify Jessie, Ryan, Nick, Vic, and Joe and tell them to be at our place by noon tomorrow to start running drills. After dinner we will all try to get a few hours' sleep until about 1 a.m., and then we will start our operation. Make sure they all dress appropriately for night ops and bring the weapons they use for three-gun competition."

Mark jotted down the specifics on a notepad. "Anything else?" he asked.

"Yeah, bring at least two medical kits, all the body armor we have, and the thermal imager. Also, make sure everyone keeps it quiet. We don't need this getting out."

"Why not Lou and me?" asked the chief.

Doug looked him in the eye and said, "I can't risk losing you two. If things don't go as planned, we need to keep continuity of leadership for the good of the town."

Not happy about the answer, Brad knew it made sense.

"But I would like you out at my place while we are gone," said Doug. "You can monitor the ham radio and have a small reaction force assembled and ready to go just in case things go bad for us. I would also like you out there with my girls, until I have a chance to tighten up the security around the property."

"I can do that," said Brad, knowing that Penny and Maddy were his friend's top priority.

"Thanks," said Doug, saying far more with his eyes that his friend fully understood.

CHAPTER 26

Ding! Ding! Ding! Maddy was consistently hitting the metal silhouette targets at fifteen and even twenty-five yards. Satisfied with her shooting and surprised at how accurate the Sig 9mm pistol was, Maddy reloaded the pistol with a fresh magazine and secured it in her shoulder holster. It would take a little while to get used to the weight distributed across her shoulders, but it was far more practical than wearing a gun belt around her pregnant belly. She grinned to herself as she recalled one of her dad's many sayings: "A firearm is meant to be comforting, not comfortable."

Maddy would have preferred to get some practice in with her AR-15; however, due to her pregnancy she didn't want to shoot the much-louder rifle. Well into her second trimester, she didn't really want to shoot the pistol either, but under the circumstances it was essential for her to familiarize herself with the new weapon.

Taking off her hearing protection, she turned to walk up the dirt path toward the house. She smiled as she saw Baxter doing a low crawl across the yard to sneak up on the chickens. She was surprised at how gentle he could be. She had never seen such a good-natured animal and was happy her child would have a good dog in their life.

As she got closer to the house, Baxter abandoned his chicken friends and hurried over to walk with her the rest of the way up the trail to the house. The two stepped up onto the deck of the house, and Maddy sat in one of the patio chairs next to Penny. She noticed her mom had her rifle resting across her lap rather than leaning against the wall. While they both were taking home security much more seriously, she was concerned her mother was having deeper issues with the new threats they were facing.

"When do you want me to take over the security shift?" asked Maddy.

"I'm good to go for a while still. I was kind of hoping your father would get home before Mark left for work. I'm just more comfortable with them around. I'm kind of hoping Brad and Kimberly do come out to stay with us," said Penny.

"You sure you can handle that?" joked Maddy. "When the two of you shared a hotel room last summer on your ladies' vacation, you swore that was the last time."

"Yeah, she can be a bit much, but I would feel more comfortable having more people here to help with all the chores and especially the security shifts."

Maddy looked over the top of her sunglasses at her mother, "You really think Kimberly Peterson is going to stay up at night pulling security?"

"Well, if she is going to live under our roof and eat our food, she sure as heck is going to pull her weight. The time for fancy social functions is over," said Penny.

As the two sat on the deck chatting, they heard the buzzer indicating someone was at the gate. Before they could get out of their chairs, Baxter was already running into the house and up to the front window. Apparently, he thought it was some sort of game or family activity when the buzzer sounded. As the girls walked inside, he was already looking out the window with his front paws up on the sill. Both girls had their rifles handy, and both wore holstered pistols. It was clear they did not want to be caught in a compromised situation again.

After waiting about two minutes, they finally saw Doug's Ram pull around the tree line. Penny let out an exhale in relief, not even aware she had been holding her breath. Baxter let out a single bark of excitement when he saw Doug's truck, then turned and ran back out to the deck to greet him when he pulled in.

"Who is that?" asked Maddy when she saw a second truck pull around the corner behind her father's.

"That's a state game warden truck," said Penny. Interested, they both went out back to see who Doug brought home.

As the two trucks parked, Doug and Scott got out and walked up to the deck. Before they could step up, Baxter ran down the two steps to check out the new friend. With his tail wagging, he checked out Scott to verify he was friendly. After a fast sniff and a friendly head scratch, Scott was approved.

As Doug introduced Scott to the girls, he explained the matter with the biker gang and that Scott would be staying with them for a few days. While Penny was happy to hear another lawman would be at the house, even for a little while, she was also concerned about the assault her husband was about to lead on the armed gang of cop killers.

"So, we are both starving, and Scott is about out of food. Do you think you can whip something up for dinner while I show him the property?"

"Sure, dinner will be ready in about an hour," said Penny.

"Great," said Doug, and the two turned to walk the property while establishing a plan for the assault.

"Is he even old enough to be a cop?" whispered Maddy when the men were out of earshot.

"I guess so," said Penny. "Either way, he seemed confident, and game wardens go through a lot of training. Your dad always spoke very highly of them."

"Well, he's not too hard on the eyes, that's for sure," said Maddy, and both women giggled.

As the two men walked the perimeter of the land, Doug explained the security enhancements he was planning to make as soon as he had a free moment. Scott was impressed at the level of thought Doug put into everything, as well as his foresight to see the collapse coming and prepare his family.

Doug walked over to a fresh dirt field adjacent to Penny's garden. "This is an area where we planned to expand our garden, but the collapse came too fast. For now, we can use it as a makeshift sand table and map out our assault plan so everyone can see it."

"Great idea," said Scott, now understanding why Doug had been carrying a three-foot-long stick that he picked up on the walk.

Using the stick, Doug copied the sketch from Scott's notepad into the soft dirt. The front side of the motel faced to the south. Each of the eight rooms had a single entrance door as well as a single large window adjacent to the door. The rear of each motel room only had a single, small vent window located at the upper portion of the bathroom wall. Adjacent to the rental rooms, on the east side of the building was the small, one-room manager's office. The office had a single door and a large window similar to the rental rooms.

The motel was a single-story wood structure with a parking lot to the south. A single paved road led to the lot. A dirt walking trail extended to the west from the motel, through a wooded area, ending at the shore of the lake about one hundred yards away.

To remain concealed while making the approach, they would have to utilize the dark of night as cover. Once the sun started to come up, they would need to be already concealed in the tall grass or the wood line. A typical military or SWAT operation would take place in the dark as the operators would have night-vision capabilities, giving them an advantage. Without the benefit of night vision or a trained and experienced tactical team, Doug felt they needed daylight to pull it off.

As with any assault, especially with untrained warriors, friendly fire casualties were a primary concern. Doug would use a strategy that would minimize crossfire incidents as much as possible; however, as someone would need to breach the rooms, the possibility could not be avoided completely.

Assaulting at sunrise would provide the best advantage as they would have enough light to differentiate targets, and the gang members would probably be asleep and, hopefully, hung over. The element of surprise is often the decisive component in battle. To achieve it, the first step would be to take out the guard sitting in the truck across the parking lot. If he were to get off a warning shot and alert the gang members, his officers would lose the advantage. Doug had already decided he would need to silence the look-out personally.

CHAPTER 27

Once the assault plan was formulated, Doug and Scott returned to the house in time for dinner. As they walked inside, Scott could smell the aroma of several of his favorite foods. He could not recall the last time he had a home cooked meal. After getting out of the Army, he went directly to the warden academy. After that he came straight to his assignment in Calumet County.

"Is there someplace I can wash up for dinner?" asked Scott.

"Of course," said Penny, and she showed him to the guest bathroom.

Once in the bathroom, it was the first time Scott had seen himself in the mirror in several days. He was a little shocked to see his appearance as he looked tired and filthy. He had about two weeks of scruff on his face and he just realized he smelled rather ripe. Now he was embarrassed to go have dinner with this nice family in their home. Washing up as best he could, he was ready for a long-awaited meal.

As he came out of the bathroom, Mark was just walking into the house with Jessie. He had met them both about an hour earlier at the fire station, but he didn't realize Mark was married to Maddy and also Doug's son-in-law. He watched as Penny and Maddy got up and gave Jessie a hug. It was apparent the girls were close but that Jessie was not part of the family. Just like at the station house, she captured Scott's attention. Now that he was about to have dinner with her, he really wished he had cleaned up a little more.

As they all sat down to eat, Maddy asked her husband to help her get the dinner rolls out of the oven. Mark knew she didn't need any help with the rolls but assumed she wanted to ask why Jessie had come over for dinner.

Once they were both in the kitchen, Maddy whispered to Mark, "Why is Jessie here?"

Mark smiled and said, "Well, she said she wants to perform well on the arrest team and wanted extra time to go over the plan with Doug."

"Really?" Maddy asked in a surprised tone.

"Yes, she really did say that, but if I had to guess, I would imagine it had more to do with that blond game warden sitting in the dining room."

"I knew it," said Maddy with a whispered tone of excitement. She was a few years older than Jessie and thought of her as a little sister. Although they came from completely different backgrounds, they had become unlikely friends over the last three years after Jessie joined the volunteer fire department with Maddy's husband and father. Maddy had actually known her before that during her time as a new teacher while Jessie was in high school.

Maddy loved being a matchmaker and often looked for someone to introduce Jessie to, but she was a hard girl to match. While she was very attractive, she had a pretty big chip on her shoulder. She was tough as they came, which meant a lot of the guys in her age group treated her like one of the boys. While everyone knew she came from a bad family, they also knew she was working hard to set herself apart. She often felt people were prejudging her based on her family, which was one of her shortfalls as she was prejudging others in the process.

Mark, wearing an oven mitt, pulled the dinner rolls out of the oven. "Jessie seemed to be interested in him when he came into the station earlier. She was kind of falling all over herself, very unlike her. I guess because he is a good-looking guy?"

"Is he good looking? I didn't notice. He's alright, I guess," said Maddy.

While putting the rolls onto a serving tray, Mark looked at his wife with a "yeah, right" smirk on his face. "Jessie has been around good-looking guys before. Wonder what makes this guy different?"

Maddy gave her husband her own familiar smirk, indicating that he was a typical man and not able to see the bigger picture. "I suppose a big factor is he is not from around here. He doesn't know who her family is or their history."

"Why would that matter?" asked Mark.

"It doesn't," she said matter-of-factly. "But it matters to Jessie."

"Is that why she is acting strange? Trying to be more feminine?"

"It's called flirting, Mark," said Maddy.

"Well, she's not very good at it," he said with a chuckle.

"No, no she's not," said Maddy, with her mind working overtime on how she could help her friend along.

Mark brought the rolls into the dining room, set them on the table, and took a seat. The spread in front of them was a welcome sight as none of them had eaten a good meal recently due to all the commotion. More importantly, it was comforting to share the time with family and friends. They had all been on an emotional rollercoaster and needed to decompress.

Doug, sitting at the head of the table, said grace. They all bowed their heads, and Baxter placed his head on Doug's lap. As Doug thanked the Lord for all they had, each one at the table took a moment to realize how fortunate they all were under the circumstances.

"Amen. Let's eat," said Doug.

There wasn't much of the table visible under all the food, serving trays, and plates. The girls had prepared a lot of the perishable foods as they were not sure how much longer they would have electricity to run the refrigerator. Frankly, they were all surprised it had not gone out already, forcing them to use generator power.

The group had good conversation and even shared some laughs while making short work of the ham, mashed potatoes, rolls, and the many side dishes. Penny brought out her famous cherry cobbler for dessert. The cherries were from the tree on their property. The dinner was a necessary break from the reality of the situation they were in. In just twenty-four hours, some of them would be getting into position to battle a heavily armed biker gang.

After dinner, Maddy collected some of Mark's clothes, judging him to be about the same size as Scott. "You have been in the field a long time," she said to Scott. "Why don't you go upstairs and take a hot shower and put these on? Get me your dirty clothes and any you have in your truck, and I will do a load of wash."

Scott was reluctant, not wanting to impose on his new friends. But more importantly, he didn't want to offend them with his odor, especially now that Jessie was there. He graciously accepted her offer.

After dinner, they all sat on the deck to relax for a few hours before bed. They needed a good night's sleep to prepare for the next day's activities. Everyone would be there by noon tomorrow to start the preparations. Penny would need to put together a large group meal while Doug, Mark, and Scott briefed the assault plan. They would need to perform weapons checks on the range, conduct dry runs of the assault, and review multiple contingency plans.

The conversation around the deck was surprisingly lighthearted. Everyone needed a mental break from all that had transpired the past week. As they were discussing future baby shower ideas for Maddy, Scott walked out from the house, all cleaned up. Wearing a pair of Marks Levi's and a Blue Rockport Fire Department T-shirt, he felt relaxed and refreshed. The thought of sleeping in an actual bed later that night was incredibly appealing as he had been sleeping in his truck for the past two weeks.

As he selected the open chair next to Jessie, Maddy and her mother exchanged glances with one another. Maddy transitioned the conversation over to how Jessie was the only female in the fire department and was just a semester away from graduating from the University of Wisconsin–Green Bay. Both Maddy's husband and father shot her looks to stop playing matchmaker, which she readily dismissed.

As the evening went on, Jessie said she was going to take a walk down to the small pond on the back side of the property. After a long pause, she awkwardly asked if Scott would like to join her.

"Sure," he said in an equally awkward manner and stood up to go with her. Baxter, assuming he was also invited, stood up and followed after them.

Once the two walked out of earshot, Penny laughed and said, "Well, that was hard to watch."

"Brutal," said Doug. "Kids today are used to interacting through texting and social media. They are going to have to learn how to communicate face to face again." Turning his attention to his daughter, he said, "And you need to stop playing matchmaker. I need them both focused on the mission. If their heads are not in the game, that can have deadly consequences. Don't forget your child's dad and grandpa are going into combat with them in thirty hours."

Her dad's comment brought her back to the weight of their current situation. While it had been fun to relax and forget for a couple of hours, the reality was incredibly serious. Her father was correct: both her child's father and grandfather could be killed. Maddy then told Mark she was tired and wanted to go to bed. The reality was, she wanted to hold her husband tight because she didn't know what tomorrow would bring.

After they excused themselves and went upstairs, Penny looked at her husband and said, "Way to kill the mood, Mr. Serious."

Doug exhaled. "Well, I didn't mean to ruin the party, but the fact of the matter is, things are serious. I need everyone's head in the game now more than ever. I am about to lead an inexperienced cast of characters against a larger, brutal gang who has already killed several people. There is a good chance we will take casualties, and with the state of our medical facility, now is not a good time to be wounded."

Penny, who had stood by her husband's side during many dangerous operations over the years, knew he felt he had the weight of the world on his shoulders. She thought about it in a different light now based on their new situation. If she were to lose him or Mark now, it would affect them even more significantly than normal. As the matriarch of the family, would she be able to provide for and protect her daughter and grandchild? She wasn't so sure of the answer.

CHAPTER 28

Baxter, running ahead of them to the pond, playfully barked at the ducks sitting on the water's edge. The ducks casually stepped into the water and swam to the middle to avoid him. Baxter looked back at Jessie and Scott, who were walking slowly, to ensure they were still coming.

"That's a pretty good dog," said Scott.

"Yeah, it's hard to believe he has only been here for a day." Jessie went on to tell him the story of the Schmidt fire and how Baxter came into their lives.

As the conversation reached the inevitable awkward pause, Jessie broke the silence by asking, "So, have you always wanted to be a game warden?"

"Yeah, I guess so. I grew up in Ashland County where drinking and hunting was about all there was to do. I got into some trouble as a kid, and a game warden sort of put me on the right path. I joined the Army after high school because I was too young to be a warden. After my four years' service commitment, I applied and got accepted to the DNR."

Jessie was a little surprised that his story was not altogether different from hers. Brad had straightened her out and led her to a position as a firefighter. "What kind of trouble could a kid get into that only a game warden could straighten it out?"

Scott got an embarrassed look on his face and said, "It was a long time ago, and I was just a stupid kid."

Jessie stopped walking and turned to look at him. "Well, you have to tell me now," she said with an interested tone.

Exhaling, Scott said, "OK, I'll tell you, but I don't want Doug to know. I don't need him thinking I'm an idiot."

Now intrigued, Jessie simply had to know the story.

As they slowly walked around the pond, Scott shared the story. "I was about fourteen years old, and my friend Tony and I started spreading rumors that we saw Bigfoot."

"Bigfoot?" asked Jessie with a laugh.

"Yeah, I don't know why, we just thought it would be funny. It started off as a joke to mess with a gullible kid in our class, but it grew out of hand pretty quick. One thing led to another, and I ended up in the woods at night wearing a Chewbacca costume."

Surprised at the shocking turn of events, she asked, "What?"

"Yeah, I was walking in front of a guy's trail camera to further the Bigfoot story. I thought it would be funny. Unfortunately for me, a couple of drunk guys were out poaching deer out of season and mistook me for a bear. As I was trying to run away, an arrow went through the back of my upper thigh."

Jessing stopped the story to clarify. "You got shot with an arrow in your butt while pretending to be Bigfoot?"

"It was the upper thigh," corrected Scott. "But yeah, I told you it was embarrassing." He continued, "Anyway, when I started to scream in pain, the poachers knew they'd shot a man and ran off, leaving me there to die. I was bleeding a lot and started to panic. I called 911 on my cell phone, but the local cops couldn't find me in the dark woods. Eventually a game warden tracked me and saved my life. He later went on to find the men who shot me."

"How am I supposed to keep a thing like that to myself?" asked Jessie, laughing.

"I don't know, but you better," he said, looking her in the eye.

She stopped laughing and returned the look. It was clear they were sharing a personal moment, and she wasn't sure how to proceed. She desperately wanted to take his hand and say something witty and meaningful, but all she was able to say was, "Don't worry, I have done my share of stupid things as well. I can't say I ever got shot in the butt while wearing a Chewbacca costume, though," and burst out laughing once again.

"OK, OK, I know it was pretty stupid. In my small town, you just can't outlive a story like that. That's one of the reasons I left and joined the Army after high school. I didn't want to be judged for the rest of my life for something stupid I did as a kid."

Jessie completely understood not wanting to be judged for past mistakes or which family they came from.

"I can see that," she said and decided to share a personal story as well. "When I was about fifteen, I was pretty messed up and mad at the world. I was spinning out of control and making horrible decisions. I had been suspended from school for fighting, which made me even angrier. I broke into the school over the weekend and spray-painted some graffiti on a girl's locker who I didn't like. It turned out the football coach was in his office at the time. When he came out to see what was going on, I hid in the girl's bathroom. Trying to wait him out, I lit up a cigarette without even thinking. When the smoke alarm activated, I panicked and tried to run. When I opened the door, he was standing there waiting for me."

"I guess that is pretty bad," said Scott. "What did the coach do to you?"

Smiling as she remembered the story, she said, "Actually, he was pretty great. He turned off the fire alarm and told the dispatcher he was just testing the smoke detector. After he helped me clean off the graffiti, we had a long talk in his office about life. He was the first person to actually listen to me and not judge me for who my family was."

"He sounds pretty great. Did he turn you in?" asked Scott.

"No. He didn't turn me in as long as I joined the volleyball team and attended after-school tutoring sessions to get my grades up. That day was a turning point in my life, and that coach is the reason I was going to college."

"Interesting. Were you planning to follow in his footsteps and be a teacher? asked Scott.

"I was going to school for psychology, but that coach was also the town fire chief."

"Brad?" he asked, intrigued at the turn her story just took.

"Yeah. I never told anyone that story before. I'm not sure why I am telling you."

"Well, thank you for sharing it with me. Your secret is safe with me." After a brief pause, he added, "Well, as long as you keep the Bigfoot story quiet, that is," and they both laughed.

CHAPTER 29

Waking up at 6 a.m., Doug got dressed and strapped on his pistol belt. He was tired from pulling the security shift until midnight, when he was relieved by Mark. Walking from the first-floor master bedroom through the living room to the kitchen, he saw Jessie sleeping on one of the sofas with Baxter curled up at her feet. He smiled to himself while shaking his head. While he was happy to see Jessie coming out of her shell, he was concerned that her mind would not be on the game.

Once in the kitchen, Doug prepared breakfast for everyone. He was making a huge stack of pancakes, eggs, and bacon when Penny walked into the kitchen and gave him a good morning peck on the cheek. He was used to seeing her wearing her robe in the morning, but today she was fully dressed and wearing her gun belt.

"It would be nice if we could get some help with security around here and all the other chores," said Doug.

"Have you heard from Brad and Kimberly about staying here?"

"Not yet, but they will be over here in a little while for the planning stage. I asked Brad if he could stay here while we are out on the operation."

"Thanks. That will make me a lot more comfortable."

Penny pulled her World's Greatest Mom coffee mug down from the cupboard and poured herself a cup of the coffee Doug had just brewed. She smiled and said, "What are you going to do when you run out of your favorite coffee?"

"I'm trying not to think about it," he said with a sour look on his face.

"What do you think about Scott staying here longer to help out?" she asked.

"So far, I like him, and he has plenty of valuable skills we could use. But let's get to know him a bit better before we make that offer. If we did, I think we would have Jessie around here a lot too," he whispered, nodding to the living room.

Penny grinned and said, "She and Scott sat up talking after we all went to bed. I told her the gate was locked and she should just stay with us tonight. I gave her a blanket and a pillow."

"She is pretty handy with weapons, and she is a solid EMT and firefighter. She would be a good asset as well. I think she would rather be out here with us than with her roommate in that apartment complex. What about asking her to stay?" asked Doug.

"I think that's a great idea!" she said, wanting more people to share with security.

"Where would we put everyone?" asked Doug, assuming Penny would already have the living situation coordinated in her head.

"I got all that worked out," she said, and took a seat at the kitchen island to share her vision while Doug cooked. "We stay in the master bedroom on the first level, of course. The large bedroom upstairs would be Brad and Kimberly, and the two small bedrooms would go to Jessie and Scott. Mark and Maddy would move to the large guest room in the finished basement, and we would turn your office into a nursery."

"My office?" Doug asked in protest. His office was his sanctuary.

"We can set you up a new sanctuary in one of the rooms in the large outbuilding," said Penny.

While Doug liked having his office, Penny's plan did make sense. And having eight adults on the property would certainly help out.

"Going from four to eight adults would really impact our food supply. We will need to get that second field planted as soon as possible and come up with a better plan for hunting and fishing. Winter will come fast," said Doug.

Penny nodded her head and said, "I think we can easily feed eight people and a dog with what we have. We can always step up our hunting and fishing a bit, but with the extra hands it should be very doable."

"Do you think we can expect any compensation for all of our work with the fire and sheriff's department? It's not fair that you all risk your lives and spend so much time helping out the rest of the community while neglecting your families' duties."

"Maybe down the road we can come up with some sort of barter system for compensation. Maybe get some food or crops for public service. But right now, I just want to maintain order and community as much as possible."

"I can see that," she said, "but it just doesn't seem fair that a handful of folks are working for the community without any form of compensation. Volunteering your time is great, but you all have taken on a much larger responsibility than most people."

"I know, but now is not the time for that. We need to hold the community together before we think of some sort of taxation proposal. But I agree, we can't keep asking people to volunteer a large portion of their time for the community while their own families go without. For example, the caretakers at the retirement home. We can't expect them each to volunteer all their time for free while they have their own families to provide for. We will figure something out, but now is not the time to do it."

CHAPTER 30

The sun was high in the sky as noon came around. All of the participants had arrived and were collected around the makeshift sand table drawn on the ground in the empty field. Doug handed each one a printout of Scott's sketch to supplement the large map in the dirt.

"OK, here is the plan," said Doug, switching to his commander's voice as he explained the mission. "The assault will start exactly at sunrise. That will be at 5:22 tomorrow morning. That should give us an element of surprise and hopefully catch them sleeping or hung over. We will all be in position long before sunrise because we need the cover of darkness to help our infiltration.

"At eleven o'clock tonight, the Observation Team, consisting of Scott and Joe, will get into position in the tree line. They will stay at least 150 yards away and collect pre-assault intelligence. They will be our eyes on the ground and can alert us of things we need to know about. They will be able to see all the doors and front windows of the rooms as well as the manager's office. When the assault starts, they will provide cover fire from the south (shooting to the north). Scott will have his AR-15 patrol rifle, and Joe will have his scoped .30-06. The rifle rounds will easily penetrate the motel and exit to the north. The Observation Team will use the fire department thermal imager. This tool is used to search for heat sources inside smoke-filled buildings, but it can also be used to identify a human body in the dark. They will scan the woods to look for any additional sentries they can't see.

"At 4 a.m., the two cover teams will get into position. Cover Team One is Vic and Ryan. They will position in the tall grass to the northeast of the motel." Doug made eye contact with each of them. "You will cover the northeast corner and the back side of the motel during the assault. If all goes as planned, you two will be called up to take control of prisoners as we take them into custody. Vic will have a shotgun, and Ryan an AR-15. You both will carry ten sets of flexicuffs each, and Ryan will have the medical kit.

"Cover Team Two will consist of Nick and Jessie and be positioned in the tree line down on the beach at the end of the dirt trail." He looked at the two of them. "You will not be able to see the motel from your location as it is one hundred yards away over a small hill and through the trees. The hill and trees will provide you cover as we will be shooting in your direction. You need to stay low until we give the all-clear. If anyone escapes the assault, they will likely run toward the beach. The Observation Team should be able to give you a heads-up if we have runners. Nick will have a shotgun, and Jessie an AR-15. You both will carry five sets of flexicuffs, and Jessie will have the second medical bag.

"At 5 a.m., the Assault Team, consisting of myself, Mark, Sheriff Decker, and Deputies Brown and Sampson, will move into position in the tree line to the east. The sheriff and I will approach the sentry in the parking lot. Once we take him out, if successful, Mark and the two deputies will move up to the pickup. Mark and the deputies will take custody of the prisoner and drag him far off into the tree line and secure him to a tree, bound and gagged. Mark will stay with the prisoner and control the road leading to the motel. We don't need any more bikers rolling up on us from our rear. The two deputies will return to the pickup and use it for cover.

"At exactly 5:22 we will start the actual assault. The sheriff and I will remain mobile to have the flexibility to adjust as needed. We will move room to room, attempting to take them into custody a little at a time and reduce their total numbers. Once they get alerted to what we are doing, expect a fight. If that happens, select a target and take it out. I don't want any random fire in a general direction.

"That's the plan, and things never go as planned," said Doug. "I expect some heavy resistance that will result in gunfire. Let's keep all our rounds going to the north or west to avoid cross fire. If we can take them alive, we will. That said, we are not going to take any unnecessary chances. I will serve as the operation leader, so I may need to make changes on the fly. If I go down, Sheriff Decker will take charge. If we both go down, Warden Connolly will take charge, followed by Deputies Sampson and Brown."

Once everyone understood their positions, they all moved down to the shooting range to perform weapons checks and to ensure their sights were on target. Doug checked everyone over personally and ensured they all were prepared for their mission.

After ensuring everyone understood their portion of the mission, Doug directed them to stand by their respective partner. "Look at the person next to you. When the sun comes up tomorrow, you will be in battle alongside that person. They are your battle buddy. You are responsible for their life, just as they are responsible for yours. The two of you are one. You will stay together at all times and operate as a single unit."

Each person made eye contact with their partner, sharing the moment and feeling the gravity of their situation. They were all committed to bringing their battle buddy home safe.

CHAPTER 31

The hours ticked down like minutes, and 10:30 p.m. came quickly. Doug made his way to the upstairs guest bedroom to awaken the Observation Team. Both Scott and Joe were fast asleep on top of the covers before the operation. Doug paired the two together because they both had Army experience and both were calm under pressure. While the much younger Scott was a cavalry scout and lawman, the more mature Joe had been a communications specialist with the Wisconsin National Guard. Scott would make the observations, and Joe would relay essential details to the team over the radio.

Waking up, the two veterans put on their gear and covered their exposed skin with black, brown, and green face paint. This would prevent the moonlight from reflecting off their skin and exposing their position.

"Any questions?" asked Doug.

They both answered no.

"Good. When you get into position, give me a communications check. After that, if you have anything significant to share, do so. Otherwise, let's try to maintain radio silence until the teams start to get into place at 4 a.m.," said Doug.

"Roger that, sir," said the young warden as he and Joe left to get into position.

At 11:14 p.m., Doug's radio came to life. "Observation Team to Command."

"Go ahead, Observation Team," replied Doug.

"We are in position with a good eyeball on the target. Four or five of the motorcycles are not present at the location. The subjects are drinking heavily and playing loud music at this point in time. One sentry is in the designated security post and armed with an AK-47. Estimate eight to ten subjects at the target," relayed Joe.

Doug wondered where the four or five unaccounted-for gang members were and what they were doing. He replied, "Roger that, Observation Team. Please give an updated situation report as things develop."

At 3 a.m., Doug woke up the rest of the team. They were sleeping anywhere they could find a spot, from guest rooms to sofas and even an inflatable mattress Penny had set up. Within fifteen minutes, they were all geared up, had applied their face paint, and had conducted weapons and communications checks. They were nervous but eager. Each was mentally prepared for their portion of the mission, and especially the chore of bringing their battle buddy home safe.

Once Doug was convinced they were ready, they loaded into vehicles, and he asked the Observation Team for a situation report, or sitrep.

"Command to Observation Team."

"Go for Observation Team."

"Assault Team and Cover Teams are in-bound to target. Can you provide an updated sitrep?"

"Target is quiet. The single sentry is partially asleep in the bed of the pickup. All others are inside the rooms. One room has a light on. Four to five motorcycles still unaccounted for."

Everyone sitting in the vehicles listened intently to the situation report. Inside the house, Penny, Maddy, Kimberly, and Brad also monitored the radio traffic, as did the three on-duty public safety officers at the fire station.

The drive to the drop-off location took only about fifteen minutes. Once there, the teams dismounted and moved in pairs the last mile and a half on foot. The last one hundred yards required a low crawl in the tall grass. Doug reached his position and waited a few extra minutes to give the others time to get in place before calling for a sitrep.

"Command to Cover Team One for sitrep."

"Cover Team One in place," said Vic.

"Command to Cover Team Two for sitrep."

"Cover Team Two in place," said Jessie.

"Command to Observation Team for sitrep."

"Observation Team in place," said Joe.

Doug replied that the Assault Team was also in place. They all held their positions intently, waiting for the assault to begin at 5:22 a.m.

At 5:16, it was finally time for Doug and the sheriff to take out the sentry, the most crucial part of the operation. The two former state patrol SWAT members had worked together many times before and were very familiar with each other's moves. They communicated through hand signals known only to themselves. As they approached in a low crawl to the pickup, Joe at the observation point had his scoped bolt-action rifle trained on the guard just in case the situation went bad. Scott had his rifle trained on the doors to the motel just in case anyone came out.

Joe watched the two seasoned lawmen disappear behind the far side of the truck and heard a faint noise as one of them tapped on the fender. The guard leaned over the side of the truck bed to investigate and rapidly disappeared out of the truck headfirst. Seconds later, Joe watched as the sheriff silently filled the empty seat in the back of the truck in case anyone peered out of a window. Next, he saw Doug drag the unconscious guard back into the tree line, where he was to turn him over to Mark and the deputies. So far, so good.

Joe keyed his microphone to provide the update to the team. "Observation Team update: phase one of the assault successful. Stand by for green light."

Far back into the woods near the entrance road, the deputies secured the prisoner to a tree with his hands and feet bound and a gag in place. While they did this, Mark slid onto the dark road and laid down two sets of Stop

Sticks, designed to deflate vehicle tires during police pursuits. This would slow down anyone who tried to enter while the operation was going down. Once back in the tree line, he knelt next to the bound prisoner and covered the road while the two deputies returned to the pickup.

When the deputies returned and got into position behind the truck, Doug gave Joe the designated hand signal indicating the second phase of the operation would begin.

"Observation Team sitrep, green light! Green light!" he broadcast to all members of the team so they would know the assault phase of the operation had begun.

The two deputies took covering positions behind the pickup while Doug and the sheriff moved to the manager's office on the far right side of the building. Joe watched through his rifle scope as the two warriors moved swiftly and silently. He watched as the two slipped into the unlocked manager's office and cleared it without incident. Seconds later, they exited the office and moved on to room eight. Doug stood on the hinge side of the door and placed his thumb over the peephole while the sheriff stood on the other side of the window at an angle. Doug tried the knob, but the door was locked. He then used the back of his knuckles and gave the door a gentle knock. As the gang member inside opened the door unsuspectingly, Doug rapidly forced his way into the room, thrusting the muzzle of his rifle into the man's sternum like a spear. Joe watched through his rifle scope as Doug and the sheriff disappeared inside room number eight and closed the door behind them.

Inside the room, the sheriff rapidly searched for additional occupants while Doug dealt with the man who had opened the door. A second strike to the head with the butt of his rifle rendered the man unconscious. Using flexicuffs, Doug secured the man's hands behind his back and then his feet together. He rolled the man onto his stomach, bent his knees back, and, with a third set of flexicuffs, secured his feet to his handcuffed hands, like he was hog-tied in a rodeo. Doug then rolled the man back onto his side so he wouldn't suffocate from the position. Doug had four pieces of duct tape precut to ten inches each stuck to one leg of his pants. Pulling off one of the strips, he used it to secure the man's mouth to make it difficult to alert the others once he regained consciousness.

As Joe watched intently through his rifle scope, he saw the door to room number eight open and watched the two lawmen silently move on to room seven. Once again Doug knocked on the door and took the gang member by surprise when he opened it. As Doug and the sheriff entered the room, the door again closed behind them.

Inside room seven, Doug grappled with the man who'd opened the door while the sheriff slipped past them to clear the room. The sheriff was briefly caught off guard as he encountered an unexpected motorcycle parked inside the dark motel room, blocking his path. Apparently, the bikers had brought the motorcycle inside the room to work on it. This obstacle bought the second biker, who was brushing his teeth in the bathroom, a moment to react. The man dropped his toothbrush and drew the pistol from his waistband. As he exited the bathroom, he briefly saw the muzzle of the sheriff's Glock as it barked to life, sending a 124-grain 9mm bullet through his brain.

Everyone inside the motel, as well as the officers on the perimeter, heard the shot. Seconds later, the door to room four opened, and two partially dressed gang members, armed with rifles, ran out to investigate. They were met with a hail of gunfire from the two deputies behind the truck as well as Scott and Joe from the observation position. The two criminals fell to the ground, lifeless after receiving several rounds each.

CHAPTER 32

Inside room number three, the combat-hardened war veteran didn't panic. He just sat up in his bed waiting for the end. He knew he had been living on borrowed time for years, long before joining his older brother's motorcycle gang. He felt numb, even dead inside since the war. After his discharge from the Marines, he served a short stint in prison and completed two in-patient treatment sessions at the Veteran Affairs facility in Tomah, Wisconsin. He was resolved to die this morning as he just wanted the pain to end. The drugs and alcohol could only medicate him for so long. As a warrior, however, he still felt the need to fight in the process of his death. He would rather die in combat than by his own hand. He had attempted suicide many times but could not bring himself to pull the trigger. He felt he needed to die in battle to once again be with his war buddies in Valhalla.

Picking up the AK-47 resting against the wall next to his bed, he crawled to the corner of the window so he could see outside. He knew it was still darker inside his room than outside, so it would be difficult for the police to see him. He observed the shots coming from men using the pickup as cover. While he could not see them, he scanned the areas of the truck for where he thought they would be. A moment later he saw, from his low position, one of the deputy's boots exposed under the truck as the deputy knelt on the other side behind the rear wheel. Taking aim at the boot, the only target exposed, the gang member fired a single round, which decimated the bones in Deputy Sampson's right foot.

As the shattered bones of his foot no longer supported his body weight, Sampson collapsed to the ground unexpectedly. This, in turn, allowed the gunman to see the deputy's head and torso under the truck as he lay wounded on the ground. A volley of follow-up shots from the AK-47 would end the deputy's suffering while simultaneously ending his life.

While no one could see the gunman inside room number three, they knew he was inside that room as the window exploded when he fired out of it. Scott and the remaining deputy both fired blindly into room number three, hoping to take out the shooter.

The members of the two cover teams could not see the action from their positions, but they could hear what sounded like an endless barrage of gunfire. Moments later, they heard Joe's voice over the radio: "Officer down! Officer down! Behind the pickup."

Worried that one of his medics would leave their assigned positions and expose themselves trying to get to the downed man, Doug barked over the radio, "Hold your positions!" Both Doug and the sheriff exited room number seven and took up prone positions on the ground at the corner of the manager's office. This new position gave them a low profile and allowed them a clear lane of fire to the west as gang members exited the rooms.

Without notice, the door to room number one flung open and three gang members exited rapidly, firing at the pickup and the observation post and causing the officers to take cover. As they ran to the west on the dirt path leading to the beach, Doug and the sheriff had only a brief moment to fire before losing sight of them around the corner of the building. They both scored hits; two of the men collapsed before making it to the nearby tree line.

"We have a runner to the west!" shouted Joe over the radio. This alerted Nick and Jessie, waiting in a crouched position at the far end of the trail. Jessie held the red dot of her rifle scope on the trail opening just thirty yards from her concealed location in the tall grass. The seconds seemed like hours as she waited. She could feel every beat of her heart as the adrenaline pumped through her veins. Finally, the gang member came into view. The image wasn't what Jessie expected to see. The man running toward her was barefoot and wearing only boxer shorts and a leather gang vest. He didn't seem evil and hard like she had visioned in her mind, but rather vulnerable and scared. He was young, probably a teenager.

"Police, drop the weapon!" shouted Nick.

The young gang member was caught by surprise, but rather than obey the command, he raised a pistol at the voice shouting at him. Jessie watched as a mist of crimson exploded from the biker's chest before he collapsed to the ground.

She had not even seen the gun in his hand until the last second. She was not sure what happened or who took the shot. Her ears were ringing from the loud rifle blast, and she was experiencing tunnel vision as she watched the motionless teen lying on the ground in front of her. She could hear a radio transmission off in the distance. "Runner down, runner down." A moment later she realized the radio transmission was coming from the microphone clipped to her collar. She then felt a hand on her shoulder. As she looked over, it took her a moment to realize it was Nick, wearing his dark face paint.

"Are you hit?" He asked.

"What?"

"Are you hit?"

Snapping out of her brief shock, she said, "No, are you?"

"No" he replied. "But I was about to be. That was a great shot! Everything happened so fast."

Jessie wondered who made the shot and why Nick was talking like she had. Looking at the chamber of her AR-15, the dust cover was in the open position as if her weapon had been fired. Looking to her right, she saw a spent shell casing lying on the ground. Had she fired her weapon? Everything had happened in slow motion, yet it also happened so fast. As she thought about it for a second, she realized she had felt the recoil of the rifle against her shoulder when she saw the puff of blood leave the man's body. She realized she had taken the shot.

Once again in the moment, she said, "Cover me," and low-crawled to the downed biker with her medical bag. Checking his pulse for a sign of life, Jessie placed her hand over the hole in his chest while searching her bag for an Ascherman chest seal. She intended on saving the man's life.

CHAPTER 33

Back at the motel, all the shooting had stopped. Four bikers lay motionless on the ground in the parking lot while a fifth was dead inside the bathroom of room number seven. One was down at the far end of the trail, and three others were in custody and hog-tied. That accounted for nine. Doug knew a tenth shooter had been in room three, but it was unknown if he was still a threat. He evidently possessed superior skills as he had been able to utilize cover and concealment to take out the deputy.

"Cease fire," Doug commanded over the radio. "Observation Team, you will provide cover fire as Deputy Brown pulls Sampson from behind the truck to Cover Team One's position for medical aid."

"He's already dead," Deputy Brown spoke into the radio in a somber voice.

"Are you positive?" asked the sheriff, heartbroken at the loss of another one of his men.

"Yes, I am positive."

"Roger that, Brown. Observation Team, provide cover fire as Brown moves from the truck to our location," said Doug.

Brown ran from the truck to the northeast corner of the motel and took a position on the ground next to Doug and the sheriff. Now they had the motel in a cross-fire position.

Doug shouted loudly, "Anyone inside the motel, exit now or you will be killed!"

There was no answer.

Doug looked over at Wes. "There is no way I am risking any more lives searching room to room." The sheriff was in full agreement.

"Command to Observation Team, provide cover while we extract the prisoners."

"Copy," replied Joe.

Doug provided cover from the east corner while Wes and Deputy Brown carried out the two bound men from rooms seven and eight and brought them over to Cover Team One's position.

Doug shouted again, "Anyone left alive inside the motel, come out now or you will be burned to death! The motel is on fire!"

No one came out or responded to the command.

"Cover me," said Doug to the sheriff. Doug moved close to the building and stood up. He knew that the two rooms to the east had been cleared, and if he stayed close to the wall, he was not visible to occupants in the farther rooms based on his angle. Doug walked into room seven and pulled a small bottle of lighter fluid out of his cargo pocket. After squirting the flammable liquid onto the old curtains and carpet, he opened the gas tank of the motorcycle, then knocked the heavy bike onto its side with a front kick. He then bent down and pulled a piece of paper out of the trash can and lit it on fire with a lighter from his pocket. Using the burning paper, he ignited the puddle of gas that was leaking out of the bike onto the floor. He then turned and ignited the curtains. As both areas started to burn rapidly, Doug walked into the bathroom and broke out the small window with the barrel of his rifle. Walking back to the front, he broke out the large front window of room number seven. As a firefighter, Doug knew that this would allow the wind to flow through the room, feeding oxygen to the fire and causing it to spread much more rapidly.

Returning back to where the sheriff and Deputy Brown lay on the ground, he said, "Now we just pull back fifty yards and wait."

It wasn't long before the motel was fully engulfed in flames. The old wood structure was poorly maintained and went up fast. Doug was not surprised he did not hear the sound of fire alarms activating inside as they probably hadn't had new batteries in years or had been deactivated by occupants who wanted to smoke in the rooms.

As the fire traveled down the row of rooms, it started to engulf room number three. This was the room that contained the man who killed Deputy Sampson. Doug waited intently with his rifle trained on the door, half expecting the man to come out shooting. Moments later he heard gunfire from the back side of the motel.

Speaking into his radio, he called out, "Cover Team One, sitrep."

Moments later, a reply came back: "Someone broke through the wall on the back side of the motel. I think I hit him, but I lost sight due to the smoke from the fire."

Looking to the sheriff, Doug said, "Keep an eye on the front of the motel until it burns to the ground. I am moving to the rear."

Keying the microphone to his radio, Doug said, "Command to Observation Team and Cover Team One."

"Go for Observation."

"Go for Cover Team One."

"Command is going mobile to the rear of the motel. Hold all fire from south to north. Sheriff Decker will cover the front of the motel shooting to the west. Cover Team, keep your eyes open and call out anything you see. I will be operating in your field of fire."

"Observation Team copies."

"Cover Team copies."

Doug stood up and quickly moved to the rear of the building. Never breaking into a run, he moved with a sense of urgency but at a controlled speed. He walked in a tactical manner, rolling each step from heel to toe. His rifle pointed forward as he walked. As he moved near the smoke, he pulled the second thermal imager from his pocket, the one Mark had brought from Milwaukee. Scanning the smoke, he could see a heat signature moving from the motel to the north.

As Doug sidestepped to his right, he kept the smoke between them to conceal his position. Once he reached the tall grass, he crouched and started to move forward toward the heat signature. Now out of the smoke, he could see the man's footprints in the mud as he moved toward him. The prints were unique as the right foot had the print of a motorcycle boot, but the left foot was completely smooth. As he closed in on the heat signature, he could make out the form of a man sitting on the ground facing away from him. Switching his focus from the thermal imager back to his rifle, he moved through the last portion of the tall grass that was concealing him.

As the man now came into view, Doug could see that he was covered in blood. He had obviously sustained multiple injuries from the gunfight and from ramming his body through the wooden wall of the motel. He was on the ground as his prosthetic leg had come loose in the mud. Sitting up, he stopped struggling when he sensed Doug behind him.

"I am ready to go see my brothers now," the man said.

"It's not your time, son. Place your hands on your head."

"My time is long overdue," he said in a voice that communicated peace with his decision to die.

As the man slowly reached for the AK-47 that was laying in the mud next to him, Doug could see the USMC tattoo on his forearm.

"Please don't do it, son!" said Doug.

"Till Valhalla," said the biker as he picked up the rifle.

As the motel continued to burn, a single gunshot was heard from the tall grass north of the structure. "Shooter down," was broadcast over the radio and heard by all.

CHAPTER 34

It was a strange feeling for the firefighters to watch a building burn to the ground and not try to save it. It went against all of their training and instincts. While they knew it was the best course of action, each person had to come to terms with their own transformation from firefighter to public safety officer. Just a few days earlier, none of them would have dreamed they would be in a sheriff's posse taking on a gang of cop killers, let alone using fire as their weapon.

Looking down at the lifeless body of Deputy Chad Sampson, the men were both numb and shocked at the tragic loss of life. It was apparent that although he died brutally, he didn't suffer long. A 7.62mm bullet from an AK-47 had entered his skull and done a massive amount of damage.

The sheriff spoke softly. "Chad was forty-three years old. He has a wife and a teenage son. He has only been a deputy for about three years. It was a second career for him. He was a good cop and an even better father and husband." Wes was getting choked up, so Doug took over to give his grieving friend a reprieve.

Doug cleared his throat and said, "The book of John tells us that greater love hath no man than this, that lay down his life for his friends." It was a Bible scripture he knew all too well as he had spoken over fallen brothers too many times. He continued, "Let us not weep for how he died, but celebrate how he lived his life. In Ecclesiastes, Solomon says there is a time for everything, a season for every activity under the heavens: a time to be born and a time to die, a time to plant and a time to uproot, a time to kill and a time to heal, a time to tear down and a time to rebuild, a time to weep and a time to laugh, a time to mourn and a time to dance." They all bowed their heads and said a short prayer for their fallen friend.

Doug turned to Vic and said, "Take Ryan and go get two of the vehicles. We will need to transport the three prisoners to the county jail in Chilton. I want to give the sheriff and Deputy Brown some time to deal with Sampson's body and to speak with his family." Vic understood and went about his task.

Turning to Scott, Doug asked him to go assist Mark with his prisoner and watch the road. "Make sure you pull up the Stop Sticks when Vic and Ryan pull the trucks around," he stated so they would understand the assignment.

Doug instructed Joe to come with him down to the lake to check on Jessie and Nick. He had sent Scott away primarily to get rid of him while he went to check on Jessie. He didn't need young love and emotions getting in the way just yet.

As Doug and Joe walked down the dirt path, Doug said, "Nice work on the Observation Team. You brought it all together." Doug had selected Joe for the key position to work with Scott due to his age and experience. At forty-five years old, the veteran of the Wisconsin National Guard was calm under pressure and maintained his radio composure under even the most chaotic circumstances.

"Thanks," said Joe. "And those were some nice words you said back there for Deputy Sampson. Especially the line from *Footloose.*"

Looking at Joe, he replied, "I'm pretty sure King Solomon said it before Kevin Bacon did."

Once Doug and Joe neared the beach, they called out to alert them of their presence.

Nick replied, "Come on down."

When they came through the woods, Doug saw Jessie kneeling at the water's edge looking out over the lake. Nick was kneeling next to the dead body of the biker, who was now wearing just boxer shorts. Next to the body was a leather vest cut off of him during lifesaving measures. From the amount of medical packaging on the ground, Doug knew a lot of precious resources had been expended trying to save a man with an obviously fatal wound.

Figuring what happened in his mind, Doug looked down at Nick and asked in a low voice, "Jessie shoot him?"

"Yeah, he was about to shoot me. I tried to fire but forgot to disengage my safety. I was struggling to flip it off when she fired, saving my butt. She didn't even realize she had fired for a few seconds, kind of in shock." Nick paused before continuing. "I knew it was a fatal wound, but it took a minute for his heart to run out of blood. She worked feverishly to try to save him. I think we both knew it was of no use, but she had to try. I finally stopped her from using up all of our medical supplies since we would certainly need them later. She just got up and went over to the water. I wanted to go check on her but needed to keep cover on the trail."

Doug evaluated the situation and instructed Joe and Nick to carry the dead body up to the motel with the others. He then walked over to Jessie and took a knee beside her. Neither made eye contact as they looked over the water at some far-off place toward the horizon.

Doug spoke. "The human body does a lot of things to protect us during times of heightened danger, both psychologically and physiologically. The adrenal glands dump the chemical cortisol into the bloodstream, initiating the fight or flight response. This adrenaline provides energy to the large muscle groups to run or fight, but at the expense of other functions such as fine motor skills. Likewise, the brain protects us by forcing our attention toward the threat but at the expense of less important senses. You likely had tunnel vision and a loss of peripheral vision. Time probably slowed or sped up. You likely suffered auditory exclusion and could not hear things close to you. This is normal and happens to everyone in a combat situation. Many police officers involved in a shooting do not remember shooting their gun, and if they do, do not know how many rounds they fired. Many did not hear their partners calling to them from just a few feet away. It is the body's response to counter the stress and help you keep focus and survive the confrontation."

Jessie nodded as this made sense and helped her understand her body's response to the situation.

Doug continued, "Soon you will experience extreme fatigue as the cortisol wears off. You will need to sleep. Over the next few days or weeks, you will experience a series of other symptoms such as sleep problems, periods of crying, nausea, appetite loss, numbness, guilt, and more. I share this with you because as a medic, you understand how the body and mind react.

"But the most important thing for you to remember is that the killing was just. It was necessary. Of that there is no doubt. He was responsible for the deaths of several police officers. He was responsible for terrorizing the people of Harrison. He took an oath to be a member of an outlaw organization, just as you took an oath to be a defender of those who cannot defend themselves."

Although she was still experiencing high emotions, she was better prepared to handle the days to come.

Doug placed his hand on her shoulder and said, "Be thankful you got him before he got Nick. Survivor's guilt is a whole other bag of emotions to deal with. Trust me."

Thankful for his words and sharing of some of his personal demons, she reached up and gave his hand on her shoulder a squeeze.

As the two stood up, Doug thought for a moment before speaking further. "This probably isn't the time, but Penny wanted me to ask you if you would consider moving out to our place. We could really use the extra help with security and all the new chores."

Doug was happy to see her smile, even if for just a moment, as a tear rolled down her young face. "I would like that very much," she said, grateful for a bit of security as her entire future had been called in question over the last week.

They walked back up to the motel, which was still smoldering and putting off a tremendous amount of heat. Vic and Ryan, who had returned with the vehicles, had loaded the three prisoners in one and the six dead gang members in the second. The prisoners would be transported to the jail in Chilton, and the dead ones would be buried in the lot behind the maintenance yard in Rockport. The body of Deputy Sampson would be loaded into a separate vehicle and taken back for a proper burial in Chilton. They found ignition keys to one of the pickups and two of the motorcycles among the dead and the prisoners. Doug made the call to seize these vehicles for public safety use.

As everyone was ready to leave the area, Sheriff Decker walked over to thank Doug.

"Thanks for stepping up, Doug. If it weren't for you and your posse, this would not have been possible."

Doug looked at his old friend and said, "We are in this together, brother."

The two looked over the burning rubble, then back at the sheriff's vehicle while the others loaded up the fallen deputy.

"I don't know what the future holds for us, Doug. We can't keep doing law enforcement the way we used to. Things have changed. The rules have changed."

"I agree, we can't follow the same letter of the law we did before, but I think we need to follow the intent of the law as much as possible."

Wes looked down at the ground to prevent Doug seeing his eyes tear up. "If we had just lit the motel on fire to start with, Chad would still be alive."

Doug took a long breath in and exhaled while trying to think of the right thing to say. "That may have been the case this time, but it's a slippery slope when justice just turns into revenge. I don't have all the answers, but I think we need to try to keep the lines from blurring as much as possible. It's far easier to have a lynch mob than to give someone a fair trial. If the police start doing it, it won't take long for anyone with a perceived injustice to start doing it. If we hope to maintain a civilized society, we need to maintain the rule of law."

"I know, Doug. It's just times like these, where we are the only ones playing by the rules, it gets hard to swallow. It's even harder when I have to go tell a woman she is a widow and has to raise her son all alone in a time like this."

Doug gave his friend a pat on the arm and shook his hand to say good-bye. Wes then climbed into the front passenger seat of the silver Calumet County Sheriff Explorer. Scott had formed everyone into a line near the front of the squad that was carrying their fallen brother. He ordered, "Present arms," and everyone rendered a hand salute as the vehicle passed by. Once the squad left the parking lot, Scott gave the command "Order arms," and everyone dropped their salute. It was an emotional time for all.

Clearing his throat, Doug rallied everyone together. "Great job, guys. Let's wrap this up. But remember, there may still be four or five of them out there somewhere, so don't let your guard down. Nick and Ryan, you drive the dead guys back and put them in a hole. Vic and Joe, I want you to follow them and provide cover in case they get ambushed. Stay at least one hundred yards behind them so you don't get caught in the same kill zone. Scott and Mark, you will drive the prisoners back to the jail in Chilton and drop them off. Jessie and I will follow you and provide cover. Any questions?"

As nobody had questions, they all loaded up and proceeded to their respective locations.

As Doug drove his Ram, he had Jessie ride in the passenger seat. He wanted to keep her mind occupied, so he gave her continuous tasks. "Roll your window down and be ready for action. I will watch for threats on the left, and you are responsible for threats on the right. If you see something, call out."

After about ten minutes of searching for threats, Jessie asked, "Are you sure Penny wants me to stay out at the house?"

"Of course, she does," said Doug. After an awkward pause he said, "And so do I."

Although she was turned away from him as she scanned for threats to the right, he could tell she was happy. He could see her wipe away a tear.

CHAPTER 35

The trip to the county jail was uneventful, and the prisoners were turned over to the corrections officers. On the trip back to Rockport, Mark and Scott stopped off at Mark's place to pick up some more things to bring out to the house. Doug thought that was a good idea, so he stopped by Jessie's apartment to do the same. Doug was a bit surprised at how few possessions Jessie had to bring out to the house. Everything she wanted to keep in life fit into two duffle bags. She'd left her old life behind years ago, and as a struggling college student, she didn't own a lot.

Within a few minutes, they were pulling through the gate to the property. Jessie locked it behind them. As they drove around behind the house, there was a group of friends waiting for them on the deck. As Jessie stepped out of the truck, Baxter came over to greet her, as expected. She knelt down and enjoyed the attention, amazed how the love of a dog could help heal the soul. Jessie went upstairs to get cleaned up, as she was filthy from the operation and had some blood on her clothes from the man she killed.

While she was upstairs, Doug stepped up onto the deck and sat in a patio chair across from Penny, Maddy, Brad, and Kimberly. He looked down at his watch and was surprised to see it wasn't even 10 a.m. yet. They had experienced a lot in just a few hours.

As he filled them in on all that happened, they were on the edge of their seats. Kimberly was the most shocked by far. It was clear she was just starting to realize the gravity of their situation and that their world had changed forever. She could not believe that people she knew were engaging in gunfights and disposing of dead bodies. The world she had built in her mind was a façade of social media and magazine covers. This terrified her, as she simply had no idea what they were going to do or how they could survive.

Kimberly reached over and took hold of Brad's hand and squeezed it. Brad was surprised by this as his wife was not overly affectionate, especially in public. He looked over at her and returned the squeeze.

Kimberly cleared her throat and said, "Brad and I have talked about coming to stay with you until things settle down a bit. If that offer is still available, we would like to take you up on it."

This surprised Brad. The last time they'd spoken of the matter, she was not sold on the idea. The realization that her world was no longer safe and that they were in real danger must have finally hit home.

"Of course it is," said Penny with a sense of glee. She scooted her seat closer to Kimberly's so they could discuss all the details of living together.

Brad made eye contact with Doug and gave him a wink, which Doug knew meant thanks. The situation was certainly the best for everyone.

"On another note," said Doug, "I have asked Jessie to stay with us also, and she accepted. She will bring a lot of resources, from emergency medicine to firearms skills to youth. She can pull more than her weight with all the tasks in front of us."

"That's great news," said Penny.

"I agree too," said Brad. He viewed Jessie as the daughter he'd never had and wanted the best for her. He also liked the fact that she would be closer to him as the world collapsed. His relationship with her filled an unspoken void in his life, and he needed her as much as she needed him.

Penny looked over at him and said, "Doug, why don't you go get cleaned up while we make supper? That face paint is creeping me out."

Doug had completely forgotten he was even wearing face paint as they had the conversation. Embarrassed, he excused himself and went to get cleaned up.

About an hour later, everyone was freshened up and enjoying a good meal together. The mood was much lighter as they did not have a pending mission in front of them. After dinner, Scott and Jessie took another walk down to the pond, again with Baxter in tow. While they were away, Doug called everyone into the living room for a family meeting.

"OK, I wanted to speak to everyone while Jessie is not here. Normally, Jessie would be part of this discussion, but I think it best she sit this one out. What are our thoughts about inviting Scott to stay here with us? We have the room for him, and he brings a unique skill set to the group. He was an Army cavalry scout, attended the DNR academy, and is young, strong, and able. Brad and I are not getting any younger, and having an extra person for security and labor would really help out with the workload."

Everyone seemed to nod in an approving manor. "Would anyone like to discuss the matter?" asked Doug.

Kimberly indicated she had a question. "Won't that impact the food we have on hand?"

"Of course," replied Doug. "But I think his value is worth the trade due to his skill set. Just the extra manpower would reduce the workload on everyone else as its one more person to work the garden, cut firewood, fish, and pull security."

It was at this point Kimberly was figuring out she would be expected to contribute to the community. While she was not opposed to helping out, she hadn't expected she would need to help with manual labor or pull a security shift. She nodded in approval while smiling unconvincingly.

Nobody had any more questions, so Doug called for a vote, which was unanimous in favor of asking him to stay.

"OK, that was easy," said Doug. "I guess the next step is to get Jessie's take on the matter. Brad, she looks to you as a father figure, so it may be best for you to have a chat with her and see what she thinks about it. Her life is an emotional rollercoaster right now as her world has collapsed, she is interested in a guy, and she just killed a man and watched him die. She could use a father figure to lean on right now."

Realizing the burden before him, Brad said, "Yeah, I guess I need to speak with her. When I can get her alone, we will have a chat."

Penny chimed in. "You'd better have more than a conversation about Scott staying on. You need to have the dad talk with her. She needs that in her life right now. You are the rock she has built the foundation of her life on. Your approval is what she craves most."

Kimberly, watching the back-and-forth between her husband and Penny, was a little shocked and concerned. While she knew Brad had been Jessie's teacher in high school and now her fire chief, she didn't understand why she would view her husband as a father figure. Further, she didn't understand how this seemed to be common knowledge while she had no idea. Kimberly always viewed herself as the social coordinator of the group, and she didn't understand how she was so far out of the circle on this.

Meanwhile, Penny was excited that her ideal group was close to developing. She was preparing a chore schedule, and the difference between seven and eight people was significant. As Maddy's pregnancy progressed, she would be far less productive, and as Doug, Brad, Mark, Scott, and Jessie all had additional public safety responsibilities, they would be less available.

A short while later, Baxter trotted up onto the deck and sat directly in front of Kimberly. After a few moments of her not acknowledging his presence, he leaned forward and placed his head onto her lap.

"Good dog," she said, and patted him on the head a couple times with her left hand, hoping he would leave soon.

Baxter looked up at her with his sad dog eyes, communicating as only dogs can do that he wanted a bit more attention. She patted him one more time before he reluctantly walked over and sat next to Penny.

Maddy watched the awkward interaction through the window from inside the kitchen. She grinned to herself, thinking this would make a good sitcom: *Kimberly versus the Apocalypse*.

Not far behind Baxter, Jessie and Scott returned from their walk. Wanting to get them separated so Brad could have his chat, Doug asked Scott to accompany him into town to do a fast patrol and check on the town board's progress. Scott eagerly accepted and was honored that Doug wanted him along.

As the two rode into town in the Ram, Doug gave Scott a fast tour of the little town. About a block from the fire station was the town square. It was the picture that comes to mind when a person thinks of a town square. Quaint, simple, like something from a Norman Rockwell painting. In the center of the green park was a white pavilion used for speeches, festivals, and all sorts of community activities. Today, the activity was a bit different. Doug watched as about a dozen people stood looking at a bulletin board posted next to the pavilion.

Doug thought to himself that it must be one of the information kiosks where people could read information from the town board. He was impressed the board was so on top of things. Parking the truck, the two lawmen walked over to the board to take a look. It was difficult to read the paper as everyone who had gathered there turned to greet Doug and ask him a flurry of questions. He spent about fifteen minutes answering questions and working to ensure people knew the local government was still operational. But the longer he stayed and talked, the more people were gathering around. It was clear that in addition to the posted news, they needed to get the town hall meetings up and running as soon as possible.

Looking for an escape, Doug eyeballed the Rockport Methodist Church on the corner across the street. "Sorry, folks, but I have business with Pastor Campbell across the street. We will have a town hall soon where we can take more questions." Doug and Scott excused themselves and made their way across the street to the old white church that had served the community of Rockport since the Second World War.

"Do we really have business here?" asked Scott.

"Not exactly, but I wanted to get away from all our fans. I wasn't prepared for a news conference just yet."

"Do you go to church here?"

"No, we go to a Christ the Rock community church up in Harrison, but Pastor Campbell is a pillar of this community, and he will be an essential figure if we are to maintain a civil society. People will need faith now more than ever, and he is the man best suited for the job."

As the two entered the church, they were impressed by the rays of sunlight entering through the stained-glass windows. The church was picture perfect and complemented the ambiance of the town square perfectly. As they walked past several rows of empty pews up to the pulpit, Doug turned and opened a door to the right leading to the back office of the church. Doug was familiar with the layout as he had completed the last fire inspection on the house of worship.

"Pastor Campbell, are you here? Its Doug Chapman," he shouted down the hall.

They heard a friendly voice reply, "In my office."

The two walked down the hall to the simple office and found Pastor Campbell sitting at his desk struggling to reassemble an old double-barreled shotgun.

"I'm glad you are here, Doug," he said with an embarrassed and defeated tone. "I thought it wise to have something for defense, and I was given this by a member of the congregation. I took it apart to clean it, and for the life of me, I can't get it back together."

"No problem," said Doug, who took the receiver and showed him how to align it with the barrels and lock them together. The pastor was a bit embarrassed at how easy it seemed to go together for Doug. Setting the shotgun down on the desk, Doug asked, "Do you have any shells for it?"

"Yes, it came with a box." Pastor Campbell pointed to an old box of birdshot.

"Well, pastor, that might be OK for putting a little food on the table, but you will want something a bit larger for defense. I will bring you a box of buckshot next time I stop by."

"So, what can I do for you two?" he asked, as people didn't tend to stop by the church just for friendly conversation.

Doug introduced Scott and shared the information about what transpired over the past couple of days. The chaplain was shocked by all the news Doug shared. As the new lawman for the community, Doug wanted to team with the chaplain to help resolve issues before they developed into larger problems.

"I appreciate the sentiment, Doug, but I need to maintain confidentiality with my congregation."

"I understand, and I would never ask you to violate the trust of your flock, but I think there will be times we can work together to keep the community safe. Just consider me a partner and share what you think I need to know, and I will do the same to you," said Doug.

"That sounds like a good arrangement. Consider me a partner. That said, there is a matter you may need to be advised of, now that I think of it."

Interested, Doug listened intently.

The chaplain continued, "A couple days ago there was a party out at the big mansion where a girl was sexually assaulted."

"I'm aware of the matter," replied Doug. "I arrested the suspect, but the jail only has the capacity to hold the most dangerous prisoners."

The pastor nodded his head and said, "That's what I heard. The issue is that the girl's family and friends may be taking justice into their own hands. They are upset it has not been taken care of to their liking."

"I expected something like that may happen. Any idea what they are planning to do?" asked Doug.

"I have no idea; I just know they are very upset, and not all of them are of the 'turn the other cheek' mentality."

"Thanks, Pastor. We will look into it," advised Doug.

Walking back out to the truck, Doug explained the Stuart situation to Scott.

Laughing, Scott asked, "Was that the guy walking barefoot with the broken nose back from Chilton?"

"That's him. If he were smart, which we all know he isn't, he would have packed up and left town. I know of at least two girls' families and a guy he beat up who may be looking for revenge. That's not to mention the meth dealers who lost their stash because of him. Without his father's money or attorney, I don't think his friends will be as loyal as he thinks they are. Let's drive out to his place and motivate him to leave town," said Doug.

CHAPTER 36

Sitting at the patio table out at the deck, Jessie had her AR-15 disassembled and the parts spread out across it. She cleaned it meticulously, just like Doug had taught her. Brad walked out and had a seat next to her rather than across from her. This conversation had the potential to be difficult for the both of them, and he felt it may be a bit easier if they were not looking directly at one another.

"So how are you doing with everything?" asked Brad, awkwardly trying to start an uncomfortable conversation. Even though the two had a special bond, neither one was comfortable expressing emotion about it.

"You mean about shooting that guy? It needed to be done, and I was in the best position to take the shot," she said as if it was not a big deal to her.

Brad paused for a moment before replying, "Yeah, shooting that guy, but with everything else as well. A lot has changed for you the past few days. The university shut down, you became a cop, the thing with the bikers, the boy, and moving out here to Doug and Penny's."

Jessie smiled while focusing on the gun part she was recleaning to avoid eye contact. "I like how you just worked the boy in the middle of that list."

"Yeah, I've always been pretty smooth with words. Anyway, I'm glad you found someone who you seem interested in. But I am a bit worried that with the rollercoaster of emotions you are on, you may not be in the right place to make sound relationship decisions."

Jessie, listening to what he said, didn't have the words to respond.

After a moment of silence, Brad continued talking just to fill the silence. "I have to warn you, I've heard relationships based on intense experiences never work."

This caused Jessie to laugh out loud, and she turned her head to look at Brad. "Dude, did you just quote Keanu Reeves from the movie *Speed*?"

Caught off guard, he replied, "Oh, you are familiar with that film?"

"Well, yeah, you showed it to us in social studies like three times in one year. Every time you had a football game to prepare for, you popped it in the DVD player," said Jessie.

"Well, you get my point. You have been through a lot of intense experiences the past few days, and, well, I just want you to know I'm here for you."

Jessie set the gun part down and looked at Brad. "I know you are. You always are. It's the one thing I have always been able to count on in my life. You know I have a hard time talking about stuff like this, but you have always been the man I looked to as a father."

As both of their eyes were starting to get moist, Brad moved the topic along. "So, since this is the first time I will be living under the same roof with you, and a boy is sleeping in the next room, do we need to chat about it?"

She laughed and said, "Slow your roll, old man. I said '*like* my father.' I'm a big girl, and Scott and I are not in a relationship. I probably will never see him again after tomorrow."

"That brings me to the next topic. How would you feel if he were to stay here with all of us?"

Jessie looked up, trying not to appear anxious. "Did Doug offer him to stay?"

"Not yet, but he thinks he would make a good addition to the group. He wanted me to talk to you about it first. But if you are against it, it's a nonstarter."

Jessie, looking back at her gun parts and recleaning the same piece for the third time, said, "Well, it makes no difference to me if Doug wants him to stay here. I have no issue with it."

Grinning, Brad said, "So I can tell him you are neutral on the matter?"

Working even harder at not making eye contact, she replied, "I guess it would make sense to have him stay here. He would bring a lot to the group. He is pretty handy with a rifle and can help cover security shifts."

Smiling, Brad said, "OK, I will tell Doug to ask him."

As Brad stood up to walk away, Jessie called to him. "Chief!"

Brad turned to look back at her.

As she wiped a tear away from her eye, she said, "Thank you."

Brad smiled and gave her a wink before walking back into the house.

CHAPTER 37

As Doug and Scott were leaving the town, Doug pointed to a plume of smoke rising above the tree line adjacent to Lake Winnebago. "Well, that can't be good. I can't be sure yet, but I would bet that is Stuart's place."

Keying the microphone on his radio, Doug called the on-duty officers at the fire station.

"Deputy Chapman to Rockport Fire."

"Go for Rockport Fire," Vic replied.

"I have smoke showing above the tree line on Lake Winnebago. Heading there now to investigate."

"Roger that. We will roll in Engine 41."

As Doug and Scott drove around the trees, they could see the large house engulfed in flames. By the time they could get enough resources on scene to battle a fire of this size, it would be far too late to save the structure. Doug wondered if Stuart's body was inside the house. There were certainly enough people with a motive.

Doug had Engine 41 continue on, just to ensure the fire didn't spread and burn out of control. Doug continued on to the next house up the road to see if they had witnessed anything pertinent. A midsize ranch house was about a half mile up the road and had an elderly couple sitting on the porch in rocking chairs. It was apparent they had been watching the fire. Doug pulled the Ram up into the driveway and gave them a friendly wave. As the man waved back, Doug and Scott stepped out of the truck and walked up to the porch.

Doug was unfamiliar with the couple and introduced himself as he approached.

"Good afternoon, I'm Deputy Doug Chapman, and this is Warden Scott Connelly."

The wife spoke for the couple and said, "Come on up and have seat. I'm Bernice, and this is my husband, Alfred." She leaned closer to Doug and whispered, "He doesn't hear too good."

"Thank you," replied Doug as the two had a seat on the porch.

"Can I get you boys a pop?" she offered in a thick Wisconsin accent.

"No, thank you, we just had lunch."

"So, I guess you are here about the Griffith place?" she said, in the form of a question.

"As a matter of fact, yes. What can you tell us?" asked Doug, using an open-ended question to prompt her to speak freely.

She took a sip of her ice tea and said, "I have been sitting on this porch for a lot of years. This was a quiet little parcel of land until the Griffiths built that house down the road. The last few years have been worse since their boy started driving. That kid is a little terror, always has been. It was a nice break when he was away at college, but since he came home for summer, he has been having a lot of parties. I guess his dad isn't around because I don't think he would go for all those kids parking on his lawn. He had a huge party a couple days ago. I didn't see any cops, but I know the fire department was out there."

"Yes, ma'am, that was my department. With all the issues going on right now, we merged the fire and police departments. What can you tell me about the fire?"

"There was all kinds of commotion down there about an hour ago. A pickup truck with about four people in the back drove down there. A couple minutes later I heard a gunshot, then a minute or two after that the Griffith boy flew by in his father's fancy sports car."

"Was it a red Corvette?" asked Doug.

"Yeah, that was it. His father's car. A few minutes later we could see smoke rising from the place. Once it was burning pretty good, the truck left and drove back past."

"Did you recognize who was in the truck? Or what the truck looked like?"

"No, I was wearing my reading glasses and couldn't make them out from a distance."

Doug and Scott thanked them for their time and returned back to the Griffith house. The fire engine was on scene, and the crew was monitoring the fire to ensure it didn't spread and ignite the nearby woods. Vic was standing next to the engine while the other two firefighters stood on the other side of the burning house.

As the Ram pulled up next to Engine 41, Vic walked over to chat with Doug through his open driver's side window. He took off his helmet and said, "The fire was roaring when we arrived. It was burning hot and had already flashed over. I don't think anyone could have survived, and we didn't have the resources to send firefighters inside. It was my call."

"It was the right call, Vic," Doug reassured his friend. "I would have made the exact same call. The fire had burned another five minutes before you arrived on scene."

Vic nodded in a manner of thanking him for his support. "It was arson," he said matter-of-factly.

"That's what I figured," replied Doug.

"I found at least two obvious burn trails leading from the yard into the house. It looks like someone poured an accelerant from outside the home to the inside and lit it up. From how fast and hot it burned, I would bet there was a lot more accelerant poured inside the home. The fire spread faster horizontally than it did vertically," said Vic.

Watching the fire smolder, Doug replied, "Stuart had a lot of enemies. The neighbors up the street saw a pickup with several people in the back headed this way moments before the fire started. They heard a gunshot, then saw Stuart fly by in his daddy's Corvette."

"Probably one of the girl's families," suggested Vic.

"Yeah, that's what I'm thinking also."

"One more thing," said Vic, as he held up what appeared to be a branding iron. "I found this in the front yard. It was still hot to the touch."

Looking at the iron, Scott asked, "What's the symbol on the brand?"

Vic replied, "It's just the letter *R*. I don't know of any ranch or farm around here that just uses the *R* brand."

Doug looked at Vic and said, "The *R* stands for rape."

CHAPTER 38

The two teenagers flinched as the bottle exploded on the wall behind them, showering them with beer and broken glass.

After throwing the bottle out of a sense of rage at the stupidity of his idiot sons, Tommy Wolf shouted, "How do you lose five grams of meth?"

Not sure what version of the story would get him in less trouble, Brett told their father that a couple of rouge cops robbed them at gunpoint.

"What cops?" asked their father in disbelief. He knew law enforcement was almost nonexistent in rural Wisconsin nowadays, and his older son had a habit of embellishing the truth.

"They didn't wear police uniforms or have police cars. One of them was huge and had on a fireman T-shirt, I think. The other one had on civilian clothes, but they both had gun belts with badges. They just pointed their guns at us and took my backpack."

"That sounds like Deputy Chapman and Fire Chief Peterson," said Dale Tucker from the far side of the old auto repair shop. "Those are the same two cops that raided my place after that biker died."

Tommy Wolf decided that maybe his son was telling the truth about the cops after all. If Tucker could corroborate the story about the renegade lawmen, maybe they actually had taken the drugs from his boys. "Where did this alleged robbery take place?" asked Tommy, still not convinced his son was credible.

"It was out at Stuart Griffith's house," said Brett.

"That rich kid?" asked their father in a surprised tone. "I told you to stay away from him. He only has time for the likes of you two idiots if you have something he needs. Don't tell me you took my drugs over to his place!"

The two teenagers looked and each other then back at their father, unsuccessfully trying to think of a response that would help the matter.

Tommy clenched his fists and looked up to the ceiling trying to contain his anger. "Do you two have any idea what kind of jam you put us all in? Those five ounces were part of the deal we made with Dale's biker friends. We were already behind schedule, and these are not the kind of guys we want to be on the outs with. They already ambushed a bunch of cops, so I don't think they will think twice about putting a bullet in your useless skulls."

Looking over to Tucker, he asked, "Where can I find these two cops?"

"They are working out of the fire station in Rockport. Chapman made all the firefighters his posse members, and they are all armed now. I know Chapman lives a couple miles outside of town someplace. Probably better to hit him at his house than at the station full of cops."

"Can you find out where he lives?" asked Tommy.

"It will be hard. I am not supposed to be anywhere near there. If you want to find out where he lives, I would check with Jessie."

"Who is Jessie?" asked Tommy.

"Your brother's girl, Jessie Wolf," replied Tucker.

Tommy looked confused. "Didn't she go off to college someplace? How would she know where this cop lives?"

Tucker replied, "She goes to college up in Green Bay, but she still lives in the old apartment building in town. She is a volunteer firefighter, and now she's on Chapman's sheriff posse. She was one of them that raided my place and took the dead biker away."

"That little girl is a cop now? I haven't thought about her in years. She always did think she was better than the rest of the family. I think when the sun goes down, we will pay her a visit and find out where that cop lives," said Tommy.

The conversation was cut short by the sound of a high-performance engine approaching the compound. Tommy and his boys walked to the front of the old auto shop and watched as a red Corvette pulled into the compound and parked next to Brett's old Camaro.

"Who the heck is that, and why is he here?" asked Tommy.

Hesitating a minute, Brett finally said, "It's Stuart Griffith. I have no idea why he is here. We were going to trade him some meth for his dad's Corvette when the cop busted—I mean, robbed us."

They watched as Stuart opened the driver's door of the car and fell to the ground. As he slowly stood back up, it was apparent he had taken a beating. He held a hand over his forehead as he stumbled toward the men.

Stuart made his way up to the open garage door and tried to enter, but Tommy unexpectedly punched him directly in the chest, knocking him to the ground. "You have an invitation I don't know about?" he asked.

As Stuart lay on his back clutching his chest, Tommy and the boys could now see the letter *R* branded on his forehead. Tommy shook his head while looking down at Stuart. "Son, it looks like you are just full of bad decisions."

"What is the *R* for?" asked Brett.

Tommy explained to his older son, "In the Civil War, they would brand soldiers with the first letter of the crime they had committed so everyone would know what kind of man they were. Cowards would be branded with a *C*, deserters with a *D*, and so forth. I would suspect someone thought that Stuart here was a rapist."

Stuart felt his head, just now realizing the long-term ramifications of his brand. He had just thought it was a brutal act committed by some girl's father.

"What are you doing on my property, rich boy?" asked Tommy.

Still on the ground, he said, "I didn't know where else to go. A bunch of people attacked me and set my home on fire. After they branded me, one of them hung a noose over a tree branch. They were about to hang me, but a girl fired a gun in the air and made them stop. She told me to leave or else they would kill me. I jumped in my dad's car and took off. I thought that Brett would help me. I need a doctor."

Tommy wasn't a man known for compassion. "Ain't no doctors here, kid, and you were not invited. The last thing I need is a punk like you bringing his troubles to my doorstep. In fact, it seems to me, you already owe me one Corvette for all the meth I lost. It was your shenanigans that brought the cops out to your place while you were expecting my two knuckleheads."

"But it's all I have. They just burned down my house," pleaded Stuart.

"You know what they say, life is hard, and it's harder if you're stupid. The last thing I need is your stupidity rubbing off on my boys. They got enough problems," said Tommy.

Stuart was at a loss and started to cry. "I don't know what to do," he pleaded.

"That's your problem. Now git!" said Tommy, drawing a Smith & Wesson revolver from a holster on his hip.

As Stuart looked down the barrel of the Magnum, he struggled to his feet and started to back up.

"Run!" shouted Tommy, firing a shot into the ground near his feet.

Stuart turned and ran from the compound holding one hand over his forehead and the other over his chest.

Tommy looked back at his boys. "Now, let's go pay a visit to your cousin Jessie.

CHAPTER 39

The pain from the brand was not as bad as he thought it would have been. The third-degree burn must have damaged the nerve endings in his skin. The pain from the other injuries he sustained during the beating became much more prominent during his long trek back to town.

A three-hour walk provides a lot of time to be alone with one's thoughts, and Stuart's thoughts were dark. He was developing a deep feeling of hopelessness and couldn't see any possible way his life would improve. There was no solution to his problem.

Stuart had studied Maslow's hierarchy of needs while at college, and he knew he was lacking in even the basics of shelter, food, and safety. While he was not particularly close to his parents, they had provided him with all of the physical needs for survival as well as social belonging through their affluence.

Now with no home, money, skills, or family, he had lost everything in less than a week. Although he had many acquaintances due to his social status, he had no actual friends or people who cared about him on a personal level. He had mistakenly assumed Brett Wolf and his little brother would be happy to help him as they were well beneath him on the social ladder. He could not find solace even on the wrong side of the tracks.

With the realization that the brand that disfigured his face would lead others to shun him the rest of his life, he knew he would never find work, social status, or the love of a woman. His situation was truly hopeless, and suicide was a realistic possibility to him when he started his journey. Three hours later the possibility had strengthened.

As he crafted a plan to end his own life, he couldn't think of any method that was fast and painless. As all of his possessions were either burned down or stolen, he didn't have access to weapons, vehicles, or drugs. While he was walking on the county highway, he could see a vehicle approaching from a distance. Vehicles typically traveled around 65 miles per hour on this road and could easily take his life if he were to jump in front of one.

Stuart crossed over to the left side of the road so he would be closer to the oncoming pickup truck. When it was about one hundred yards away, he finally built up the nerve and prepared to jump in front of it. Suddenly, the truck slowed down and stopped about five yards in front of him. A man wearing a green army uniform climbed out of the bed of the truck and jumped down to the ground. Pulling a green duffle bag out of the bed, he thanked the old couple in the cab for giving him a ride.

Stuart, not sure of what was happening, just watched as the couple drove away. He couldn't even catch a break trying to commit suicide. The man in the army uniform was young, probably still in his late teens. As he walked up to Stuart he smiled and asked him how he was doing.

"I've been better," he replied, wondering what the soldier would say about the brand on his forehead. Stuart, looking over the young man's uniform, saw a name tag on the right breast pocket. It bore the name Schmidt.

"Are you in the military or something?" asked Stuart.

"I used to be. My family is from around here. I'm just passing through and checking on them."

Looking to his left and right, Stuart didn't see any houses or farms nearby. "Why did you get out of the truck right here?"

The soldier just smiled and said, "My family's place is over yonder a bit. I thought I would cut through this field right here."

Looking in the direction the man indicated, Stuart still couldn't see a house in the distance.

The soldier looked up at some birds flying overhead. "Look at those doves. They don't sow or reap or store food in barns, yet the heavenly father provides for them. Are we not more valuable than they are?"

"What? I don't follow," asked Stuart.

The soldier looked back at Stuart and said, "While you may feel like you have nothing left in this world, God will provide if you let him." He then picked up the duffle bag and slung it over his shoulder.

Stuart didn't know what to say to the soldier. He just watched him as he turned and started walking away through a farmer's field. Perplexed by the situation, Stuart continued on toward Rockport, not knowing what tomorrow held.

CHAPTER 40

As it was getting near dinner time, Doug headed back to the property so they could grab some food and check in. He also wanted to talk to Brad and see how the chat with Jessie went. If she was in favor of having Scott stay on, he wanted to talk to him about it soon, knowing Penny was anxious to complete her work rotation schedule.

As Doug pulled around behind the house, he noticed the parking near the deck was starting to get congested with all the new vehicles. He would need to come up with some sort of parking plan to ensure cars didn't get blocked in. Looking at Maddy's Wrangler sitting by the house brought a smile to his face. She wanted a Jeep like her mom's when she got her first teaching job after college. Doug had been worried he was losing his little girl as she was soon to be married and move out. Although there were several Jeeps for sale in the local area, Doug intentionally found one for them to go look at on the other side of the state. This would give him one last daddy-daughter road trip before she moved out. She still didn't know he'd done that.

As they got out of the truck, Scott was concerned he was overstaying his welcome at Doug's house. He knew food was a limited commodity, and he did not want to impose on his new friends. He said, "Well, the operation with the bikers is over, so I better get moving on."

Buying some time, Doug said, "No hurry. You should stay for dinner and can move on in the morning."

"That would be great, thank you," replied Scott.

Seeing Brad walking out of the house, Doug told Scott he needed to speak with the chief before he left for town to fill him in on the fire at the Griffith place. Scott said he was going inside to help the girls with dinner.

Once they were alone, Doug asked how the chat with Jessie went.

"Pretty good, I think. She is going through a lot but handling it relatively well under the circumstances."

Doug nodded. "What did she say about having Scott stay on?"

Laughing, Brad said, "She told me she was indifferent to the idea."

"Indifferent? What does that mean?" asked Doug.

"Well, I got the idea she was a bit more than indifferent, but she didn't want to seem too eager."

"OK, I will talk with Scott about it and see what he thinks. Where are you off to?" asked Doug.

Brad replied, "The high school. We are having a town meeting at 6 o'clock this evening. You should be there, too, unless you have some pending dragons to slay."

"Oh, there are plenty of dragons that need slaying. Stuart Griffith is on the list yet again."

"He still hasn't learned his lesson?" asked Brad with a tone of surprise.

"I think life keeps teaching him lessons; just not sure how much he is retaining. Anyway, he seems to be the victim in this case. A group of concerned citizens burned his house down and possibly branded him."

"Branded?" asked Brad.

"Yeah, Lou found a branding iron in the yard in front of his house," said Doug.

With a surprised look on his face, Brad said, "I don't even know what to say about that." Turning the conversation back to the meeting, Brad said,

"Mark is going in to replace Lou at the firehouse, and this is Jessie's regular shift. Once Penny gets a rotation worked out, I will make sure they are on different rotations at the fire station to ensure we have better coverage here at the house."

Doug said, "That would be great, thank you. Let me talk with Scott and check in with Penny, and I will meet you up at the school in a while."

"Sounds good. See you there," said Brad as he climbed into his Suburban.

Doug stepped up onto the deck and looked inside the house to see Scott helping his wife and daughter set the table for dinner. It felt right asking him to stay as he just seemed to blend right into the family. Then, looking beyond the dining room into the living room, he saw Kimberly sitting on the sofa attempting to read a book. Baxter sat up on the sofa next to her, staring directly at her while she worked to actively ignore him. Doug laughed at the situation and also wished Kimberly would fit in half as well as Scott had.

Doug took a seat in one of the patio chairs and motioned for Scott to join him. Scott, wiping his hands on a kitchen towel, excused himself from assisting and joined him on the deck.

Doug started off the conversation. "So, what plans does our area game warden have now that the renegade biker case is closed?"

Scott scratched his head and said, "I really have no idea, sir. I have no way to communicate with my leadership down in Madison, and after what I witnessed in Milwaukee last week, I seriously doubt they even exist anymore. I feel like I need to uphold my oath and serve as a lawman, but without getting any sort of compensation, I have no place to live and nothing to eat."

Doug nodded and said, "Sounds like quite the quagmire you've got there."

"I know. I have been taking it one day at a time, putting all my focus into getting the gang that ambushed the deputies. Now that that's done, I'm not sure exactly what to do. Under the circumstances, it doesn't seem logical to go around busting folks for hunting out of season or fishing without a license."

Doug looked him in the eye and said, "Well, let me run this option by you."

Scott looked at Doug with interest.

Doug continued, "How about you base your state game warden office out of Rockport? I will get the sheriff to deputize you like he did me. Until then, you can serve under me on the sheriff posse, but you also have statewide authority under the Department of Natural Resources (if they still exist). I will get Brad to make you a firefighter as well."

"I love that idea," said Scott. "Do you think the chief would let me bed down at the fire station until I find someplace to stay?"

"Yes, I suppose he would. But if you are interested, I would like to offer you to stay here with my family. Of course, that would mean you would need to pull your weight. Things like covering security shifts, working the garden, hunting, fishing, and so on. As the eighth member of the family, you would be more than just a hired hand. I would expect you to give your life to defend my family. And we would do the same for you."

Scott looked down at the ground as he was starting to get emotional from the offer. He nodded in approval. "Yes, sir. I would like that very much."

Doug extended his hand, and Scott gladly shook it.

"That will make my wife happy," said Doug. "Let me tell her the news so she can finish the chores schedule. After that, I need to run back to Rockport for the town hall. We are short staffed tonight, so I need you to get some sleep as you will be relieving Maddy on security duty tonight at midnight. I will swap out with you at 6 a.m."

"Can do," said Scott. "What does it entail?"

"I will formulate a better security plan tomorrow as we need to enhance things around here. For now, just try to hang out around the perimeter and near the gate as much as possible. The main goal is to alert the others in the house if there is something out of the ordinary. Between you and me, I am worried that the group of guys in the white Ford will return," said Doug.

"I will watch over them like they are my own family," said Scott in a reassuring tone.

"That's good," said Doug. "Because now they are."

As they walked into the dining room, Penny, Maddy and Kimberly were already sitting at the table and eating. "There is chili in the crockpot. Grab a bowl and sit down," said Maddy.

The two scooped a bowl of chili each and took seats at the table. Doug said, "I need to eat and run. I should really be at the town hall with Brad tonight."

"I figured as much," said Penny. "You know, Doug, the list of tasks that need doing around here is piling up."

"I know," he replied. "I have some good news, though; Scott here has agreed to stay on and help us out."

Maddy reached over and squeezed Scott's arm while Penny told him how excited she was. Even Kimberly smiled in approval.

Doug said to Maddy, "Scott will relieve you for his security shift at midnight, and I will relieve him at 6 a.m."

Maddy tapped the Sig pistol in her shoulder holster and said, "I think we got a handle on it, old man."

He smiled. "I'm sure you do, but don't take any chances. If you see or hear something out of the ordinary, call Scott on the radio."

Maddy winked at her father and said, "Will do."

CHAPTER 41

The white Ford pickup truck circled the block for the third time before parking in the dark alley behind the only apartment complex in Rockport. Built in the 1950s, the two-story building was small and only contained sixteen units, eight on each floor. It had two entrances, one on each end of the building, leading to the inside corridor where the individual apartment entrances were. Most of the occupants were in the low-income level, an equal mix of young people and elderly.

At 11 p.m., the building was quiet, and nobody stirred about. The four men, dressed in dark clothes, walked to the rear entrance of the building. Tommy attempted to pull open the glass security door that led inside but found it locked. Examining the thirty-year-old security keypad adjacent to the door, he observed four of the nine buttons were worn more than the others, indicating the building manager hadn't changed the combination regularly. The worn buttons formed an "L" shape and consisted of the numbers one, four, seven and eight. Entering that combination unlocked the door on the very first try, and the men entered.

At the other end of the corridor, just inside the front door, there was a series of old mailboxes built into the wall. Tommy scanned the names on each box and stopped at apartment 4A. The small handwritten name card next to it read Jennings/Wolf.

Moving back to apartment 4A, located adjacent to the back door they had just entered, Tommy reached up and unscrewed the lightbulb that was illuminating the back portion of the hallway. Knowing that his niece Jessie might remember him even after several years, the tall, bearded man instructed his son Brett to knock on the door. She hadn't seen her cousin since he was a child and likely would not recognize him.

After knocking and waiting for an answer, they heard a female voice from inside say, "Just a minute." The person inside the apartment fumbled with the lock, and the door finally opened, exposing a tall, dark-haired woman in her mid-thirties, wearing a bathrobe. She instantly had a look of fear on her face as the tall, bearded man pushed past his son, forcing himself through the door. The three others followed.

Panicked, the woman turned to run but was quickly knocked to the ground from behind. The much-larger man forcefully held her head to the ground while looking at her face. "This ain't her," said Tommy. "Check the bedrooms."

Tucker searched the back rooms and said, "No one else is in here."

"Where is Jessie?" asked Tommy.

Crying and wincing in pain, the woman on the ground said, "She moved out."

"Where to?"

"Please don't kill me," pleaded the woman.

Tommy applied pressure to her neck and asked again, "Where to?"

Still sobbing, the woman said, "She moved in with a retired state trooper that works as a volunteer fireman."

"And where does this man live?"

Working to catch her breath as she was starting to hyperventilate from fear, she said, "He has a place a couple miles east of town on the county highway. You turn left through some trees and follow a gravel road a ways to a security gate. I have never been past that."

Tommy's eyes widened with the realization he knew exactly where that was.

"That sounds just like the place where Merl got killed!" said Brett. "You sure we want to go back there?"

Tommy looked at his son and said, "Oh, we are going back there. But this time we are not using the front door."

Looking down at the sobbing woman, Tommy applied pressure to her throat and held it until her heart stopped beating. His younger son, Jaxon, was crying and begging his father to stop. Brett held his younger brother back to protect him from their father's wrath. He had been looking after his brother since their mother died many years earlier.

Tucker was terrified by the site before him. His fear of Tommy was now equal to his fear of the motorcycle gang. He didn't know how he had gotten himself into such a situation and was wishing he had gone to his sister's place in Manitowoc.

CHAPTER 42

The three ladies sat at the dining room table examining Kimberly's Beretta Silver Pigeon 20-gauge, over-under shotgun. Their group had often shot sporting clays together out at the Woodfire Lodge, where Kimberly typically dressed in a Scottish tweed vest and looked like a character from *Downton Abbey*. But regardless of her fashionable appearance, she was an exceptional shot with her double-barrel shotgun.

"It is a beautiful shotgun," said Penny, "but it may not be the best choice for security here at the house. I'm sure tomorrow Doug can find you a pistol and a long gun that are better suited for out here. We can take you down to the range and get you familiar with them."

"I suppose you are right," said Kimberly. "It's just that I am very comfortable with my Beretta."

Maddy chimed in. "Yeah, you are crazy good with that thing, but the light bird shot you use for shooting clay pigeons won't sufficiently penetrate a person after just a few yards. It will only pepper them with shallow wounds."

"I guess I have to be open to new things. I'm willing to try something new if you all think it's best."

"Good night, ladies," called Scott from the living room. "I'm going to get a couple hours of sleep in before I take over security for the rest of the night. I will have my radio on, so call me if anything seems out of place."

"Will do," said Maddy.

Scott went upstairs, and Baxter followed close behind.

Maddy said, "I'd better go and do an exterior patrol; it's been a while."

Maddy picked up her AR-15 with pink accents and slung it over her shoulder. As she walked out of the house, Penny could not help but smile at the sight of her daughter wearing her father's old shoulder holster. She remembered many years ago when, as a child, she would wear the empty holster and walk around the house doing *Charlie's Angels* poses. Now at six months pregnant, she still seemed like that little girl at times.

Stepping down from the deck, Maddy stood by her Jeep and fondly remembered the road trip her father tricked her into taking when they bought it. There were several for sale in the local area, but her dad tried to convince her the one three hours away was a much better deal. She'd loved that he wanted to spend one last day with her before she got married, and she never did let him know she was onto his little ruse.

Standing by the vehicles, she looked out into the night to allow her eyes to adjust to the dark before her patrol. She fondly remembered the day her father was a guest speaker in her class and somehow got on the topic of pirate warfare of the eighteenth century. He explained to the students that pirates wore eye patches to protect their night vision in one eye. That way they could fight above deck in the sunlight using the uncovered eye and switch to the other eye when moving below deck to battle in the dimly lit areas.

Once her eyes were properly adjusted to the dark, she started her foot patrol. She slowly walked through the woods toward the front gate. Every so often she would stop, close her eyes, and just listen. That was another trick her father had taught her. At night, you can hear farther than you can see.

After her walk around the gate, everything seemed to be in order. Next, she walked over to the garden, then down to the shooting range and pond. Everything seemed secure there as well. There was a full moon, which provided enough ambient light to see pretty well, now that her pupils were fully dilated.

As she walked over toward the chicken coop, she thought she heard something on the other side near the parking area, but she wasn't sure. Just to be on the safe side, she keyed the microphone on the small radio. "It's probably just a deer, but I heard some sticks snap in the woods out behind the chicken coop. I'm going to check it out."

"Roger that," said Scott. "Give me a couple minutes to get dressed and I will come down."

"I got this, Scott. Just wanted to give you a heads-up. I will let you know if I need you."

Maddy stopped and closed her eyes to listen to the dark, but the sound of the chickens clucking prevented her from hearing anything else. As she opened her eyes, she heard a deep voice directly behind her.

"Hello, Jessie. Remember me?"

Startled, she turned abruptly to see a large man with a beard looking back at her. Then everything went black.

Tommy reached down and picked up Maddy's AR-15 and slung it over his shoulder. Next, he picked up her unconscious body and held her close as he walked backward, dragging her into the woods to his truck parked down on the highway.

All of a sudden, Tommy heard a gunshot from about fifty yards away and felt a burning sensation in his left shoulder. As he started moving faster into the dark, he heard a second shot, and his right shoulder started to burn.

Penny worked the lever of her cowboy rifle, ejecting the spent shell and loading a third round into the chamber. She was taking careful aim at the man dragging her daughter, so as not to hit the young woman by accident. She was aiming at the edges of the man that were not concealed behind her daughter's motionless body. In the dark of night, it was very difficult to see where one body started and the other stopped.

As Penny took aim for the third time, she was trying hard to see the front sight of her rifle against the edge of the dark shadow blending in with the woods behind them. Suddenly, she felt extreme pain and collapsed to the ground. The bullet had come from somewhere in the dark and penetrated her left leg. Falling to the ground, Penny tried desperately to get her rifle pointed back at the shadow dragging her daughter away, but she could no longer find the target.

Penny screamed in agony, not from her wound but from the thought of losing her child. Her screams were interrupted by the sound of two shotgun blasts fired in fast succession. Trying to roll over to engage the new threat, she saw Kimberly standing by the chicken coop with her skeet gun. She was firing to Penny's left, presumably at the person who had just shot her.

Kimberly was focused on her target and reloaded and fired the shotgun with incredible speed. She was able to get six shots off before the men disappeared into the dark. As she reloaded for the fourth time, Scott ran past her in just his underwear and T-shirt, with his rifle in hand. Baxter was close behind him, barking wildly. Penny pointed to the area where she'd last seen her daughter and shouted, "They have Maddy!"

Scott ran in the direction Penny pointed, but once he got inside the woods, the moonlight was no longer able to penetrate the tree canopy. It was very dark, and he had no idea who or what he was chasing. Moments later he heard an engine start up not far to the west. Scott ran in the direction of the sound and eventually came out of the woods onto the county highway. He could see a pickup truck driving away at a high rate of speed. He aimed to fire, then thought better as Maddy was most likely in the truck.

Scott ran back through the dark, navigated only by the sound of Baxter barking. When he came through the woods, the moonlight once again allowed him to see better. His bare feet were bleeding from several cuts and gashes he'd received running through the woods. As he came around the chicken coop, he saw Penny on the ground sobbing frantically as Kimberly struggled to drag her toward the house to treat her wound in the light.

Slinging his rifle, Scott scooped Penny up in both arms and carried her into the house. Laying her down on the dining room table, he shouted for Kimberly to hold pressure on her wound while he ran to the ham radio.

"Warden Connolly to fire station. Emergency!"

"Go ahead, Scott. This is Mark."

"Shots fired! Shots fired! Maddy has been taken by unknown persons in a pickup, they are heading away from town on the county highway. Penny has been shot and needs a medic!"

"I'm on my way!" said Mark into the radio.

CHAPTER 43

As the white Ford sped down the dark highway, Brett and his brother rode in the bed of the truck with the unconscious woman. Both teenagers were bleeding from dozens of shallow wounds after being peppered by two loads of birdshot each. Jaxon sobbed from both the pain of his wounds and the totality of the situation. Over the past two hours, he had watched their father assault Stuart, strangle a woman, and now kidnap another.

Brett had always tried to look out for his little brother, but things were rapidly spinning out of control. While he didn't know how they would live or where they would go, he finally made the decision that if they survived the night, he would take Jaxon away.

Inside the cab of the truck, Dale Tucker sat in the passenger seat, also bleeding from dozens of shallow wounds. The lead birdshot pellets, smaller than BBs, burned like fire just underneath his skin.

"I need a doctor," he said, not knowing where to apply pressure as the small wounds covered the entire right side of his body.

"Stop your whining," replied Tommy, driving the truck. He, too, could feel warm blood running down each of his arms. A .357 Magnum round had pierced each of his shoulders from front to back. While he was pretty sure they had not hit bone, he was certain there was significant soft tissue damage. He was just starting to feel the pain as his adrenaline was wearing off.

"Did you get any of them?" asked Tommy.

"Yeah, I got one of them. I shot that crazy woman who was shooting at you with that cowboy rifle. She went down but was still alive. I was about to shoot her again when someone started blasting us with a shotgun."

"Did Brett get any of them?" asked Tommy.

"No, he didn't even fire a shot."

"Idiot," mumbled Tommy to himself.

As the truck pulled through their gate, the exterior building lighting illuminated the compound. This allowed Tommy to see the five motorcycles parked between the house and the auto shop.

"Damn it!" said Tommy. "That is the last thing we need right now."

Parking near the open roll-up door of the auto shop, he saw a gang member posted outside the building to provide security for his leadership. He had an AK-47 slung over his shoulder and watched as the four bloody men climbed out of the truck.

Tommy nodded at the biker, then told Tucker and the boys to take the unconscious woman inside and cuff her to the heavy metal workbench against the wall. As he walked inside his own shop, it was apparent the gang members had made themselves at home. The first thing he noticed was that they were drinking beer taken from the refrigerator inside his house. Tommy always kept some Stone Arch beer, brewed locally in Appleton, for special occasions. The fact that these men had entered his private home angered him, but he thought better about saying something.

"Who is this?" asked the gang's leader as he pointed to the unconscious woman.

"It's my niece. She fell in with a group of renegade cops, so I had to reintroduce her to the family," said Tommy.

"Looks like she put up one hell of a fight," said Ty, and the other three bikers laughed.

Tommy looked down at the blood dripping onto the ground at his feet from his two flesh wounds, then over at Tucker and the boys as they examined each other's birdshot wounds.

"She didn't do this!" shouted Tommy, starting to lose his temper.

"Watch your tone," said the huge biker Tommy knew only as Tank.

Tommy took a breath and tried to calm himself down, knowing he was outgunned.

"Dad," called Brett from over by the bench.

"Not now!" shouted Tommy. It was not the time or place to hear from his idiot son.

"But Dad, this is not our cousin. This is Mrs. Cruz, my teacher at the high school."

A look of defeat took over Tommy's face. He could not imagine anything else going wrong at this moment. He turned and walked over to the unconscious woman lying on the ground, bleeding from her head where he had hit her with his revolver.

Looking down at her, he asked Brett, "You sure?"

"Yeah, she was my social studies teacher, and I think she is pregnant."

Tommy was again angered at the laughter coming from the four gang members behind him.

Laughing out loud, Tank asked, "You mean you guys got yourselves all shot up and you grabbed the wrong girl in the process?"

Tommy didn't have the words to respond.

"And she is a pregnant schoolteacher," said one of the other bikers as they all continued to laugh.

Looking at Tucker, Tommy asked, "Why didn't you say something?"

Dumbfounded at the situation, Tucker replied, "It was dark and it all happened so fast. This is the first good look I got at her in the light. Why was she wearing a shoulder holster and carrying an AR?"

Tommy pulled Maddy's AR-15 off his shoulder to look at it. He just realized the rifle had pink accents, which sent the bikers into another fit of laughter.

Setting the rifle down, Tommy turned back to Ty and said, "Let's get down to business. I will deal with this situation later."

CHAPTER 44

Doug's throat was getting tired after all the questions he'd answered at the town hall for the past few hours. There were some good questions, and the community was making good progress. While nobody had answers to the overarching question of how this breakdown had happened, the citizens were really coming together at the local level to help their neighbors.

As a question came in about the medical clinic, Doug passed the question off to Doc Shelby. The doc stood up from his folding chair on the stage and walked to the microphone. Doug stepped back and took his seat next to Fire Chief Peterson. Taking a drink of water, he whispered to Brad, "I think we may just come through this if everyone bands together for the common good."

Brad suddenly got a very serious look on his face as he heard a radio transmission through his earpiece. Keying the microphone, he asked the fire station to repeat the last transmission. Looking at Doug he said, "Penny has been shot, and Maddy has been taken."

Doug bolted from his seat, ran past the microphone, and jumped from the stage. He ran through the audience and out the back door of the gym. Brad was only seconds behind. As Doug ran to his truck in the parking lot, he saw the fire department F250 fly by on Main Street with lights flashing and siren wailing. Once in his truck, he started it up and squealed his tires as he left the school. Speeding down the county highway, he could see the flashing red lights about a half mile ahead of him.

Doug was gaining on the fire truck, which appeared to be slowing down. As Doug neared the turnoff to his property, he could see Jessie and Ryan jumping out of the fire truck and then running up to the gate on foot. He assumed Mark must be driving the fire truck and was continuing on after whoever took Maddy.

Doug, not having all the details, didn't know if he should follow Mark or go to his house. At the last moment, he turned hard left and drove up the access road to the gate. He used the radio in his truck to tell Brad to follow and assist Mark.

Just as he was getting to the gate, Jessie was swinging it open. Doug slowed to allow Jessie and Ryan to climb in with their medical bags. Before they could even get their doors closed, Doug was already accelerating and driving the last couple hundred yards to the house.

As the Ram slid to a stop, Doug leaped from the vehicle with his rifle in hand and moved toward the house with surprising speed. As he approached the three-foot-high deck, he bypassed the steps and jumped onto the platform in a single bound without slowing. When he entered the dining room, he saw his wife lying on the dinner table while Scott and Kimberly worked on her frantically.

It was a lot of information to take in all at once. He observed his wife's blood-soaked jeans lying on the floor, having been cut off with trauma shears. He moved around Scott to where he could see what was going on and saw that his wife was conscious and crying. She had a tourniquet placed high on her left leg, and Scott was applying a QuickClot dressing to her bullet wound. The hemostatic agent would absorb the water in the blood and increase the clotting capabilities.

Seconds later, Jessie and Ryan entered the room, ripping open the fire department medical bag. Ryan, being a paramedic, was trained to a higher level than Scott, so he took over tending to her wound.

"Doug!" cried Penny. "They took Maddy!"

"Who took her?" he asked, holding her hand tight and placing his forehead against hers.

"I don't know. There were at least two of them," she said.

Kimberly interrupted. "There were at least four of them."

Scott chimed in. "They parked down on the county highway and came through the woods."

Doug thought for a moment, and the most logical conclusion was that they were attacked by the same group that had come three nights earlier. It was a small group of men, and they were somewhat familiar with the property. They knew enough to avoid the front gate. They were probably motivated by the fact Doug had killed one of them.

Doug asked Scott, "Did you see their vehicle? Was it a lifted white Ford truck with black rims?"

"It was too dark to see it well, but it was definitely a lifted pickup. It could have been white."

The only lead Doug had was that the man he killed earlier was a known associate of Jessie's brother Rosco. The white truck with mag wheels may have belonged to her uncle Tommy. While the lead was pretty thin, it was all Doug had to go on.

"Jessie, can you tell me how to get to your uncle's place?" asked Doug.

"No, I haven't been there since I was a little girl. I would probably know it if I saw it again. It was basically a junk yard with a bunch of wrecked cars piled up. The compound had a house, a workshop, and a few outbuildings," she replied.

As Doug was trying to process all of the information in order to formulate a plan, Penny called to him, "Bring our baby home, Doug!"

"I will," he said.

Looking up at Ryan, he asked for a status check. Ryan spoke as he continued to work on her. "It looks like it was a single, small-caliber bullet. Probably a .223 based on the level of tissue damage. The projectile entered the side of her left thigh and passed behind the femur. It exited the medial side of her leg. We need X-rays to be sure the bone was not hit. There is muscle and tissue damage, but I don't think it is life threatening."

Doug processed the information and said, "Good. Get her stabilized, then get her to Doc Shelby's." He then turned to Jessie. "I need you to go with me and try to find your uncle's compound. We need to leave now."

"Of course," she replied.

Mark entered the room in a panic with Brad right behind him.

"Did you find them?" asked Doug.

Mark shook his head no.

"Get your kit. We are going after them. Jessie is going to show us where her uncle lives. It's the only lead we got."

"I'm going with you," said Scott.

Doug looked at him and said, "We are not being cops right now."

Looking down at his underpants, Scott replied, "I'm not wearing a badge."

"OK, go get your kit on. We are leaving ASAP."

Doug turned to Brad and said, "I need you to help Ryan and Kimberly get Penny to the doc. Please look after her."

"Will do," said Brad.

Doug reached down and pulled the Calumet County Deputy badge from his gun belt and placed it on the table next to his wife. He was not interested in due process while his daughter was in danger.

Doug kissed his wife goodbye and told her he loved her. He then walked to his Ram outside and opened the passenger side door. He pulled out his body armor, placed it over his head, and secured the Velcro straps on each side. He pulled out both of the spare thirty-round rifle magazines to ensure they were fully loaded. Next, he performed a press check on each of his weapons to ensure they were ready for action. Reaching into the glove box, he withdrew his Benchmade Nimravus combat knife and secured it on his belt in cross-draw fashion. While a fixed-blade knife is not a typical piece of gear utilized by law enforcement, Doug was not gearing up for a police mission.

"Jessie will ride with me. Mark and Scott will follow us. Turn your fire radios to channel four. We are headed east. Any questions?"

As nobody had questions, they loaded up into the two trucks and left the compound. The mood inside the Ram was understandably tense. Jessie said, "I haven't been there since I was a kid."

"Just do your best," said Doug, with an eerie lack of emotion in his voice. This concerned Jessie, as her friend seemed to be transforming into some kind of Terminator-like entity.

"I'm sorry about Maddy," said Jessie, feeling somehow responsible due to the familial relationship with her possible captor.

Doug replied, "It's not your fault, and they are no longer your family. But I don't expect you to battle them; just get me to their location."

Jessie had a tear in her eye and said, "Maddy is like a sister to me. I would give my life to get her back." Then she reached over and squeezed Doug's arm while he drove.

CHAPTER 45

Her eyes opened, but things were blurry, and she didn't know where she was. Her head hurt terribly, and she could hear a man's voice in the background say, "Take her over to the house and cuff her up over there. And stay with her. I don't need you two embarrassing me again." She could feel her hand being uncuffed from an object before she lost consciousness again.

Sometime later, she woke up again, this time on the floor of a filthy kitchen in an old house. Someone was holding a wet towel against her forehead and trying to tend to her wound. As her eyes came into focus, she recognized the boy sitting next to her from one of her freshman classes. His name was Jaxon, and while he was high functioning, he was clearly on the autism spectrum. A quiet and skittish boy, his only friend was his older brother, who tried to look out for him.

"Jaxon, where are we?" asked Maddy.

"We are at my house, Mrs. Cruz. Please don't be scared," he replied.

Realizing that her right hand was cuffed to the metal pipe under the sink, she started to panic. "What's going on? Why am I handcuffed?" she asked.

Jaxon said, "Please be quiet. He will hear you."

Whispering, she asked, "Who will hear us?"

"My dad," replied Jaxon. "Sometimes he gets upset. He thought you were my cousin."

Finally starting to piece it all together, Maddy recalled that Jaxon's last name was Wolf. It had never occurred to her that he could be related to Jessie. The man that hit her must be Jessie's uncle, the one they suspected of coming out to the house when she and her mom were home alone.

Realizing the gravity of her situation, Maddy scanned the area for something she could use as a weapon. Looking at the items under the sink she was cuffed to, the only thing she could find to use as a weapon was an old rusty Phillips screwdriver. With her uncuffed left hand, she concealed the tool in her back pocket until she had an opportunity to use it.

Hearing yelling from the other room, Maddy thought it must be the father shouting at Jaxon's older brother. "Who the hell is she?" the deeper, more mature voice yelled. "She was my teacher last year," replied a voice she recognized as Brett. "What was she doing at that cop's house then?" demanded the father.

The large, bearded man suddenly stormed into the kitchen and looked at Maddy sitting on the floor. "Leave her alone!" he shouted at Jaxon for tending to her wound.

Looking down at Maddy, he said, "So, teacher, what were you doing out at that cop's house?"

Realizing the man was angry with her father, Maddy felt it was best to conceal her relationship. "I am a tutor for his grandchild," replied Maddy.

"Why would a cop need a tutor in the middle of the night? And wearing this?" said Tommy, holding up the shoulder holster with the Sig 9mm.

Maddy replied, "The cop's grandson has special needs, and I was looking after him while he was out. My father made me take that gun for personal protection while I was away from home. I don't even know how to use it."

Tommy considered if what she was telling him was the truth. It didn't matter since he would kill her anyway once she was no longer of use to him. If she was just a tutor, there was no point in keeping her alive. He unsnapped the shoulder holster and pulled out the Sig pistol. As he prepared to shoot her with her own gun, he noticed the engraving on the slide of the pistol. It was a retirement gift for a Special Agent Doug Chapman. Tommy grinned as he looked at Maddy, realizing she may just be of value to him after all.

Maddy could see in his eyes that he now knew she was the cop's daughter. She watched as the man sat the pistol down on the kitchen table, far out of her reach. She knew her father and husband would come for her eventually, but could she survive long enough to see them?

CHAPTER 46

Once the Suburban had pulled up in front of the veterinary clinic, Kimberly ran to the door and started knocking frantically. After a few moments, the light came on, and she could see Doc Shelby walking toward the door to open it. The veterinarian's home was connected to the clinic, and he often opened up at night for farm-related emergencies.

While waiting for his wife to get the clinic open, Brad worked with Ryan to prepare to lift Penny out of the Suburban. Baxter was lying next to Penny, resting his head on her chest in an attempt to comfort her.

"OK, bring her in!" Kimberly shouted from the front door of the clinic. Penny was in a lot of pain as the two large men carried her into the building, then into one of the exam rooms. They placed her on a stainless-steel table, and the doc started to examine her wounds while paramedic Ryan gave a report of her vitals and condition. As the two men worked on her, Brad stepped out of the exam room and into the waiting area to check on his wife.

Once in the waiting room, he was surprised to see his wife sitting on the floor and crying. She had been through a lot, and her entire world was collapsing around her. Brad watched as Baxter walked over to her and gently put a paw on her leg. His wife wrapped her arms around the black-and-white dog that she had been working to ignore the past couple of days. It was apparent that Baxter was a comfort to his wife as she was breaking down.

Sitting on the floor next to Kimberly, he put his arm around her and pulled her and Baxter close. Kimberly looked at her husband with tears in her eyes and said, "I don't even know who I am anymore. Everything I thought was important has disappeared."

Brad pulled her tight and said, "You're wrong. Only the distractions have disappeared. Everything that's important in life is still right here."

She looked up at her husband and said, "I love you."

"I love you too."

"Brad, I want you to know I am going to change. I will be a wife you can depend on. I will be a true partner. I want to be someone you can share your feelings with."

"It's OK, babe. Let's get through tonight, and then we will tackle tomorrow.

Back in the exam room, Doc Shelby was taking X-rays of Penny's leg to see if the bone had been hit and if any part of the bullet remained inside. Satisfied that it was a through-and-through wound, he started stitching up the tissue. While there was damage to both muscle and tendons, the vet did the best he could to repair the wound.

CHAPTER 47

It took about fifteen minutes to get to the area where Jessie thought her uncle had lived years ago. It was dark, and rural Wisconsin did not have lighting on county highways. Doug was thankful for the full moon that provided a little bit of light. As they drove the side roads, they passed an old barn that seemed familiar to Jessie. It was unique as it had the words GO PACKERS painted on the side in huge letters. About a mile past the barn, they passed what looked like a junkyard. Jessie recalled a white house and a green auto garage in the compound near the entrance gate.

"That's it!" she said when they drove past and could see the familiar structures.

Talking into his microphone, Doug said, "That's the compound to your left. Scott, we need a reconnaissance report."

The two trucks drove another half mile and parked in a grouping of trees well off the road.

Doug gave commands for everyone to gear up in preparation for traveling back to the target on foot. As they approached the compound in the dark of night, Doug instructed Mark and Jessie to prone out on the ground and wait while he and Scott performed recon, Doug in the front of the compound and Scott in the back.

Both men low-crawled to their respective positions. When Doug got to a position where he could scan the front area, he pulled the rifle from off his back and zoomed in the scope to the sixth power. Shouldering the weapon, he scanned the area through his optic. The compound was well illuminated, which was both good and bad. It made it far easier to collect reconnaissance, but it would be harder to approach undetected.

Scanning the area, he could see the auto shop with the lights on inside and the roll-up garage door open. From his angle of observation, he could only view a small portion of the inside of the building. He could tell there were people inside due to the shadows being cast on the far wall. Doug stopped scanning when something inside caught his eye. Resting against the wall inside the building was an AR-15 with pink accents. That was Maddy's rifle.

About fifty yards away from the auto shop was an old two-story farmhouse. There was a first-floor light on inside; however, all the activity seemed to be taking place in the shop.

Scanning the parking area to try to get a count of possible hostiles, he saw the five motorcycles parked with the armed guard out front. The target just became harder. Scanning further, he saw the white lifted Ford truck. The tailgate was down, indicating they had recently unloaded something or someone from the bed. Looking at the driver's side taillight of the truck, Doug could see damage consistent with backing into the tree on his property the night he shot the man.

Next to the truck, he saw the blue Camaro the teenagers were driving when he took the meth from them at Stuart's house. Next to that was a red Corvette, most likely Stuart's. This was getting interesting, and fast, Doug thought. The last truck in the compound was a familiar one as he had seen it parked at the Rockport maintenance facility over the past ten years. It belonged to Dale Tucker.

Doug estimated a probability of ten hostiles, plus or minus. He radioed the others and provided a situation report. Scott's briefing indicated no movement in the rear of the compound. Doug instructed Scott to meet him back at the position where they left Jessie and Mark, and they would formulate a plan.

Once back at the rally point, Doug advised the team of their assignments. "Scott, since you are already familiar with the rear of the compound, you will cover Mark and me while we cut through the fence and slip in. Be sure to watch the rear of both the shop and the house. We will start with the shop as that has the highest probability. Jessie, you will cover the front of the compound. Keep eyes on the house as it will be to our backs and someone may come out when the shooting starts. You will be at a distance of about seventy-five yards. Mark and I will make the assault. We will cut through the chain-link fence at the rear of the compound and move up to the rear of the garage in the shadows. I will move around to the front and take out the security guard with my knife. We will then stack outside the garage and move in together on my lead. When I enter, I will close directly on the biggest threat inside and use the element of surprise and speed of the assault to our advantage. Mark, you will enter right behind me and move to the nearest corner of the room and provide cover fire from that angle. That will give them two targets to shoot at in opposite directions, dividing their firepower. It will also give us two angles to shoot at them from, reducing any cover they may have. I know this is a hasty plan, but time is not on our side. We need to get Maddy back. Any questions?"

Nobody had any.

"Good," said Doug. "You two get into your cover positions and keep low. Be ready with weapons on fire, as this will go down fast. Move out."

Doug and Mark low-crawled until they came to the chain-link fence at the rear of the compound. Doug pulled a set of tin snips out of the cargo pocket on his pants. Lying low, he snipped through the fence from the ground up for about eighteen inches while Mark covered him with his rifle. Once the hole was cut, Mark held it open while Doug crawled through. Once on the inside of the fence, Mark passed both rifles through the hole to Doug, then crawled through while Doug held it open.

The rear portion of the building was not illuminated, so the cover of darkness was on their side. As they approached the rear of the shop, Doug snuck up to the window while Mark covered him. Since it was light inside the building and dark outside, Doug knew the occupants of the building would not be able to easily see him. Looking inside, he could only see a portion of the garage. The inside was very cluttered with equipment and car parts, plenty of objects that the bikers could use as cover. Doug could see at least two bikers inside from his angle, not counting the one out front. He could also hear voices inside discussing a meth lab. He was certain one of the voices belonged to Dale Tucker.

Doug moved back to Mark and advised him of the building layout. "When you enter the building, move directly into your near right corner and start engaging targets from right to left. Watch for me as I will be moving straight into the room and engaging targets from left to right as I go. I will need to move into your field of fire to engage targets behind cover. I will take out the guard out front with my knife before we enter. If he makes a sound, just go past me into the room and start selecting targets. I will be right behind you."

Mark nodded and said he understood.

"And Mark, leave Tucker alive so we have someone to interrogate in case we don't find Maddy."

Doug keyed his microphone and advised Jessie and Scott they were about to assault the shop. "If Mark and I go down, it is up to you two to rescue Maddy."

Both Jessie and Scott confirmed the assignment.

Doug slung his rifle behind his back and drew his knife. Walking slowly from the rear of the building, he remained in the shadows. He rolled the bottoms of his boots from heel to toe to ensure silence and balance. As he slowly moved around the corner, he positioned himself behind the gang member holding an AK-47. Doug, utilizing an Israeli military sentry removal technique, wrapped his left arm around the man's neck and pulled him off balance. With the knife in his right hand, he reached around and severed the man's throat from left to right, cutting deep through his trachea and carotid arteries. He held the man off balance for several seconds until he was life-less. Slowly lowering him to the ground to avoid noise, Doug signaled Mark to move up to his position. Wiping the blood from his knife onto the dead man's shirt, he then sheathed his blade.

Transitioning to his rifle, Doug ensured the optic was once again set to 1 power, the lowest setting, as he would be engaging targets at close range. Mark came up behind him to prepare for the assault. He tapped Doug on the shoulder to communicate he was in place and ready to go.

Doug started walking in a fast but steady pace. As Doug turned the corner and entered the shop, he dipped his rifle to the left corner, clearing it of possible threats before moving past. Doug was immediately seen by two gang members, who made a move for their guns. Before they were able to reach their weapons, Doug had delivered two rounds into the center of each man, dropping their lifeless bodies to the floor. The sounds were deafening as the report of the rifle reverberated between the walls of the shop. As Doug moved further into the shop, he saw movement up ahead as another gang member was taking cover behind a fifty-five-gallon barrel. Hoping that the barrel was empty, or at least partially, Doug fired three rounds into the upper half of the barrel. The gamble paid off as the bullets penetrated the barrel and hit the large, bearded man hiding behind it. As the man fell to the ground, Doug fired two rounds into his center mass.

Moving around the debris, Doug searched for additional threats just as a barrage of gunfire erupted from a dark corner to his left. Doug felt multiple bullets impact his ballistic vest and left arm. Staying focused, Doug turned toward the threat and fired several rounds into the corner until a gang member fell to the ground. Doug recognized him as the gang leader from the booking photo the sheriff had showed him.

Following right behind his father-in-law, Mark entered the shop and moved to the right corner of the room. The first person he encountered was Dale Tucker, who had his back turned to him. Startled by Doug's gunfire, Tucker reached for a pistol on the workbench next to him. Mark held low and fired two rounds to his lower body as instructed.

Mark held his position while Doug cleared the rest of the building.

"Maddy?" asked Mark.

"Not here," replied Doug.

Walking over to Tucker, who lay motionless on the ground, Doug rolled him onto his back so he could interrogate him about Maddy. Once he got him onto his back, he could see the blood draining from his face. Looking down at his legs, he saw several liters of blood pooling on the concrete floor around his lower extremities. He said, "You severed the femoral artery. He is a dead man. Let's take the house."

CHAPTER 48

Inside the house, Maddy waited until Tommy left the kitchen, then asked Jaxon if he knew where the key to the handcuffs were.

"My dad has the key in his pocket," said Jaxon.

"Do you know what bolt cutters are? Do you have one?"

"Yes, but they are in the shop, and Dad told me to stay in the house."

"How about a pipe wrench or something that I can use to unhook the pipe I am cuffed to?"

"Let me check," said Jaxon, and he stood up and left the room. A few minutes later he returned, looking very guilty, and pulled a pipe wrench out of his pants that he had concealed from his father.

Maddy took the wrench and attempted to loosen the pipe, but with the use of only her left hand, the effort was futile.

She looked at Jaxon and asked, "Can you help me?"

He took the pipe wrench from Maddy and tried to loosen the plumbing; however, he could not get it to budge.

Now that it seemed like escape was a futile option, she switched her thought process to defense. She had a concealed screwdriver, but using it with her left hand from a seated position did not seem very effective. Looking at Jaxon, she whispered, "Do you know where your dad put my gun?"

"I think so," he said, and left the kitchen one more time. When he returned, he had the Sig pistol concealed in his waistband under his shirt.

Maddy felt like she had won the lottery. As she reached out for the weapon, Jaxon looked back to make sure his father was not coming before he handed it to her.

Once she took the pistol, the first thing she did was check to see if a magazine was in place. Her heart sank when she observed it was not. Maddy put the pistol between her knees and used her left hand to pull the slide back enough to see if Tommy had left a round in the chamber. To her surprise, she saw brass inside the chamber when she performed the press check. She had one bullet.

Maddy struggled with the decision before her. Should she use the bullet to try to shoot the handcuff chain to free herself, or save it to shoot Tommy to defend herself? She wasn't sure if a 9mm bullet would actually break the chain or if it would break her wrist in the process. She didn't know if she could kill the large man with just one bullet, fired left-handed. What if she shot him but there were other dangerous men in the house? She came to the conclusion it was best to save the bullet to defend herself when the time came.

Her thoughts were interrupted by the sound of gunfire nearby. It sounded like it was right outside the kitchen window. Maddy knew it was her father and husband coming to rescue her. The rifle fire came in fast pairs, what her father called a double-tap. He always said, "If someone is worth shooting once, they are worth shooting twice."

As Maddy was saying a prayer for her dad and husband, she was interrupted by Tommy as he burst into the kitchen with a rifle in his hands. He ran past her to the kitchen window to look out. He must have seen someone to shoot at because he raised the rifle to his shoulder as if he was about to fire. To Maddy, if there was someone Tommy felt needed killing, it would most likely be someone she would want to protect.

Time slowed for Maddy as she viewed the image before her. The large man was wearing a dirty flannel shirt with both shoulders saturated with blood. As he raised the rifle to his shoulder, he took a wider stance with his feet to stabilize himself for the recoil.

Maddy pulled the Sig pistol from behind her and aimed it at the back of the man's head. As she was right-handed, trying to aim the gun with only her left hand made a very shaky platform. Not wanting to miss with her only bullet, she lowered her front sight toward the center of the man's back, a much larger target.

Bang! The gun fired and ejected the empty casing onto the kitchen floor. He didn't fall, and she wondered if she had missed him altogether. She could see a small patch of blood start to form on his shirt that was growing in size. It was about two inches to the right of his spine. While it did not incapacitate him, it prevented him from firing on her family.

Tommy turned, with a look of pain and anger on his face. Maddy pulled the trigger again, but the hammer dropped on an empty chamber. The sound of the click was louder than the recoil, Maddy thought to herself. She knew her life was about to end, but her thoughts were for her unborn child.

Jaxon stepped in front of Maddy in an attempt to prevent his father from shooting.

"Move, you idiot!" shouted Tommy as he raised the rifle and pointed it toward the two of them.

Suddenly the kitchen window exploded, sending pieces of shattered glass across the kitchen. A bullet had come from somewhere outside the house, striking Tommy in the side of the face. Tommy dropped to his knees with a horrific wound. The bullet had entered the left side of his jaw, and the exit wound on the right was massive. Teeth and blood spattered the cupboard.

Even though the wound looked horrible, he was not yet incapacitated. Maddy was hoping he would bleed out or lose consciousness before he could shoot her. She could see the life leaving his eyes, but it was not fast enough. As Tommy raised the rifle in her direction, she frantically struggled to free her hand from the cuff.

Just as the barrel of his gun was leveled to her head, she closed her eyes and waited for the end. She could feel Jaxon holding her tight and screaming for his father to stop. The shot came, but she did not feel the impact. When she opened her eyes, Tommy was slumped back against the wall with a small hole just below his left eye.

Looking back over her shoulder, she saw Jaxon's older brother Brett holding a pistol. He had a blank stare on his face. He just killed his father to save her and his little brother.

As Maddy made eye contact with the teenager, she mouthed the words, "Thank you."

Brett looked at his dead father, then at his little brother, who was crying frantically and holding onto Maddy.

Looking back at Maddy, Brett said, "Please look after him."

A moment later she heard the sound of the front door of the house being kicked in. She knew her father would kill everyone standing in a matter of seconds. She yelled at Brett to drop the gun, lie down on the floor, and spread his fingers. Brett repeated his request—"Please look after him"—then turned and exited the kitchen with the gun in his hand.

Maddy looked at Jaxon and instructed him to lie down on his stomach right now and put his hands behind his head. Afraid and in shock from seeing his father killed, the confused young man did as she instructed.

CHAPTER 49

In the shop, Doug removed the partially full magazine from his rifle and inserted a fresh one from the pouch on his tactical vest.

"You're bleeding," said Mark, nodding his head toward Doug's arm.

Looking down to rapidly assess if his wound would prevent him from continuing, Doug opened and closed his left hand to ensure it was operational. He then breathed in and held a deep breath to verify the bullet had not penetrated a lung, causing a pneumothorax. Satisfied the gunshot was not immediately critical, he decided he could continue on.

"On me," he said to Mark as he started moving in a methodical manner toward the residence. Once they exited the shop, a gunshot rang out from within the house. Doug and Mark took cover back around the corner of the shop. Just as Doug was about to radio for cover fire from Jessie, a single shot rang out from the tall grass where she was positioned. At the same time, a window shattered in the house.

"One shooter down, first floor, southeast corner, kitchen," said Jessie in a calm voice over the radio.

Doug gave a thumbs-up in her direction, knowing she was watching over them. Doug said again to Mark, "On me," and continued moving on before any shooters inside the house had a chance to regroup. As the two men closed the distance between the auto shop and the house, another shot rang out from within the kitchen. It sounded like a pistol. Having no cover, Doug pressed on toward the house.

Moving up the steps to the front, Doug continued onto the porch and kicked in the front door without losing stride. The two men rapidly searched the front room for threats. Doug looked at Mark and gave him a hand signal instructing him to cover the uncleared kitchen and stairway while he cleared the back of the house. As Mark covered his area, the kitchen door opened, and a man exited with a pistol raised. Mark fired two rounds in rapid succession into the center of the man's chest. The man dropped the gun and collapsed to the floor.

Doug returned to the front room and asked, "Are you good?"

Mark nodded and said, "I'm good!"

Doug instructed him to cover the stairwell while he cleared the kitchen. Once inside the kitchen, he saw his pregnant daughter sitting on the floor with her hand secured to the plumbing under the sink. She had dried blood on her forehead. There was an obviously deceased man against the far wall, and blood spatter covered most of the kitchen. Lying at Maddy's feet was one of the teenagers he had taken the drugs from at Stuart's house. He was lying face down with his hand behind his head.

"Daddy, he helped me, don't shoot him!" yelled Maddy.

Processing the information in a mechanical fashion, Doug backed out of the room and looked over to Mark. In a calm voice, he said, "Tend to Maddy while I clear the rest of the house."

Doug moved to go up the stairs while Mark moved to enter the kitchen. Mark was experiencing a lot of emotion, not knowing what to expect when he turned the corner. As he entered the kitchen, Maddy told her husband not to shoot the boy on the ground as he had helped her. Seeing the pieces of broken glass and the blood-spattered kitchen, Mark tried to process what had happened in the small room. He could not easily determine what kind of horrors his wife had lived through, so he simply moved to secure the scene. Slinging his rifle across his back, Mark placed a knee on Jaxon's shoulder as he secured his hands behind his back with a flexicuff. He then turned to his wife and asked, "Where are you hurt?"

"I'm not sure, just uncuff me," she said, more concerned about the health of her unborn child than of her own well-being.

Pulling a handcuff key from his pocket, Mark unlocked the mechanism, freeing her hand.

Maddy hugged her husband tight and said, "Help me up. I am so uncomfortable."

"No, lie back on the floor so I can assess you," said Mark, the paramedic in him overruling the emotion of the husband.

As her husband checked her over for signs of injury, Maddy turned her head and looked at Jaxon, whose face was about fourteen inches from hers. She could see the fear in his simple eyes. She reached over and brushed his hair gently, telling him that it was over and everything would be alright.

As Mark examined her head wound, she heard her father's voice come over the radio on her husband's vest. "The house is clear. Scott and Jessie, move into the compound and clear the outbuildings."

Hearing that the house was secure, Mark picked up his wife and carried her into the living room and placed her on the couch. He wanted to remove her from the macabre that was the kitchen.

As Doug returned to the first floor, he saw Mark placing his daughter onto the sofa. It was at this point the emotions of the father started to overtake the determination of the warrior. She was the most important thing in his world, and the fact that she was now safe brought on a flood of emotions. He walked over to the couch and knelt down next to his daughter. He squeezed her hand and the two looked at each other, communicating in the unspoken language known only to a father and daughter.

CHAPTER 50

As he placed the dressing over the freshly stitched wound, Doc Shelby said to Ryan, "She will need the bandages changed regularly. Watch for any signs of infection."

"Will do," he replied.

Looking at Penny, he instructed her to keep off her feet with her leg elevated, as it would take time for the wound to heal. "Once the stitches are out, we will need to develop a physical therapy plan to get you back into shape."

As Penny was thanking the veterinarian for helping her, they were interrupted by the sound of commotion coming from the waiting room.

"Excuse me," said the Doc as he went to check it out.

As he walked out of the exam room into the waiting area, he watched as Scott held the front door open so Mark could carry in Maddy.

"You still open?" asked Scott.

"Apparently," replied Doc. "Bring her into exam room two."

Mark followed the Doc to the examination room and sat Maddy on the table.

In the waiting room, Scott continued to hold open the door for Jessie, Doug, and Jaxon.

As Doug went into the exam room to check on his wife and tell her Maddy was safe, Jessie took Jaxon to the far side of the waiting room and sat with him.

Scott leaned against the wall, not wanting to intrude on the special moments that were taking place in front of him. He watched as Brad consoled Kimberly and Jessie looked after her newfound cousin.

Jaxon, still in pain from the birdshot wounds, felt safe for the first time since losing his mother years earlier. Jessie held his hand and asked, "Do you know who I am?"

Jaxon nodded his head and said, "You are cousin Jessica."

She was surprised he remembered her because she hardly remembered him. It must have been eight years since she'd last seen him—or since she went by the name Jessica. She would have been fifteen years old, about the same time Brad came into her life and got her involved in sports. It was right after her Aunt Rose, Jaxon's mother, passed away from a drug overdose. Since her own mother left when she was a child, her Aunt Rose was the closest thing she'd had to a mother figure growing up. Jessie was just now recalling memories she had repressed about her childhood.

Jessie looked at him and said, "Wow, you must have only been seven or eight years old the last time you saw me."

Jaxon, looking straight ahead, said, "I remember. I always remember."

Jessie thought that was an odd way to phrase it. In her last semester at the university, she had taken a psychology class where they discussed autism. The professor explained that sometimes people on the spectrum can display extraordinary memories. She wondered if her cousin was some sort of a savant.

"Jaxon, do you remember the last time you saw me?"

He replied, "Two thousand nine hundred sixty-two."

Confused by his response, she said, "I don't understand."

"Two thousand nine hundred sixty-two days."

"What is the last thing you remember about me?" asked Jessie.

Still looking forward, he replied, "The day of Momma's funeral. Uncle Bobby brought you and your brothers to the funeral home. You wore a dark blue dress and sang the song 'I Will Remember You.' You had to stop singing because you started to cry."

Jessie was vaguely starting to recall that memory, which had been lost to her for years.

Jaxon continued, "After the funeral, everyone came over to our house for food. You kept crying and went into my brother's room to be alone. My dad was drinking a lot and went into the room to check on you. He closed the door. Something bad happened in the room, and you started screaming. Your dad went into the room and got into a fight with my dad. You all left after that."

Jessie, just starting to recall short flashes of repressed memories, asked, "Was that the last time you saw me?"

Jaxon nodded his head up and down. "Two thousand nine hundred sixty-two days."

Jessie, now starting to understand herself a little better, realized what kind of life Jaxon must have lived over the past eight years. The fact that she had put a bullet into his father's head was somehow therapeutic to her. It was like she closed the door to a dark chapter of her life she hadn't even realized existed.

She squeezed his hand tight and told him she would take care of him now.

A tear rolled down his face as he replied, "I would like that."

CHAPTER 51

The rays of the morning sun were shining past the church steeple, creating a warm, calming feeling in Doug as he stood in front of the veterinarian's office. He was thankful that his daughter was safe and his family had come through the ordeal mostly intact. While he couldn't explain it, he felt something calling him to go to the church.

Turning back to the clinic, he saw Brad and Ryan ready to carry Penny out to the waiting Suburban to take her home. Doug held the door open for them as his stitched-up shoulder prevented him from helping lift her. Scott had already driven the others back to the house. Once she was in the Suburban, Doug gave her a kiss and said he would be home in just a bit.

"Don't be long," she told her husband.

"I won't," he replied, causing Penny to shoot him the "yeah, right" look.

He smiled and said, "Love you."

She returned the smile as he closed the door.

Doug tapped on the top of the Suburban, indicating they were good to drive away.

Looking at his watch, he saw it was almost 7 a.m. Doug walked to his Ram and opened the passenger door. His rifle sat in the passenger compartment, where he'd placed it after rescuing Maddy. In his right hand he carried the heavy tactical vest he had worn into the vet clinic hours earlier. Placing the armor on the passenger seat, he could see where two rounds had impacted the front plate, saving his life.

Doug closed his eyes and said a prayer, thankful for all the gifts he had been given. He was truly a rich man, not because of money but rather his faith, family, and friends. He was blessed.

Closing the door to the truck, he started walking toward the church, not knowing what he expected to find. As he neared the house of worship, he heard the sound of a dumpster lid slamming shut behind the bakery to his right. Investigating, he walked around the corner to see who was making the noise so early in the morning. He was surprised to see Stuart sitting next to the dumpster, eating stale bread from the garbage.

When Stuart saw the lawman, he was both afraid and ashamed. He first thought was to run; however, in his defeated state he just sat on the ground with his head in his hands and cried. He had hit rock bottom and didn't think he could go on any longer.

Doug approached the young man and knelt next to him, placing his hand on Stuart's shoulder.

"I don't know what to do," said the young man. "I have lost everything. Everyone hates me, and I have been marked for the rest of my life."

"You haven't lost everything," said Doug. "You have only lost the things that were holding you back—the big house, the money, and the friends who only put up with you for what you could provide them. None of that matters anymore. In fact, it didn't matter last week either; it was just harder to see it."

"I don't know what that means," said Stuart.

"Remember what the Bible said about the rich man?" asked Doug.

"No, we didn't really go to church much in my house."

"It said it is easier for a camel to go through the eye of a needle than it is for a rich man to enter the kingdom of God."

Confused by the parable, Stuart asked, "Am I supposed to be the camel?"

Smiling, Doug said, "Don't worry about that right now." He reached into the cargo pocket of his pants and retrieved a protein bar. He handed it to Stuart, who gratefully took it.

"Thank you," said the young man as he tore open the packaging.

"Are you ready to start the next part of your life?" asked Doug.

With a tear in his eyes, he said, "I am."

Standing up, Doug said, "Good. I know just the man who can help you with that. Let's take a walk."

As the two walked over to the church, Doug opened the door and told Stuart to have a seat in one of the pews. He then walked down the hall toward Pastor Campbell's office.

He called out, "Pastor Campbell, you back there?"

"Yeah, come on back," came the reply.

Doug walked into the office and took a seat in the empty chair across from his desk.

The pastor asked, "Did you bring me the 12-gauge shells you talked about?"

Doug shook his head no and said, "I have them in my truck down the street, but that's not why I'm here this morning."

"OK, why are you here?"

Doug explained all that happened over the past couple days. He further explained all that happened to Stuart, including the branding incident. The pastor was shocked at all he heard.

"Are you looking for redemption for killing all those men?" asked the pastor.

"No," said Doug. "I have no remorse for that. That needed to be done, and I believe I was put in place to make that very thing happen."

The pastor thought for a moment and said, "Well, the lord does work in mysterious ways, but I don't know if that was his intent."

"The death of the men who took my daughter and shot my wife doesn't weigh on my heart—at all," Doug emphasized. "The reason I am here is Stuart Griffith. He has hit rock bottom, and I felt a calling to bring him here. I can't explain it, but I felt it was something I needed to do."

"Like I said, the Lord works in mysterious ways. The girl he assaulted is a member of my church, and her father branded him out of revenge. They are regretful for their actions and ready to forgive. I believe God has a mission for Stuart, and this is just the start of his journey," said the pastor.

Doug thought for a moment and said, "I don't know about all that, but I hope you are right. As this world falls apart, if we don't have redemption, we have nothing at all."

Doug thanked the pastor and left Stuart in his care. The walk back to his truck was tranquil, and he felt at peace for the first time in days. When he reached the Ram, he opened the door to the back seat to retrieve the buckshot for the pastor. Next to the ammunition was the small wooden box from the Schmidt farm. Doug picked up the box and closed the door. He climbed into the driver's seat, sat the ammo on the dash, and placed the wooden box on his lap.

As he opened the box, he expected to find Vietnam-era medals from Elijah's military service. Doug was surprised when he opened the box and found medals from Operation Desert Storm, Doug's first war. They must have been medals from their son who was killed in action in 1991.

As Doug examined it further, he realized it seemed to be a keepsake box Mrs. Schmidt had kept to remember her son. It contained items of significance only understood by a grieving mother. There were a handful of photographs, letters he had written home from the war, and other mementos. Doug pulled two faded concert tickets out of the box and looked at them. They were from the farewell tour of the country music duo the Judds in 1991. The box also contained the compact disc *River in Time* from the mother-and-daughter duo. He wondered what significance this had to her son.

Doug opened the CD case and removed the disc. He placed it into the CD player in his truck and turned on the ignition. As he sat and listened to the music, he watched as Pastor Campbell and Stuart crossed the street to enter Doc Shelby's office. He assumed it was to get the brand and broken nose looked at. Doug made a mental note to do something nice for the veterinarian in return for working all night looking after his family.

Doug closed his eyes as he listened to the CD. His body was finally starting to crash as the adrenaline had long worn off. He was abruptly awakened by the sound of a knock on his passenger window. Looking up, he saw Pastor Campbell standing next to his truck. Doug reached to roll down his window with his left hand, but due to the injured shoulder, his finger only made it to the door unlock button before he pressed down.

Hearing the door unlock, the pastor opened it and climbed into the passenger seat. Closing the door behind him, he looked at Doug and asked him how he was doing.

"I'm fine. The shoulder is starting to ache, but it's a small price to pay," replied Doug.

The pastor nodded. "I'm sure it is Doug, but I was talking more about how you are doing spiritually and mentally. You have taken on a tremendous load as a leader of this community."

Smiling as he thought about his words, Doug replied, "I'm not a community leader. That position falls to people like you and Chief Peterson. God's role for me is that of a protector."

"You mean an avenging angel?" asked the reverend.

Doug grinned. "No, more of a guardian angel, I suppose."

The pastor sat and thought for a minute and seemed to come to the same conclusion. "I guess the difference between a guardian angel and an avenging angel is a matter of perspective," he said. Looking down, Pastor Campbell added, "Speaking of guardian angels, I see you have Mrs. Schmidt's memory box."

Surprised he knew where the box had come from, Doug asked, "How did you know this box was hers?"

"Linda and Elijah had been members of my church since I took it over in 1988. I spent a lot of time counseling her, especially after she became ill. That box contained the memories of her late son who passed away in the Gulf

War. As her illness progressed, she believed her son was watching over her as her guardian angel, guiding her to heaven."

"And do you believe her dead son was a guardian angel?"

"Well, the Lord does work in mysterious ways, but also, people facing death sometimes gravitate to ideas that give them comfort. To Linda, the thought was very comforting and put her soul at ease. It allowed her to accept the end of her life without fear of the unknown," explained the pastor.

Opening the box, Doug pulled out the Judds CD case and held it up. "There is a song on this CD called 'Guardian Angels.' Is that why it is in the box?"

The pastor grinned and said, "Well, that's where her story gets a little odd. In 1991, she and her husband drove up to Green Bay to see a concert by the Judds in person. That song 'Guardian Angels' touched her in a special way. On the drive home she told her husband she could feel something had happened to their son in the war. When they returned to their house in Rockport, there was a Wisconsin state trooper and an Army officer waiting for them. Her son had been killed in action that same day. During her son's funeral, she had me play that song as she believed it was a sign."

"That is strange," said Doug, "but people experiencing grief often misinterpret coincidences as some sort of divine message."

"I agree," said the pastor, "which is what she did when that dog showed up on their porch."

His interest now even more piqued, Doug asked, "What's that about a dog?"

The pastor explained, "About a month before she passed away, a border collie just showed up on their porch. It reminded them of the dog their son had as a child in the 1980s. He had on a silver name tag, but there was no address or owners' information. Linda believed the dog was a guardian angel sent to comfort her in her last days."

"Did he?" asked Doug.

"Yeah, her mind was at ease when she passed. She was ready for the journey, and that dog stayed by her side until the end."

"Does God use dogs as guardian angels?" asked Doug, looking over to the pastor.

He shrugged his shoulders. "There is some scripture to support the idea. I researched it quite a bit when that dog showed up. Exodus 23:30 tells us, 'Behold, I send an angel before you to guard you on the way and to bring you to the place that I have prepared.'"

"And you believe the dog was sent as a guardian angel?" asked Doug.

The reverend scratched his head and said, "Well, not exactly, but angels are pure spirits who don't have physical bodies of their own, and I suppose they can manifest physically in whatever form would be best for the mission God gave them on earth. So, while I wouldn't say I believe that dog was an angel, I guess I couldn't rule it out entirely. There are several examples in the Bible where angels appeared in the form of a dove."

Doug nodded and asked, "Any idea why they left the box for me personally?"

The pastor smiled. "I didn't know she had done that." He explained further, "A few months ago, before you retired from the state patrol, you stopped by their farm to pay them a friendly visit. That meant the world to the old woman, who believed it was also a sign. You reminded them very much of their son. You would have been the same age, you served in the same war, and after getting out of the Army, their son intended to join the Wisconsin State Patrol."

Surprised at the situation, Doug asked, "She thought I was a guardian angel?"

"In a way, I guess. She thought God sent you to be in her husband's life and comfort him after her passing," said the pastor.

Looking defeated, Doug replied, "Well, I guess I failed at that mission, since he took his own life."

"No," replied the pastor. "Elijah made his own decision. That's not on you at all."

"Well, pastor, you have given me a lot to think about." Nodding his head toward the box of 12-gauge shells on the dashboard, he said, "Those are for you."

"Thanks," said the pastor as he stepped out of the truck and returned to the veterinary clinic to check on Stuart.

As Doug pulled away from the curb to return home, track ten on the CD began to play. The song was 'Guardian Angels.'

CHAPTER 52

As Doug pulled the Ram into the parking area next to the other vehicles, he couldn't help but wonder about the dog. Surely, Baxter wasn't an angel. He could see how an old lady on her deathbed wanted to believe in a divine sign from above, but the dog showing up on her porch was certainly just a coincidence.

With a dog's big eyes and gentle nature, Doug could see how people found comfort in them. Dogs are known for their loyalty to families or to a special person. But were dogs simply more perceptive, able to sense a person in need, or were they assigned a mission by a higher power? Dismissing the thought, Doug walked up onto the deck and into the house.

In the kitchen, he was surprised to see Kimberly making breakfast for everyone while Brad assisted. Doug was pleased she finally seemed to be assimilating into her role as part of a team.

As he continued on to the living room, he could see Jessie was having a personal conversation with Jaxon. They were both crying, and she was holding his hand. Not wanting to interrupt them as he walked through to the master bedroom, he chose to turn left and go up the stairs. As he got to the second floor, he could hear soft music coming from the nursery. He wasn't sure if the tune was "Twinkle Twinkle Little Star" or the alphabet song.

As he entered the room, he found Maddy sitting in her rocking chair while Mark was leaning against the baby dresser next to her. The song was coming from the mobile that hung over the crib. It was clear they were focusing on their future family now that she had survived.

"How's the arm, old man?" asked Maddy, minimizing the whole ordeal just as her father would.

"I'll live," he replied with a smile.

Looking around the nursery that Penny and Maddy had been assembling for months, he asked, "You guys ready to relocate this stuff to my office?"

"Yeah, I was just getting ready to start bringing it all down," said Mark.

"You sure you are OK with losing your office?" asked Maddy.

"Yeah, I will be fine. Well, I need to get some things done before you put me to work too," said Doug, excusing himself.

He walked down the stairs and encountered Jessie standing at the bottom, waiting to speak with him.

Looking nervous, she asked, "Doug, can I talk to you for a minute?"

Knowing what was on her mind, he beat her to the punch and said, "Jaxon will have to bunk with either you or Scott. You work it out."

She smiled and wrapped her arms around him, giving him a tight hug. Realizing she was hurting his bad shoulder, she let go and said, "Oops, sorry about that. And thank you."

"No problem," he replied as he walked toward the master bedroom to check on his wife. As he approached the room, he could hear the song "Footloose" playing. Instantly, Doug knew she was going to use her injury as an excuse to binge-watch all her favorite girl movies.

Penny was lying in their bed with her bandaged leg elevated on pillows. Baxter was lying at her side. Doug could see a pile of DVDs waiting to be watched on the nightstand next to her.

"I see you had Maddy bring up some of our old DVDs. Any chance there is a Clint Eastwood or Chuck Norris film in the stack?" asked Doug.

"Hmmm, I'm not sure about that. There might be one between *Dirty Dancing* and *Titanic*," said Penny with a giggle.

"That's what I figured."

"Are you going to take a shower and join me finally?" asked Penny.

Smiling, he said, "Soon, babe. I just need to run into town and take care of something first."

Looking at her husband with a familiar smirk on her face, she said, "Yeah, right."

"Love you," he said with a smile.

"Love you too," replied Penny.

As Doug turned to leave, Baxter jumped off the bed to follow him. Doug stopped off in the kitchen and opened the cupboard. He removed an empty mason jar and a lid, then closed the door. Walking out of the house to the bottom of the deck, he stopped and picked up a set of rubber garden boots and a small shovel, which he placed in the bed of the truck. He opened the driver's side door, and Baxter jumped in ahead of him.

"I guess you are going with me, then?" he said to the dog.

Baxter lay down in the passenger seat and rested his head on the center console, looking up at Doug. His eyes spoke to Doug in a way that made him feel like he understood him—as if the dog could see into his soul. As Doug climbed into the driver's seat, he scratched Baxter on the head and told him, "I'm not an impressionable old woman." He laughed to himself as he drove out to the Schmidt farm. Once there, he parked the truck near the burned-out house and put on the rubber garden boots. Taking the small shovel and mason jar, he waded into the ashes to search for the remains.

In the center of what was the living room, he found what appeared to have been a hospital bed. It was likely where Mrs. Schmidt spent her last days. Next to the bed, he found the burned remains of the couple. After filling the mason jar with some of their ashes, Doug returned to the truck, but Baxter was no longer there. As he looked around, he heard a bark coming from a clump of trees off in the distance. He tossed the shovel into the bed of the truck, then climbed into the cab with the jar of ashes. Driving the truck down the dirt trail, he rounded a corner exposing an open pasture behind the clump of trees.

On the far side of the field, Doug could see a ray of sunlight shining onto a small family cemetery. Baxter was sitting in the cemetery and gave a single bark, as if to call him over. Doug drove over to the cemetery and put the truck in park next to where Baxter was waiting for him.

Stepping out of the truck with the mason jar, he said, "What's this, Baxter?"

Baxter walked over to the one headstone that was different from the others. Doug recognized it as a standard military grave marker. Doug followed the border collie as he walked to the marker and sat down directly in front of it. Doug took a knee next to the dog and read the inscription on the tombstone.

Baxter Schmidt

US Army

June 7th 1971

Feb 1st 1991

Bronze Star

Purple Heart

Doug had a lump in his throat as he read the name written in the stone. He set the mason jar containing the ashes next to the granite headstone, then stood at attention and rendered a hand salute. In the background, the CD in his truck rotated to the tenth song and played "Guardian Angels."